Joanne Burn was born in Northampton in 1973, and now lives in the Peak District where she works as a writing coach. Her first novel, *Petals and Stones*, was published in 2018. *The Hemlock Cure* is her second novel.

D1386915

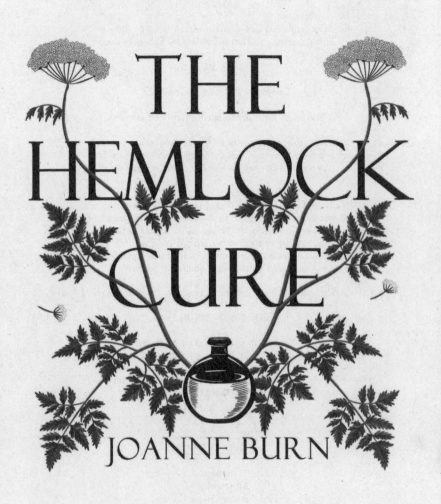

THE HEMLOCK CURE

JOANNE BURN

SPHERE

SPHERE

First published in Great Britain in 2022 by Sphere
This paperback edition published by Sphere in 2023

3 5 7 9 10 8 6 4 2

A CIP catalogue record for this book is available from the British Library.

ISBN 978-0-7515-8193-5

Typeset in Garamond by M Rules
Printed and bound in Great Britain by Clays Ltd, Elcograf S.p.A.

Papers used by Sphere are from well-managed forests
and other responsible sources.

Sphere
An imprint of
Little, Brown Book Group
Carmelite House
50 Victoria Embankment
London
EC4Y 0DZ

An Hachette UK Company
www.hachette.co.uk

www.littlebrown.co.uk

For my parents.

Character List

Wulfric Housley
married to Florence Housley

Florence Housley
died 1660

Leah Housley
daughter of Wulfric and Florence. Died 1662

Mae Housley
daughter of Wulfric and Florence

Marshall Howe
married to Joan Howe

Joan Howe
married to Marshall Howe

William Howe
infant son of Marshall and Joan

Isabel Frith
married to Johan Frith

Johan Frith
married to Isabel Frith

Frances Frith
daughter of Johan and Isabel

Gabriel Frith
son of Johan and Isabel

Harry Frith
son of Johan and Isabel

Edward Frith
son of Johan and Isabel

Elizabeth Bradshaw
married to Francis Bradshaw

Francis Bradshaw
husband of Elizabeth. Died 1659

John Bradshaw
son of Elizabeth and Francis

Jacques Claridge
brother of Katarina

Katarina Kitts
sister of Jacques

Rafe Kitts
son of Katarina

Sam Chapman
apprentice

Thomas Stanley
Rector of Eyam 1644-1660

William Mompesson
Rector of Eyam 1664-1669

Catherine Mompesson
wife of William. Died in Eyam in 1666

PROLOGUE

*T*he baby, when eventually it came, slipped from her body like St Margaret from the dragon's belly. Mother's groan was death itself. And the little scrap, like a skinned rabbit, lay lifeless on the linen between her legs.

The year is 1650, and this is my earliest memory.

'Open the shutters, Leah,' Isabel said to me, and my tiny fingers fumbled with the catch and hinges, pulling back the wooden panels, opening the casements. I felt a trickle of air against my cheek and wondered whether it was the new day coming in or my brother's spirit leaving; and if it was his spirit why it was in such a hurry to get away.

I wanted to go to Mother, but the chamber was full of trouble and I failed to see a way from where I stood to where she was.

'By your divine providence . . .' she was muttering. 'Through your infinite grace . . . some miracle . . . my soul . . .'

At first glance she was an angel, beatific and praying. The next she was an animal, damp and lamenting. Either way, she was unreachable.

Isabel held out a bundle of herbs.

'Get them burning,' she told me.

I held them to the candle flame, my gaze flitting from the herbs to Mother, to Isabel, and back again. I drifted to Isabel's side.

'Like this,' she told me, grasping my wrist and wafting the smouldering herbs over the baby's body. I repeated the action, watching her thread a piece of wool through the centre of a hagstone and wrap it about the infant's lifeless chest.

'Bone to bone, sinew to sinew, vein to—'

It was then I felt Father behind us. He had entered the birthing chamber uninvited, and I knew, without looking, that fury would be pouring off him.

CHAPTER ONE

Late Summer 1665

Mae reaches beneath her bolsters and pillows for the coiled strip of linen, letting it unspool between her thighs. She wraps it around her naked chest – once, twice – swaddling the mouse-soft flesh, ignoring the needling pain in her baby breasts, tugging the knot beneath her armpit. She pulls a shift over the top, a bodice over that, and looks down to see whether it will do for another day: her soon-to-be-womanhood disguised beneath the layers of linen.

Pulling on stockings, petticoats and apron, she glances around for her slipped shoes. They have been kicked beneath the bed and she crouches for them.

After washing her hands and face at the basin she brushes her hair, pins it up and covers it with her coif, tying the straps beneath her chin.

Already, she perspires.

Chamber pot in hand she pauses at the door, listening for sounds of Father praying in his own chamber. He paces when communing with God, naked as a newborn, as if he hasn't a thing to hide. In the winter his lips are blue by the time he's finished, his hollowed cheeks mottled as if the saints have been slapping him about the face.

A warm draught rushes beneath the door, across her feet. And Mae holds her breath as she listens for Father, calculating his whereabouts in the house. She prefers to make a start on the day before he has roused himself, to please him by getting ahead. But sometimes he hardly sleeps at all and she'll find him at dawn, hunched in the kitchen by a guttering candle, more intractable than ever. It is not just his irritation she's forced to endure on those days but his bitterness; it is God that bestows a good night of sleep, and Father must juggle with his conscience when rest is denied.

There are no remnants of a sleepless night, though, when she descends into the kitchen; nothing to suggest he spent the night poring over *Malleus Maleficarum*: *The Hammer of Witches*. That tattered book is never far from his thoughts, the oft-thumbed pages tearing from their stitching.

Moths flutter at the kitchen window, and the mice are unhurried in their searching of the pantry floor for the tiniest of crumbs.

At the hearth, in amongst the ash, Mae finds the tiniest of trembling embers. A loose pile of dry grass, a breath or two, and the fire is started. She arranges some kindling, a faggot, then she stands, lulled for a moment by the sight of the flames: comforting even on a summer morning. She's reluctant to turn away to her morning duties of dough-making, hen-feeding, vegetable-chopping. But she coaxes herself with the promise of herbs and alchemy later on; the proper work of the household will begin after breakfast and prayers: the grinding of Jesuit's bark, millipedes or senna, the pressing of pills, the soaking of woodlice in boiled oil. She will be the hands that Father cannot do without. And with every turn of the pestle in the mortar she will toil with the task of convincing him that she would make a worthy apprentice.

The dough is proving by the time Father comes down the stairs. He has to stoop through the doorway into the kitchen, his greying hair falling in front of his face as he does so. He pushes it behind his ears, rubbing gingerly at his hands. Mae fetches him a mug of ale from the pantry, and then she brings two slices of bread and butter – one for each of them. They sit together at the table and eat, and when they have finished Father administers a tincture which he fetches from the pantry: several drops beneath her tongue. He never, these days, announces what he has chosen for her – in what way he perceives her humours require adjustment. He simply comes towards her with the earthenware jar in one hand and a bone spoon in the other. And she is careful not to flinch from him.

The taste of it spreads in her mouth, all burgundy and blood red.

'Lemon balm and nettle,' she says, just loud enough for him to hear.

They walk the cobbled street in silence past Little Edge, Fiddler's Bridge and Hawk Hill to church. Its great wooden doors are closed but unlocked, its parishioners encouraged to offer God their prayers at any time of day or night. It is empty inside, as it often is so early in the morning, and Mae stands at Father's elbow as he lights a thin tallow candle.

'Glory to you, O Lord,' he intones, ' . . . who gave me sleep to refresh my weakness and repay the toils of this weak flesh. To this day, and all days, a peaceful, healthy, sinless course, grant, O Lord.'

It is a shame she looks so much like him. I was made from Mother's mould – rounded on all the edges, and fair. Mae has Father's angular face and jutting bones, the dark hair of his youth. I watch her on occasion regarding herself in the looking-glass at the clockmaker's cottage, thin lips pressed together to stop them from trembling, perturbed it is Father's eyes staring back at her. If she had Mother's blue eyes – *my* blue eyes – then she might not be so afraid of forgetting us.

She is made in Father's image but she was always Mother's *little mouse*, and the temptation was always too great for me: claws out, waiting to pounce. There had been something about her sensitivities – her strange abilities – that enraged me. And her ridiculous hair – a nest of loose, teasing snakes – had always been too much to resist. I would swipe for a fistful and lead her about the kitchen until she screamed merry murder. Mother would throw us into the garden until the fury was out of us, and on a hot day she might follow with a pancheon of dirty water, determined to bedraggle us both.

In the cool church, they kneel and pray and Mae finds, as she often does, that her prayers are not to God at all, but to

Mother: . . . *in your wisdom, guide me. I am blind, even though your light is all around. Give me grace in my heart, purpose in my character, vigour in my actions.*

She stumbles on *your light is all around*, and repeats it beneath her breath. She tries to make it real – trying to *feel* it, as if that might bring Mother back from the dead. Everything changed when she died – the temperature in the house, the shadows in the garden, the timbre of our voices. Most of all, *Father* changed. The village speaks of this at times – how grief ruffles some, disassembles others.

They stop at our grave on the way home. Mae's coif fastenings are damp with sweat, chafing beneath her chin. She holds her shawl about her and kneels, brushing the simple stone with her free hand, cleaning away a few dry leaves, a tumbling of desiccated moss. She runs her fingertips over the lettering of Mother's name, and then backwards from the last letter of my name, to the first. It is five years, almost to the day, since Mother died. And three since *I* was taken. When Mae is here alone the graves are more peaceful than sombre – we stir up her soul as she kneels in the grass getting her stockings dirty, bringing us to mind: a spatter of freckles, the curve of an eyelash, the smell of warm milk.

She says my name beneath her breath: *Leah*, like a sigh, too quiet for Father to hear. But perhaps he senses her longing, for he grasps her elbow and lifts her to her feet.

Marshall Howe stays his shovel, the grave knee-deep, and observes them. His face is wet with sweat, itchy beneath his whiskers, salty when he licks his lips. He presses his shirt sleeve against his forehead and wipes his damp hands one at a time on the back of his breeches. He watches Father and

Mae, but he thinks of Joan because she is never far from his thoughts, and he can remember the taste of her that morning and how she'd been looking down at him when he'd opened his eyes. She had bitten his lip playfully, painfully, dipped her tongue in his mouth. Then baby William woke, and though Marshall had closed his eyes in disappointment, it was not long before the child was making him laugh.

Mae scrubs the table with salt and crushed rosemary. She fetches the jars Father asks for from the shelves that line the walls of the kitchen. Ground snake skin, agaric, sarsaparilla. He sits by the hearth, nursing his hands, massaging the great lumps where his knuckles used to be.

'I can wrap them for you,' she offers, thinking of warm salt water, of tamarind decoction, senna-tea, cream of tartar. But he does not respond.

She gets the pestle and mortar, knives and spoons.

'Bring vinegar,' he says. 'And turpentine.'

She moves briskly, without fanfare, demonstrating her usefulness. *You need me*, she is trying to remind him. She hopes. She looks to the goodness in him – but it's a memory she's looking at, faded and unreliable. And so she looks to something else: the fact it is only the two of them left, and there is always so much to be done, and each winter his bones grow more troublesome. He needs me, she tells herself.

Mae drags the steps across the kitchen floor, leans them against the wall and scales them for the liquorice and the aniseed. At the table she waits for him to tell her to chop the short stub of grey valerian root. To grind it, to tip it into a brass cauldron. She imagines a jug of water, a few raisins and a pinch of powdered liquorice. It would be so much quicker if she did not have to wait for his instruction; if she didn't have to feign ignorance so as not to betray herself.

When eventually she sets it to boil, hanging it over the fire, she has to lean in front of Father to do so, aware of his clasped hands almost touching the fabric of her petticoat. She can hear the breath in his nostrils – a whistle like the wind in the joints of the house, like the faint, thin sound of a newborn rat – and the hairs lift on her arms, neck prickling.

Mae lifts the heavy iron knocker – a coiled serpent – at the great door of Bradshaw Hall, and lets it fall three times. Then she tips her head backwards to regard the majestic stag carved in stark relief above the entrance. She turns in the direction of its faraway gaze – towards the moors of Bleak Low and the heights of Longstone Edge – as if they might observe something there together.

A shriek tells her that Isabel's two youngest sons are playing together on the hillocks of sandstone at the back of the hall, chasing one another round the stacks of rotting timbers and joists, playing hide and seek in the phantom wings that were half-built years ago when Elizabeth Bradshaw's husband was still alive. Now they crumble, imagined but never finished, darkness where there should have been windows, wild flowers growing from the abandoned masonry. Some say this is what happens when a woman is left in charge of a great house. It belongs to Elizabeth's sons, but those boys still wet the bed at night and need their meat cutting for them at the dinner table.

Mae is brought through the Great Hall with its familiar

tapestries and vast table long enough for twenty-four guests. She knows the housekeeper from the rear better than she knows her face: her rump as wide as any mare, her plaited hair the colour of toffee, the quick, rhythmic slap of her boots on the stone. Always the same gesture as they reach the corridor to the kitchen: a sweep of her hand, as if Mae might forget where she is going and follow the housekeeper onwards to whatever task has her occupied elsewhere in the house. However perfunctory that little hand gesture, no matter the lack of conversation, they are bound together as allies; Mae's presence at Bradshaw Hall every Monday evening is not to be spoken of outside these walls. Elizabeth Bradshaw has given her staff strict instruction on the matter.

It is the end of the day and the kitchen is scrubbed clean, the floors are swept, Cook's apron is filthy. The room has the settled feeling of a creature readying itself for sleep. Cook is finishing a Lombard pie for tomorrow, sliding a knife beneath the top crust – steam rushing out – and Mae slows to watch her ladle cream and eggs over the meat and spiced dried fruit.

Through a door, she leaves the quiet of the kitchen behind and enters the stillroom. The place is awash with the scent of roses. Tall windows flood the chessboard floor with the evening light, and amber sunbeams bounce from the copper stills. She looks to the glass objects on the long shelves that run the length of the room: bottles and flasks lined up like shapely soldiers. Something within her settles at the sight of everything in its place. Her eyes skim the pestles and mortars, the scales and weights, the gallypots and graters, strainers and sieves, the two dozen tin vessels – diverse in size with a multitude of spouts. She passes the cold furnaces and braziers, then the heat of one that is gently bubbling.

She eyes the two women – Mother's closest friends – deep in conversation at the far end of the room. Isabel's hand is clenched around Elizabeth's upper arm as if they are discussing something earnestly, something of gravity. But then they erupt in laughter and grasp one another to steady themselves.

Isabel looks up at Mae as she draws close. She stretches an arm wide so Mae can lean against her momentarily. It is all soft, all warmth – Isabel's body like a new pillow stuffed with the lightest down. Her thick waves of silver hair (she is not yet thirty-eight) tickle Mae's face. She smells of lavender and cinnamon pastries. But then the moment is gone and Isabel squeezes Mae's arm accusingly through her shawl and shift – as if the arm has no right to be there.

'Skin and bone,' she says, her brow furrowing. She looks Mae up and down, appraisingly, as if she can see right through the layers of linen to Mae's collection of bones: the undulations of her ribs and hips.

'Your mother was never so thin,' she says, as if believing Mae guilty of some conspiracy.

If she cared to, she could go on: *your mother was never so small, her hair was never so dark, her eyes were never so close together.*

'Dear Florence,' says Elizabeth then, pushing a wisp of red hair behind her ear. Their attention falls to reminiscing about Florence in the way that is simple once a person is dead: speaking only of virtues. Mae listens eagerly to Mother's friends for any new droplet that she has not heard before. *Tell me more*, she used to say. *Tell me more.* She would scrape that jar of memories if she could, lick them sticky from her fingers, savouring the taste for days afterwards.

Sometimes the women talk of me, but not so much; they struggle, you see, to speak of me warmly.

They speak easily though, then, of unguents and waters, balms and cordials. And Mae fiddles with the small brass alembic waiting to be put to good use on the long wooden table – upending its funnel, tapping the glass receiver. Sometimes she gives the appearance of not listening, but she does not miss a word. The evenings she spends at Bradshaw Hall – with these women that remember Mother and care to speak of her, these women who do not think Mae's education a folly – are a potent therapeutic.

Isabel opens her receipt book: recipes of all kinds hoarded in a bulk of loose, stained, well-used pages – gathered, sought and bequeathed. Sometimes the poorest women of the parish who cannot afford to pay directly for her midwifery services offer Isabel a cherished receipt in lieu of payment – some secret remedy passed down through the woman's family.

From the heated cupboard on the wall behind them, Elizabeth brings forth dried earthworms.

'They were soaked in vinegar before being dried.'

She fetches bitter almonds, dust of Spanish steel, and white wine, speaking all the while of the green sickness and how to diagnose it. Virgins, wives and widows are all susceptible.

'If she has it, she will be so pale she is almost green,' says Isabel. 'She will be fatigued, in want of appetite, suffering with cold sweats and low spirits. That her courses will have ceased is the thing that tells you it is the green sickness she has, and not any number of other ailments. A physician might suggest that such a woman is in need of a man, that she is wanton and vigorous chamber-work the only cure.' After a pause – 'But that has not proved itself a reliable remedy.'

She says this last as an aside to Elizabeth who laughs quietly, and Mae cannot help smiling, looking between the women, wondering whether they will share the joke with her. Sometimes they do, sometimes they don't.

'Have either of you had the green sickness?' she asks, hoping to draw them on the subject.

Elizabeth passes Mae a pestle and mortar, then pushes the pile of withered worms across the table. They are the colour of bruises, and Mae drops them into the mortar, crushing them beneath the dry grind of the pestle.

'I know women who have,' says Isabel. 'Often the sickness comes after a child, especially if the birth was particularly troublesome. Exercise is helpful. As is the warmth of the summer, plenty of meat and perseverance in the prescribed medicine.'

Isabel pauses, waiting for Mae to make a good job of crushing the brittle corpses. Then she pushes Mae's receipt book towards her, along with a quill and ink. 'Write it all down.'

Mae feels Isabel's eyes upon her as she concentrates on writing neatly. Learning to read was never a problem, but her hand – so the women constantly remind her – looks as if a spider has fallen into the ink and dragged itself across the page. *You need to be able to read it again in the future, or there is no point in writing it down!*

They crush the bitter almonds, adding them to the pow-dered worms and dust of Spanish steel. Elizabeth pours in a few splashes of wine to form a paste.

'A small spoonful can be taken every morning and evening, in a quantity of warmed wine, or ale.'

Mae writes, and blots.

'Of course, if you know the right merchant, and your woman is rich enough, then a single dose of powdered uni-corn horn will cure the disease entirely,' says Elizabeth.

'Shall I put that?'

'Well, at forty pounds an ounce . . . ' says Isabel.

Elizabeth shakes her head. 'Don't waste the ink. Some ingredients are so rare they are a cure for all that ails us. They are not difficult to remember.'

Mae always leaves plenty of time to be home before Father, so she can settle herself down at the hearth with some sewing. Enough time to re-tie her coif, to smooth down her petticoats. Enough time to numb her flesh against the hard chair in the corner of the kitchen. To remember that *that is there* and *this is here.* One day she hopes to impress him with all she has secretly learned. But for now, she must remember her ignorance – the length and breadth of it, the weight of it.

They are like clockwork, the two of them, returning from their secret arrangements. But still Mae hurries from the hall as if she might have misjudged it. As if Elizabeth's pocket watch is not to be trusted and this will be the week Father catches her. It is not the thought of him finding her out on the street or fumbling at the door that she is afraid of – she could think of some excuse if she really needed to. It is the notion of betraying her arrangement with Elizabeth and Isabel. Of somehow bringing the stillroom home with her – the scent of roses and cinnamon pastries clinging to her hair.

CHAPTER TWO

Late Summer 1665

The unrelenting August heat has abated for an afternoon. The skies are thick with heavy cloud and rain pours, filling the air with a fine grey mist. When Johan answers the door to the post-boy, the child is as sorry-looking as a drowned kitten. Johan brings him in and fetches him a piece of tart from the kitchen. The boy chunters on about the size of the puddles on the road from Bakewell (*big enough to drown a horse!*) and all the while Johan fingers the thin package the boy has handed over – the tattered paper folded in on itself, secured with a faded black ribbon and a dollop of wax. His eyes trace the looping, inky letters of his friend's hand, and he feels an impatience rising as the boy starts a comparison of one road, one ditch, one puddle with another, and which side of Derbyshire is worst afflicted.

'And now I have a puddle of my very own,' says Johan, looking down at the stone flags beneath their feet, water running from the boy's sodden cloak. He seems to take the hint at that, looking up at Johan with apologetic eyes, cramming the last of the tart into his mouth.

Johan closes the door behind him and takes his package into the parlour. He clears a space at his worktable – lifting away carefully, piece by piece, the inner workings of a deconstructed lantern clock, scooping a pile of screws and spirals of metal ribbon into a small tin box.

The light coming in at the window is rain-blurred and feeble, and so he takes the time to light a candle. He sits, draws breath, checks the postmark. The package was posted on the 24th August, and Johan feels a familiar relief, not only at the knowledge that Jacques has kept well enough for another month to write and post a letter, but at the broader comfort of knowing the General Letter Office continues its business with vigour and pertinacity; the city of London is not yet on its knees.

He pulls gently at the ribbon that keeps the package together.

Just two days ago Jacques held this very parcel in his hands.

Unwrapping the paper Johan exposes a sealed letter and, beneath that, the July edition of the Royal Society's monthly journal, *Philosophical Transactions*. He fingers Jacques' letter momentarily, postponing the moment of opening it, his thumb pausing on the dark red seal: the colour of congealed blood. He raises the letter to his face, pressing the smear of wax to his nostrils, breathing in the musky scent of ambergris and bergamot. Leaning back in his chair, he puts the still-sealed letter aside and lifts the journal, opening it out on the table.

Just as Johan has over the last months taken comfort from the letters that arrive, so too has he felt encouraged by the Royal Society meeting still; that these men of natural philosophy persist in their endeavour to provide an account of the *undertakings, studies and labours of the ingenious.*

He turns the pages of the journal, scanning the titles of each article: *A way to Break Easily and Speedily the Hardest Rocks; Progress to be made in the Breeding of Silk Worms; New American Whale Fishing about the Bermudas.*

His heart sinks, then, as he notices an announcement at the very back: *The reader is hereby advertised, that by reason of the present contagion in London, the printing of these Philosophical Transactions will now for some time be intermitted.*

He sighs, reaches for his packet of tobacco, stuffs his pipe, places the stem of it between his lips, and picks up Jacques' letter. He turns it over in his hands and thinks of calling for Rafe: *your uncle has written!* But he knows he will do no such thing. He will consume the letter in private, and hide it away afterwards if necessary, because that is what Jacques would expect of him. Every missive brings some new concern. A year ago it was the troubling news from Holland that the plague was returned. Three months later it was a rumour of two dead Frenchmen in Long Acre, at the upper end of Drury Lane. Two months after that, Jacques told of the terrible apprehensions among his friends and fellow merchants as the pestilence crept from St Giles-in-the-Fields, to St Andrew's in Holborn, onwards to St Bride's, and into Clerkenwell. In March, Jacques wrote that knavery and collusion was rife – neighbours hiding the disease from one another, the authorities manipulating the weekly bill of mortality to obscure the scale of death. And in

May, he confirmed the plague had spread beyond any hope of abatement.

Johan breaks the seal, and unfolds the letter.

My Friend,

I trust this finds you well, that Isabel thrives, and the children too. How does Rafe? Be sure to convey my love to him.

I wish I were writing with better news, but the tide has truly turned in this city. The bills of mortality are ever increasing. The authorities are shutting up homes as soon as a single person is stricken; watchmen stand guard outside whilst inside the whole family succumbs and perishes. People cry for help from their windows, begging to be let out, but no one can go to them. The physicians have left, the apothecaries have abandoned their shops. Even the clergy have fled in their multitudes.

The west part of the city has emptied out almost entirely. The better sorts have thronged away with their servants. Just last week in Whitechapel the streets were thick every day with carts and waggons weighted down with so many belongings. There was such a bustle of overwhelmed carriages, such a sight I've never seen.

There has been daily crowding at the Lord Mayor's door to obtain certificates of health, and passes to travel – without which there can be no admittance through towns on the road, no lodging at any inn, no stabling for a horse. People wait all day to reach the Lord Mayor's door only to be turned away at sunset.

The whole city is gripped by such hurry – hurrying away, hurrying to the grave, hurrying from sanity and conscience.

The people are addicted more than ever to prophecies and astrological conjurations. Printed predictions abound, all foretelling the ruin of the city in its entirety. The people are terrified. Just yesterday a man in only his drawers was running through Clerkenwell shouting, 'Woe to this city!'

I know what you will tell me, my friend – Save yourself! Retire into the country! But even if my mind had turned on that subject, I truly think I have left it too late. I was there at the Mayor's office out of curiosity. Perhaps if I had been able to reach his door I might have asked for a certificate of health and permission to travel. But even then I would have been lucky to find a horse – there is not a single beast to be bought or hired. If I were to leave now I would be forced to travel alone, on foot. How would I eat? How would I survive? And who could I trust to oversee my warehouse? There is no call for Flemish linen now, no demand for raw silk or metal thread from the east. I cannot sell what I have, and yet I dare not leave it unattended.

I know you will be distressed to hear my news, but cheer yourself if you can. I am not dead yet! And you have your paper to read. See the account of letting the blood of a healthy dog into a mangy one – I know you will be fascinated to contemplate such a thing. They say the dog was cured. Next they will propose letting the blood of a bishop into a Quaker!

Take heart, my friend. The world of enquiry and discovery continues!

Yours, most faithfully,

Jacques.

Johan reads the letter again, folds it, pushes it away. He opens *Philosophical Transactions*, turning the pages until he finds the article Jacques was referring to. In awe, he reads about the experiment – the insertion of tiny tubes into the arteries of the animals. He cannot help imagining – unsettlingly – not unconscious dogs, but his very own children, blood pulsing slowly from one small body to the other, merging together memories, humours, and all their bright differences. He knows better than to be troubled by a thing simply because it is unfamiliar, and reminds himself what he reads about – replacing bad blood with good! What a wonder! He thinks of my sister – how keenly Mae would consume the details of the experiment if she were here, and how astute her observations would likely be.

He scuffs his slipped shoes back and forth against the rush matting.

'Rafe!' he calls, leaning back in his chair, listening to the expanding silence that follows his voice through the house.

The boy is Johan's only ally in the household when it comes to matters of astronomy or natural philosophy. His own sons do not share his passion. Harry and Edward are too young to care, and Gabriel pales at the idea of medical inter- ference – once he fainted, cracking his head on the hearth, after Johan described a new process of taking skin from an animal to cover the gaping wound of an injured man.

His own flesh and blood do not see the universe as he does – as intricate clockwork. They do not think of the human body like the planets, forever circling. Not every- one, he has to remind himself, feels compelled to search out the patterns stippling the cosmos. Quite *why* the perpetual motion of life is of so little interest to his family is, in itself, a mystery. Isabel is an attentive wife, and a good midwife, but she would not care for a tale of draining blood from one hound to another. And Frances belongs to Isabel when it comes to education and the workings of the human body. Their daughter does not fall upon the hearth at the sight of blood, nor pale at the stitching of torn skin. She is not frightened by a lifeless child refusing to breathe, still warm from its mother's body. She has a strong stomach, and a quest for knowledge. But Isabel has instructed Johan more than once not to interfere; the Royal Society has little to offer a midwife in the making.

So, when all is said and done, it is Rafe who is Johan's best companion here now. He eases himself from his chair, holds a match to the candle, lights the tobacco in his pipe and pulls the hot, tasty smoke into his lungs. He walks from the room and stands at the bottom of the stairs, listening to the small sounds of his children above him. Running his hand over his beard, he presses two fingers to his moustache, smoothing it away from his lips.

He calls again for Rafe.

In the near-dark of the stairwell, he waits, wondering whether the boy is in the house at all. It is just as likely that he's not – that he's out in the woods flying Reverend Mompesson's sparrowhawk, or whiling away the hours with Mae, gathering leaf or root or bark, pretending afterwards he wasn't with her half so long.

Johan puts his pipe between his lips, and tugs on it again.

Back at his desk he writes a letter to Jacques. He does not start with any pleasantries, but gets straight to it asking his friend to find a horse – to exchange his entire warehouse of fine fabrics and ribbons, of seed pearls and spangles for a lame nag if that is all he can find. *Come to Eyam*, he implores. *Come be with your nephew – you're the only family the boy has.* He feels the betrayal as soon as those words slip from his quill;

Rafe was barely out of his nursery gown when he first came to them, and has grown alongside Gabriel and Frances ever since. Harry and Edward have never known their family without Rafe in it. Johan stares down at the words he has written. He hates the mess it will make, but crosses out the last line anyway. Then he continues:

London is not safe. I insist you listen to me for once!

By Friday morning, Johan's letter is on its way to London. It nestles with news from all corners of the country, weighty in the mailbag that hangs from the horse's crupper. Passed from post-boy to post-boy, it travels through the day, through the night. As dawn breaks on Saturday, and the post-boy announces his arrival in Bugden with a blow of his horn, he passes a cart travelling in the opposite direction. He barely sees it (busy as he is fantasising about his breakfast), but on that cart, in a wooden chest, is a bundle of cloth and used clothing from a draper's shop in Cheapside. It is damp from the downpours in Baldock and Biggleswade. Fleas rest in the weft and weave.

And it travels to Eyam.

CHAPTER THREE

Early Autumn 1665

Mae walks up Church Street in the direction of Ivy Cottage. The distinctive figure of Marshall Howe lollops down the centre of the road towards her. Shovel balanced across his shoulder, he half-heartedly raises a hand to a neighbour who bids him a good morning.

People think him curmudgeonly, but Mae fancies digging graves would make any man a little down in the mouth. He limps to the left, so subtle you could miss it. And he stands a head above any other man from here round about, even Father. Most of the village would like to look down on him, and it irritates them when they must do the opposite.

His smell is familiar, distinctive: old sweat, damp straw and clay. His boots are smeared with the stuff, and they stop their slow, steady progress down the hill when he sees Mae coming towards him. He will be on his way to dig a grave, and she wonders who it is for. She wants to ask, but thinks better of it. He pushes his wide-rimmed black hat up onto his head a little, and swings his shovel in front of him, leaning on it.

'Morning,' she says.

Marshall breathes slow and steady through his long, greying whiskers. He looks tired. Mae thinks of digging troughs in the garden, preparing them for seed. And she marvels at what it must take to dig a grave; it is no surprise the man is weary. An aromatic water would be of benefit, but Marshall has never come to Father for medicines and he certainly would not come for a spice water. Digging graves does not provide for the luxury of white camellia and cardamom seeds steeped in brandy.

''Ave some ol' bits of leather at home. Rafe might fancy making use of them, so I thought.' He nudges his hat again.

Rafe. Mae likes that he uses her friend's name. Not *Johan's stray.* Or the *Friths' foreigner.* Or *that blackamoor waif.*

'I'm on my way there now,' she says. 'I'll be sure to tell him.'

Marshall picks up his shovel, and without another word they go their separate ways.

Isabel's face brightens at the sight of her.

'*Mae,*' she says, stepping back from the door and opening it wide. Her silver hair is tied up in a bun, uncovered. She wears a simple, short-sleeved shift and petticoat. No stockings, no shoes. Mae feels uncomfortable suddenly in her unnecessary layers of clothing, her chest tight in its binding.

She steps into the house, the air cool against her skin,

and goes through into the parlour where Johan is working at his large oak table. He looks up and smiles, removes his eye glasses from the bridge of his nose and beckons her over with them, holding them up for her to see once she is stood beside him.

'All of a sudden, I can see again,' he laughs, pressing them to her eyes, blurring her vision. She blinks, recoiling. 'But look,' he says, and positions them over some tiny cogs that are laid out on the table in front of them. She bends, and peers at the magnified objects. The table is by the window for extra light; all the better to make sense of the miniature levers, gears and ratchets. Johan has explained their functions to her before – how it is that a timepiece keeps time, why it loses time, the elusive pursuit of accuracy. She took care, as she always does, to listen well.

She steps away from the table and lowers herself into a chair, noticing the faint aroma of the rush matting beneath her boots: the tremor of camomile and wormwood amongst the strong scent of the dried bull rushes.

Isabel stands in the doorway, a blur of pale linen in the corner of Mae's eye.

'So, tell me what you know,' Johan says, leaning back in his chair and looking Mae full in the face. This is the way he talks to her – with his full attention, as if she matters. His shirt balloons beneath his flannel waistcoat. His stockings are bunched around his knees, and on his feet he wears slippers the same green as his breeches.

'Tale or truth,' he prompts. 'I care not.'

Once she would have conjured something fantastical – the start of some tale he'd have accepted from her as naturally as if she'd passed him a platter of food. He would have selected some morsel from that platter and passed it back to her so they could feast together. But fantastical tales seem hard for Mae to come by these days. No longer do they spring up like weeds; she would have to forage for a tale if she wanted one.

'I'm out for plantain and chickweed,' she says, looking down at the basket slung over her arm. It is a truth, but it seems of such little consequence now she has uttered it.

Johan nods, watching her carefully.

'The house is full of moths,' she tries again. 'A plague of moths.'

'That many?'

'From nowhere, and all different kinds.'

It is another truth, but perhaps he will think it the start of a tale if she continues – that some of them are as big as her hand, that they cluster in the corners of the rooms and beneath the shelves, but do not flutter at the windows as moths usually do. That they flit through her thoughts as she sleeps.

'I'm baking, if you'd like something,' says Isabel, from the doorway.

'*I* would like something,' says Johan, shooing them out of the parlour, as if driving cattle through the country lanes.

In the kitchen, Isabel bends at the bread oven, removing the door and sliding the paddle in, scooping up the pastries with a quick, practised arm. Mae and Johan loiter by the table, watching greedily. The kitchen fills with the smell of honey, cinnamon and dried fruit – a sweet swirl of russet. And that is a truth she could discuss with Johan if she were minded to. *That* is a thing she knows: that every scent has its own colour. That the rush matting in his parlour is the deepest of blues, tinged black. That Johan himself is blue also – but paler. That Isabel is brown as a coffee bean.

If Mother's warning had been just a little less severe, then Mae might have trusted Johan with this peculiarity. And she does know it to be peculiar. Not only from Mother's stark instruction to refrain from mentioning it to a single soul (even Father), but from the time Mae once told Johan a tale about a girl who saw colours where others did not. She'd explained that because this girl saw a colour with every scent, then she saw a colour for every person she knew. How he oohed and ahhed at the *magic of such conjurations*. He had embellished the tale for the purposes of their folly, saying something of apparitions, something of oracles, and Mae's mind had leapt at once to witchcraft.

'You'll have been wanting to see Rafe, I suppose,' says Isabel.

And as if they can summon him with only their thoughts he is all of a sudden there at the kitchen door. The sparrowhawk on his wrist rouses, spreading its blue-grey wings, settling once more, head bobbing. Its eyes lock onto Mae.

'Hello, Swift,' she whispers.

She moves towards them, boy and hawk, and drinks in the striated bronze and cream of the bird's breast, the yellow legs, and chunky black beak hooked and dirty with blood. Swift ruffles his feathers again and Mae smiles. She reaches out and traces her fingers across the feathers of the hawk's head and back: soft down on hollow bone.

At times, in the dense woodland, Rafe has passed her his falconer's glove and she has slipped her hand into the rough leather and offered it to the silence of the forest. Mae likes the not-seeing — the beloved hawk wild again and lost to them as he slides through the dense trees. She likes, too, his manner of return, as if he has, like a ghost, slipped through from another world: a flurry of soot-grey and ember-orange.

'Did he eat?' Mae asks, looking to Rafe.

'A big fat thrush.'

He looks at Mae, cocks his head, tight curls of black hair falling across his face, his brown eyes flitting the length of her.

'You've grown,' he says, putting his shoulder to hers. They look at the place where they are touching; he, a whit taller.

'Since just last week, you've grown.' He says it with consternation, as if she has tricked him out of something, as if growing is a thing she desires.

'A proper young woman you're turning into,' says Isabel, sharpening a knife at the table.

A quiet, dull ache starts up behind her ribs, as if she has been too greedy with hot cakes and they have lodged in her gullet as punishment. She tries to swallow the feeling away. Looking down at herself she imagines the bound, flattened flesh beneath her bodice. Is it so obvious? If it is obvious to them, it will be obvious to Father. She is not sure why it matters, nor what it is she feels. She only knows that she wishes to avoid his scrutiny. She has come to loathe the moments of meeting him unexpectedly on the stairs by candlelight – their distorted shadows flickering on the walls. There is something that comes between them when they catch each other by surprise in that way – when they have not arranged themselves sufficiently. Some moment approaches, like the rumble of hooves on dry earth before the carriage comes into sight. It is something she is uncertain of – something she does not understand. It is something I wish I could explain to her.

'Mae?' says Isabel, gesturing to the steaming pastries.

'No,' she says, shaking her head.

I have watched her half starving herself these last months. As if by denying herself sustenance, she might cling to childhood a little longer – to the safe simplicity of not becoming a woman. Her body, though, is betraying her, a little more each day.

'Call the others,' Isabel tells Rafe, and he disappears into the dark of the house.

'I can see your bones,' Isabel says, running her fingers along Mae's collarbone.

'Leave the girl,' says Johan.

Isabel opens her mouth to speak, but after a moment of regarding Mae she says nothing, turns back to the pastries and the knife. She slices a pastry into quarters, scoops the pieces onto a platter, then cuts another one. Johan leans in for a piece and eats it noisily – with little moans and sighs of pleasure, smacking his lips.

'Become a midwife, Mae,' Isabel says, quietly. 'You and Frances would work so well together, and you are gifted with the herbs.'

This is not a new suggestion. Isabel has mentioned it

several times over the last year, trying to make it so – *her* reason for their Monday evenings at Bradshaw Hall.

'Father needs me,' Mae says. 'His hands are worse all the time.'

And goodness, she thinks, he'd never stand for it. *You know this*, she wants to say. There is no love lost between Father and Isabel. He would never relinquish her into the midwife's hands. Mae looks into Isabel's clear blue eyes, her smooth skin hardly touched by the years.

'You'd be a good midwife,' says Isabel.

'And I will be a good apothecary,' says Mae.

'You would be an excellent apothecary, but . . .'

Mae turns towards the sound of chatter – Harry and Edward barrelling into the kitchen, jumping up onto their stools and looking eagerly to their mother.

Rafe comes back to stand beside her, looking down again at the step of their shoulders, as if making a note of just how much growing is needed to keep ahead of her. When Gabriel comes in, followed by his sister Frances, they offer Mae a brief greeting before going to Swift, and running their fingertips down the bird's grey back.

'Finish cutting the pastries, Frances,' says Isabel, and Frances turns away from the hawk and picks up the knife, talking to her mother about the afternoon ahead, and the multitude of jobs that will fill their time until supper.

Mae fidgets with her basket, thinking of all the jobs *she* ought to be getting on with, and how she will have to explain herself to Father if she is out too long. Rafe's arm rests against hers, and she begins to contemplate stepping away, of leaving the ease of Ivy Cottage.

As if she has spoken her reluctance aloud, Rafe says:
'I'll come with you. I need to return Swift.'

They walk in time with one another: mute, hobnails clacking.

Swift — hood removed — watches every movement in the hedgerow, but with the lazy countenance of a bird that is already sated; a bird that just an hour ago plucked the down from a thrush's breast, and tore at the creature's flesh while it was — mouth gaping in panic — still alive. Mae once saw a blackbird's fluttering heart after Swift had stripped away everything covering that delicate beating thing. And although her love for the hawk had always been, up until that moment, uncomplicated and absolute, she hated him then.

Just kill it, she had demanded. *Kill the thing!*

On the outskirts of the woods they slow, bending for the last of the summer's bilberries. They crouch among the low bushes, staining their fingers purple, eating every berry they can find before continuing into the forest.

Beneath the canopy of branches the shadows are delicate as lace-work. The air is humid, pungent with warm sap and earthy moss.

Mae bends to collect some wood sorrel, pulling up generous handfuls, slipping the occasional leaf into her mouth. Moving from one clump to another, she loses sight of Rafe. After a while, she faintly hears him calling. She stands, glancing around, spotting him a way away. He beckons her with some urgency. Without hurrying — Rafe can get excited about all manner of things that do not necessarily warrant genuine excitement — Mae picks her way through the undergrowth towards him. When she is there at his side he gestures into a dense tangle of brambles (the berries thickening, a dull red, not yet ripe). He points, and Mae's eyes follow into the sun-deprived underworld of thorny, arched stems.

'There,' he says, and she sees it: the leafy, mossy sphere of a dormouse's nest suspended, chest-height, in the vast knot of bramble.

'Safe and sound,' whispers Mae, and Rafe turns and smiles, his face just inches from hers. She can smell his skin, the merest hint of lavender oil in his hair. He does not look away, but examines her face much as an artist might look at his subject, hungry for every contour of bone and cartilage.

He swallows, and her eyes flicker to the lump in his throat, like a walnut trapped there beneath the skin. She has an urge to reach out and touch it – to tell him she has noticed it lately, bobbing there when he eats and drinks. She wants to ask him what it feels like to have something new grow so visibly. She wants to ask whether it troubles him.

But before the words can leave her mouth she is caught by the thought of putting her lips to his. All she need do is lean forwards; his lips are *just there*.

His breath is warm upon her face.

She does not, though, lean forwards. She does not put her lips to his. But all the same, for the briefest moment, it feels as if she has done. She feels the prickle of sweat beneath her arms, and her body sways with the vigour of her galloping heart.

They have always been at ease with one another, like siblings without the rivalry. But when Rafe turns away from the tangle of brambles, when he steps backwards to put a little distance between them, Mae feels it clear as anything. Like a cloud blotting out the sun. The ease – this thing they have, this important thing – is suddenly gone.

And neither one of them is going to mention it.

CHAPTER FOUR

Wulfric's Diary

September 28th 1645

If the mind is a gateway to your infinite grace, then in my bride – my Florence! – I have surely found a new path to knowing you. Pious, and pure, with a rational mind, she has no time for mysticism, quacks or cunning folk. She recognises her calling, and understands it is only through your scriptures that we may hope for salvation. Untainted by frivolity, she has proved herself to be a good, hardworking helpmate to her parents, and how pleasing it is to rest assured of her abilities. I am proud to call her my wife, and together, in your service we shall find an ecstasy to best that of the flesh. Comeliness is of no matter to me. I only ask for a devoted wife – that she will make a bond of marriage as pure and good as Christ's bond with the Church.

Please Lord, grant us a fruitful life together, side by side in devotion, full of promise and purpose. Where else should we look for guidance, but directly to you? Our king sets no example to his people in this regard – with a queen so full of vanity and loathsome connivance. How our nation languishes, stripped of all wealth and glory, as our monarch bends like a sapling to the will of his papist wife. I shed not a tear for Charles with his popish intentions, but I pity any man who has not the strength to command the weaker vessel of his wife, let alone his country.

CHAPTER FIVE

Early Autumn 1665

A ll through the village, they ask the same question:
    '*Have you heard?*'

It is how Isabel greets Elizabeth on entering the stillroom.
But Elizabeth looks blank.

'The Hadfields' journeyman, George Viccars, is dead.
They buried him today, and Catherine Mompesson said he
died from the plague.'

Elizabeth's hand goes to her throat; Catherine is the rector's wife: a reliable source.

'It can't be true,' says Elizabeth nonetheless.

'Mary Hadfield confessed it.'

'So you think them certain?'

Isabel considers the question. They *are* certain, but it seems
too awful to say it. All day her insides have been churning,
and she steadies herself against the table as her mind flits from
Mary Hadfield's two young sons, both still in their nursery

gowns, to her own youngest sons who are still in theirs: not yet breeched, not yet studying their letters, concerned only with mischief and hiding in her coats and what tasty goodness will come from the oven next. She can hardly countenance the notion of her small sons falling ill – of *any* of her children falling ill, and she includes Mae and Rafe in that number.

'Who else is showing signs?' asks Elizabeth.

Isabel puts her hand to her forehead as she thinks the matter through all over again.

'Alexander is away,' she says. 'Mary and her sons show no sign of it as yet.'

'Then perhaps Viccars will be the extent of it. He travelled a fair amount, perhaps he recently returned from some cloth merchant, or weavers in London.'

'What fool would travel now to London?'

'There are fools enough around. When did he fall ill?' asks Elizabeth.

'I know not.'

'Has she burned his things? She must burn his things.'

'She may not wish to do that with Alexander away.'

'There is no time to lose. She must strip his bed, gather his clothes and all his cloth, everything he was working on.'

Isabel watches Elizabeth agitate herself with one instruction after another, with offers of gunpowder and aromatics for burning in Mary Hadfield's cottage.

'I can take them myself,' Elizabeth says, pacing the stillroom. Loose wisps of red hair catch the evening sunlight, as if she burns and crackles, sparks flying. 'Someone must take charge,' she says, her shoulders slumping as if doubting the tenability of her own statement.

'Perhaps Reverend Mompesson . . . ' says Isabel.

Elizabeth rolls her eyes. 'Half the village would more happily endure the plague than do as William Mompesson asks!'

'So who would do a better job? Who has a voice the entire village would care to hear?'

But there is no one; the war has divided Eyam. There are those who rejoiced at the restoration of the monarchy and the Book of Common Prayer. And there are those that grieved. There are those who celebrate the banishment of the dissenting rector, Thomas Stanley, from the village. And there are those who feel outrage at his exile, and disgust at the young vicar brought in to replace him – with his pale and sickly wife, both of them foreigners: all the way from Scalby in Yorkshire. And there are, it has to be said, those who do not care which prayer book they sing from on a Sunday. Those who weigh parliament against the king and find them both wanting.

'I'll take gunpowder to Mary Hadfield and her neighbours, and I'll do it tonight,' says Elizabeth. 'I will burn his things myself if I have to.'

The door to the stillroom opens and Mae comes like a shadow from the gloom of the kitchen. The women watch her approach.

There's something different about you, Isabel thinks.

And she is right – everything is different. All week Mae has slept badly, dwelling on Rafe, the warm humidity of the woods that day, her lips and his and whether he had read her mind as it seemed he had. There has been only uncertainty when she thinks of it all – the kind of uncertainty that stretches all the way to sorrow. She has felt the fluttering of excitement too, like a winged creature at her throat. At other times she has felt afraid. And all of it curdles deep down in the pit of her belly. One night, after she had fallen asleep ruminating on the whole matter particularly hard, she had lurched awake to a wetness between her legs. It had been too dark to see much, and she had lain there until the dawn dissolved the stars and there was light enough to discern the blood on her hands and legs and shift.

But when Isabel looks into Mae's face and sees her weariness, she assumes only: *you have heard about George Viccars*. And it is true, she has heard.

'People came all day for preventatives,' says Mae.

Isabel watches her, waiting for her to say more. Mae looks even paler than usual, her pinched features more than ever those of a little mouse.

'We need something to settle us,' says Elizabeth, turning, walking away. Her yellow stockings flash beneath her petticoats. It is reassuring to Isabel – that spark of yellow against the black and white floor, the sway of her friend's red hair. Elizabeth has always seemed invincible. In that way that some people do, as if no harm will ever come to them. Isabel watches her friend disappear into the kitchen, the door swinging closed behind her.

'My courses have begun,' whispers Mae.

And despite the fear already flooding through her, Isabel feels a new weight bearing down – as if a dish of iron has been slipped beneath her coif. Of course, it is no surprise that Mae's courses have come; she is fourteen, after all, and Isabel has had it in mind a great deal of late. She is suddenly, though, all of a rush, overcome with a feeling of powerlessness, and she starts to cry.

'What's *wrong*?' says Mae.

Isabel pulls her close.

'It is terrible news for the village, and you becoming a woman, right now in the middle of it all.' It is something of a lie, but she stumbles on with it. 'It makes me think of your mother and how much I miss her. I hate to think of you all alone.'

Isabel feels Mae sink into their embrace, like Harry and Edward do when they are particularly tired. She loves the weight of a child's limbs when they slump against her in that way; when the child is young enough, or weary enough, or upset enough to surrender fully to being held. But all Isabel can think as Mae leans into her, showing no sign of pulling away, is, *how can I possibly protect you?* An urgency presses in from all sides. She wants to say, *stay with me, do not go back to him.*

And *I* wish for her to say it. But she will not.

'Have you told your father?'

Isabel feels Mae shake her head.

'Then don't.'

Mae pulls away and looks up into her face, scrutinising her.

'But what if he asks me?'

'You must lie to him.'

'But *why*?'

Isabel shakes her head. 'He does not need to know—'

'But—'

Elizabeth comes back into the kitchen with three mugs and a sack posset in a copper cauldron. Isabel smells the sweet wine, the cream and spices. The posset will be full of nourishment, and she wishes for Mae to drink it all.

They do not open their receipt books, and Elizabeth does not fetch ingredients of any kind. They only talk of what has come to the village, and what it might mean. They drink their posset, and clasp hands across the table. And when Mae asks Elizabeth the time, when she says she must take her leave, Isabel follows her out the stillroom, through the kitchen and the Great Hall. They do not see Cook, or the housekeeper. And there is no sound at all from elsewhere in the house, only the echo of their footfall, as if the whole place has fallen into the deepest contemplation. As if, like the rest of Eyam, Bradshaw Hall is waiting.

Outside, the wind blows in sudden, angry gusts. Mae looks up at Isabel, and is just about to say goodbye when Isabel reaches for her arm, and squeezes it gently.

'Remember what I told you,' she says.

Mae stiffens.

Yes, she almost says, *of course I'll lie to him.*

There is, after all, some instinct pulling her in that direction. And hiding her courses would be a small matter, surely? She hides from him already: her secret education here at Bradshaw Hall every Monday evening; and the nights she spends in the parlour, by candlelight, reading William Bullein's *Defence Against all Sickness, Soreness and Wounds*, and Nicholas Culpeper's *London Dispensatory*, and Levinus Lemnius' *The Secret Miracles of Nature*.

But hiding the truth is not quite the same as lying. He

has, after all, never asked her, *do you go someplace on Monday evenings when I worship with Thomas Stanley? Do you spend sleepless nights educating yourself against my wishes from my very own books?*

Hiding things from him is something she does out of necessity, and her disobedience is not a thing she carries lightly. She does what she can to make amends by being a good daughter – attentive and obedient. She asks forgiveness from God for her deceit. She prays to Mother that he never finds her out.

Sometimes, she even prays to me.

Mae struggles to find the right words as the wind fights against her and Isabel – their shawls flap, petticoats snapping.

'I don't understand,' says Mae, looking into Isabel's bright blue eyes. Strands of silver hair have escaped her coif and are fluttering about her face.

'Wait here,' Isabel instructs, withdrawing into the dark doorway.

As she waits, Mae toys with Isabel's request. Questions rear up, and fall away unanswered. Father is there too, in the dark corridors of her mind. Of course he is there, he is always there. He is peering into her face, so close that she smells his sour breath. He is asking her whether she has *the benefit of nature* yet? Bleeding can alter the balance of humours; he would choose a different tincture for her, if he knew. He asked her some months ago if her courses had come, and she tries to imagine what she will tell him if he asks her again. How will she arrange her face to disguise her deceit?

Isabel does not return, and Mae continues to stand on

the doorstep buffeted by the wind, an impatience blowing through her. She would have been nearly home by now if Isabel had not detained her. She thinks of Father walking across the moors at this very moment, returning from his meeting with Thomas Stanley. She thinks of the wind in his face – whipping him up into a fury. And just as she is thinking, *I must be away, I cannot stay a moment longer*, Isabel returns. In her hands she holds a tin box the size of a boot, which she thrusts at Mae.

'Ask me no questions, and we will talk another time. But, for now, do not tell your father about your courses. Keep your rags hidden in this box – bury it outside where he will not find it.'

Mae takes the metal box, and with a sigh of resignation she looks only briefly at Isabel before walking away. As soon as she is through the gates of Bradshaw Hall, she runs.

CHAPTER SIX

Leah

*P*adding down the stairs, barefoot, in the middle of the night, I heard only the raging storm at first. The wind had woken me, whistling through the thatch. For a little while — knowing I was supposed to stay in bed right through until the morning — I had lain there, trying to go back to sleep. But my longing for Mother had started up, and it was so hard resisting the temptation to go to her when she was just on the other side of the wall, sleeping in that large, comfortable bed with Father. There was plenty of space for me, if only they had been willing to share. I had fidgeted, restless and resentful. And eventually, unable to stop myself, I'd slipped from beneath my blankets, crept to my bedchamber door and opened it as quietly as possible (I could only just manage the heavy, awkward handle that fought peevishly against its own purpose). I lost my courage as I lingered at their door, knowing Father would be cross with me. Reluctant to return to bed, I began to head downstairs in search of something to eat. I took the steps slowly. Concentrating. As if every one of them posed a great threat to me; as if each one was there to catch me out. I lifted my night-shift so there was no risk of tripping, letting it drop only when I was stood on the kitchen flags – the white moon shining through the window. The kitchen was full of shadows. And the wind was like a creature there in the house with me – some wraith or fairy that liked to dance and jape about. It rattled the doors. It shook at the casements. It sent strewing herbs, dry and brittle, shifting across the stone flags. But beyond all that – and after a moment of standing there in the middle of the kitchen – I discerned a sound that turned my limbs to stone. It was the sound of a child whimpering, right there in our house where the only child was me.

For a moment I was not certain where the whimpering was coming from. But as I stood there listening, stock still, heart of a fluttering bird, I understood that the child was hiding in the pantry. I took one small step after another, pausing at the threshold, listening to this strange, new sound. Suddenly, I was not afraid, but dreadfully sorry for this forlorn creature, and I stepped into the pantry, searching the gloom for a child I imagined just as tiny as myself. But as my eyes searched – and found – a huddled thing, crouching beneath the shelving, I saw it was not a child at all, but Father. I swallowed, suddenly afraid, unable to fathom what on earth had occurred for him to be hiding away, weeping in the corner. I wanted to ask him what was wrong, but I could not find any words at all. And then he was pulling himself to his feet and flying towards me like a demon. As if it hadn't been the wind at all – but Father – rattling the bones of the house.

This was a while before I learned Father is afraid of the wind. And years before I understood that fear transmutes so easily to fury.

CHAPTER SEVEN

Autumn 1665

For some days after George Viccars was put in the ground, it seemed that perhaps Elizabeth Bradshaw burning gunpowder, frankincense and juniper in Mary Hadfield's cottage might have chased the evil away. Mary and her two young sons remained quite well and their neighbours – in whose homes Elizabeth Bradshaw had also seen fit to burn her aromatics – persevered in good health.

Perhaps it is not here, after all, the village said. *Perhaps, God's punishment was intended for George Viccars alone* – for some sin greater than drinking too heartily or taking the Lord's name in vain. Some sin of which the village was ignorant. They sought to convince themselves of this, cultivating rumours about the Hadfields' journeyman – the sordid shape of his sins with Alexander away and him all alone with Mary.

When little Edward Hadfield sickened, then died, the village was uncertain in what manner to find fault with a three-year-old. Especially one that looked so much like an angel. Most fell silent on the matter, sorry in their hearts for poor Mary Hadfield. But there were still the huff-snuffs that clutched at straws, adamant God was pointing fingers at the fallen, rather than the village as a whole. And someone – after dark one night – painted a red cross on the door of Mary's cottage.

But then Peter Hawksworth – a miner held in good esteem, with not an enemy in the parish, who lived just across the street from Mary, who had been right as rain just the day before – could not get out of bed for his day of work below the ground. And at his neck grew lumps as large as hen's eggs. Within days of Peter being taken, strapping Thomas Thorpe was taken too, and half of Church Street heard his lamenting the night he died.

So then all the village knew for certain: it was among them.

Marshall rises early; it is barely light. All night he dreamed the same dream – with shovels for hands he'd been digging a tunnel so deep, so twisted, he was sure he would never get out of it. It is a relief to be awake, despite the two graves that need digging by the middle of the morning. He'll be digging them side by side; Sarah Syddall and Mary Thorpe were inseparable during life, and their families have agreed they should remain that way for all eternity.

Mae wakes thinking of the gap between Sarah's front teeth (as wide as a guinea). Just a month ago she had spoken with her and Mary at the village wakes. The three of them – all in new clothes – had lingered at the coconut shy, eating gingerbread. They had laughed at Mary's father, Thomas, in the boxing ring with his shirt thrown off, prancing around like a court jester. The air had been thick with the smell of roasting mutton and the jangle of Morris Dancers' bells — the rhythmic clatter of their boots, the crack of their staffs.

Now the girls are in their winding sheets, with blackened fingers and lips.

Mae looks up at the moths clustering in the eaves. It is not often she finds herself reluctant to start the day. She has never been one to stay in bed — to *want* to stay in bed. She would rather be in the woods if there is time to spare. But today she is pinned beneath the blankets by a heavy sadness, even though she never thought of Sarah and Mary as friends; she knew them, that is all. She allows herself to be transfixed by the scrabbling, fidgeting moths, counting with her fingers on the coverlet the number of friends she has in the village.

Later — after breakfast, and prayers in church, and a succession of tasks that Father meted out — Mae is sent to the woods for rampion. Because the sadness has not lifted, and a heaviness is troubling every limb of her body, and she has been so busy making preventatives under Father's instruction that she has not seen Rafe in more than two weeks (and when she did see him it was the briefest discourse on the outskirts of the woods), she runs all the way to Ivy Cottage in the hope of seeing him.

Johan takes Mae into the kitchen where Isabel and Frances are kneading dough, the table shunting to-and-fro with the vigour of their efforts. The air is pungent with yeast, and the colour of it is the richest cream; it blots out every other scent, so there is no pale-blue Johan, no rich-brown Isabel.

Harry and Edward are playing a game in Isabel's petticoats, hiding in the folds of linen, snatching for glimpsed limbs, shrieking when caught. Rafe is suddenly there at the kitchen door, in the corner of Mae's eye, fleeting, then gone without a word.

The air hangs heavy – yeasty, thick in her lungs when she takes a deep breath.

She is panting a little from running up the street and along the lane. Frances smiles apologetically as if she knows something that Mae does not. Isabel barely smiles at all, letting her gaze drift briefly across Mae's face before looking back at the dough on the table; she thuds the heel of her hand into the soft mound, stretching it thin, picking it up and throwing it down with a slap.

'So, we'll no longer meet on Monday nights?' says Mae, when it seems Isabel has not a thing to say. She had been unaware of the new arrangement – that there *is* no arrangement anymore. She had arrived at Bradshaw Hall as usual on Monday evening to be told by the housekeeper (who had shouted the message from behind the closed door) that Elizabeth Bradshaw was not accepting visitors.

'Elizabeth does not wish to gather for now, so we will not gather,' says Isabel.

'But my receipt book is there.'

'I will fetch it for you and keep it here.'

'But—'

When will I see you, now? she wants to say. *When will I see you properly? Away from here, where you're forever busy in your*

kitchen and garden? Busy with your children and Johan and the
labouring women of the parish.

Mae feels her insides sinking. No one speaks; there is just
the scuffle of the boys' game, and the loud, rhythmic crump
of the table leg against the flagstone floor. Johan takes a
chunk of bread from the food-safe on the wall and chews
on it, brushing crumbs from his beard.

'Father says it'll take us all by the time the year is
out,' says Mae.

She has been horrified by his prediction, desperate to find
someone willing to contradict it. Johan pulls at his rusty
beard with slow strokes, looking to his wife. Harry and
Edward fall against one another in a fit of laughter.

'The families of the sick should stay at home,' says Isabel.
'But they go from house to house, full of the vapours and
speaking of comets and God's wrath.'

'And if not his wrath, then his refuge,' Johan says, wryly.

'Boys begone!' Isabel commands, pushing Harry and
Edward from the folds of her petticoats; they run from the
room and thunder up the stairs.

Mae moves to the hearth, tracing her fingertips across the
oak lintel, running her nails along the cracks and grooves.

'What will become of us?' says Isabel. She lays off the
dough and looks from Johan to Mae and back to Johan. 'It
spread through the whole of London, not a parish spared.'

'But they say the city of London is steeped in sin, that
iniquity runs through the streets like a river,' says Frances.

Father has spoken big of this – all the plays and gaming
tables, the music houses and dancing rooms that have, so
he says, *debauched the manners of rich and poor.* How vexed he

becomes recounting the buffoonery of the Jack-puddings that roam the streets of the city looking to entertain. So too the merry-andrews and the puppeteers. *And the new king himself the worst of scoundrels, returned from France with a pope in his belly and lust in his loins – profanity is rife, and the plague is God's answer to that!*

'You know this is not how it is, Frances,' says Isabel, turning to look directly at her daughter. 'They say it about dead babies, too, do they not? They say it about barren women. *It is wickedness that causes it.* But you know it is not so with dead babies and empty wombs, and it is not so with the plague. There is no reason to it. Good women lose their babies and innocent children die of the pestilence.'

Isabel stands back from the table, putting floury hands to her narrow hips. She looks furious one moment, fearful the next.

'We cannot avert our attention from what is,' she says. 'Jacques wrote there are too many dead to be buried, corpses rot everywhere in the streets. It will come to pass here, just the same, I swear it will.'

Mae can smell decay when people speak of it, as if it is right there under her nose. It is the deepest green – a mould-bloom on a mouse-carcass, the thick slime of stagnant water, the wet stone in Cucklett Cave. So too when they speak of the dark tokens that appear on the skin, and the swellings that burst through the throats and groins of the ill. There is a sweetness to the smell of such dying, like the cloying scent of the house after she has made blood puddings.

'He says you can't walk the streets without sorrow weeping from the casements,' says Isabel. 'It's brought the city to its knees – king and court forced to flee – what's a tiny village to do?' She looks earnestly to Mae, as if she has the answer. 'It *will* take us all, I swear it.'

And there it is: Mae has never heard Isabel agree with Father before.

'It will *not* take us all,' says Johan, shaking his head, tearing at the crust with his teeth.

'And think of the sorrow of that!' says Isabel. 'Which of us can we spare?!'

Johan does not go to Isabel, but comes to Mae instead, putting an arm around her shoulders and pulling her towards him.

'Thomas and Mary Thorpe are dead,' says Isabel. '*Good* people. The rest of the Thorpe household are ailing with it – every one of them, so I hear.' Isabel shakes her head, wringing her hands in her apron. 'Who will dare go into such a household to help care for the sick? And what happens to the children if the parents are taken first? Can you imagine?'

Mae tries not to.

Johan moves away from her to the food-safe for another hunk of bread, and there beside her instead, stealthy as his hawk, is Rafe. He puts his hand against her back, his palm between her shoulder blades, and it feels for a moment that he is holding her up. His fingertips press a little into her skin, speaking to her through his flesh. His hand is hot, and the heat seeps into her. She imagines that warmth flowing round her body. The kitchen blurs and fades. Isabel's voice recedes. There is only Rafe, and the silent solidity of him at her back.

CHAPTER EIGHT

Wulfric's Diary

August 4th 1646

I had imagined a boy – a future apprentice. But I am grateful for the healthy child you have sent to us, and born so soon. Our spousals were fresh in our minds when Florence found herself with child. And here now the infant bellows from the bedchamber with hearty lungs. Is this your blessing upon us? Am I to believe – oh! how I wish to believe – that this child is your gift to me? An indication that you are pleased with us? I look everywhere for a sign of your satisfaction, but the doubt eats away at me. Am I blind, Lord? Is there something here I do not see? I saw in her a pious woman, and joined with her because of it. But how she has come to me hot with desire, quite outwitted by her flesh. And even with her belly swelling and full of child, night after night, so keen was she to find that pleasure again. And again! Swept away by earthly delights, sweating like an animal, eyes rolling in her head as if possessed by some demon. I am full of shame at the weakness of my own flesh, Lord, knowing that all ravishment and ecstasy belong to you. She tempts me, and I find myself drawn to her quite inexplicably. My shame knows no bounds when I think of it. All pleasure is the devil's snare. But then here is a perfect child – our Leah. And she is surely a blessing?

CHAPTER NINE

Autumn 1665

*T*he church feasts upon its congregation's sorrows. Every pew is crammed with villagers pressed shirt to shift, children held in arms to make more space for extra feet on the cold, stone floor. There are those who are absent – whole households who would not be welcome: the *Thorpes* and the *Torres*, the *Ragges* and the *Banes*. They have been told to stay away, but are remembered in prayer by Reverend Mompesson: *Lord, grant your children relief from their suffering, deliver them swiftly from the burden of their flesh, so they may find bliss and fulfilment in your eternal glory.* The village says *amen* to that – *deliver us from this evil.* And how they sing, spilling their hearts out the doors and down the paths that weave between the graves.

Mompesson – adored, detested – speaks to his newly attentive flock, smoothing the soft frills of his white collar, worrying at it with careful fingers. He speaks of prayer and repentance, and submission to God's will. *The disease will not be outwitted,* he warns, *only endured.* He is referring to those who have fled the village, and speaking directly to those who may be considering flight. There is a murmur of agreement through the congregation as he speaks, and Isabel hears *Bradshaw* mentioned once, twice, three times. Her heart sinks as the rumour unfolds – that Elizabeth will be the next to go, that right now she prepares her family to be away.

She goes north.

She has family that way.

She has land.

Another home.

'Tis all very well for some.

Isabel looks around, straining for a glimpse of the Bradshaws' pew. It is useless – she can see nothing. And even if she could see through the crowds she knows in her heart she would not see her friend worshipping with the rest of the village. An anger ignites and smoulders within her as the service continues – as she sings, and gives the appearance of praying, and as she listens to William Mompesson speak of patience, and faith and surrender. He does not, she notices, speak of *why the Lord is so enraged*, which is all the village seems to speak about these days. Some blame the boys who let the cows enter the church last summer and foul the nave. Others claim to have heard the sound of Gabriel Hounds in the steep and wooded valley of Eyam Dale: the souls of unbaptised children – roaming, full of lamentations – bringing with them bad luck and God's punishment.

After the service is finished and they have made their way outside, Isabel slips her arm through Johan's, and reaches up to whisper in his ear.

'I must go to Elizabeth. I hear she is away to York imminently.'

Johan looks at her, and Isabel does her best to hide her anger; only because at every turn recently she finds herself upset and indignant at the choices of others and she suspects Johan may be tiring of it. She has always prided herself on her equanimity, but of late it has deserted her.

'Take the children home, will you? I'll not be long. I'll be back before dinner.'

Isabel weaves between her neighbours. There is a chill in the air; last night brought the first frost of autumn. She pulls her cloak tightly about her and glances briefly through the crowds for Mae, seeking reassurance that all is well with her. She is nowhere to be seen, though, and after telling herself it means nothing, she keeps her head down as she walks away; she does not wish to be accosted and drawn into discourse, or to give advice. And more than anything she does not wish to hear of any woman newly with child. She simply wishes to speak with her friend. Although when she imagines their conversation she is not so much speaking with Elizabeth, as haranguing her.

She walks quickly through the graves and out onto Church Street. Behind her, the multitude of voices fade to a murmur, and her own chattering thoughts crowd in. *What on earth shall I do? How will I manage with Elizabeth gone?* Her worries bleed one into the other. She walks so quickly she is almost running, and as she turns onto Hawkhill Road she stops to catch her breath. Her head is thick with indecision. Is she angry with Elizabeth, or in need of a favour? What *is it* she would say, if she had the courage? Of what is she certain? What is true, after all?

Standing at the bottom of Hawkhill – a little dizzy, so tired with everything – she cannot find a way to balance the scales. And if *she* cannot weigh the matter exact, then how can she possibly confide in Elizabeth? Suddenly, it seems she has left it all too late. She hangs her head, and grits her teeth. *How dare she just run from the village because she can?*

In the walled courtyard there is the bustle of farmhands lifting wooden chests onto carts and into carriages. Horses are being fed and watered. Harnesses, bridles, bits and cruppers lie in a heap on the cobbles. From within the house, as she moves towards it, she hears only discord – the shouting of orders, quarrelsome retorts. She is grateful that no one seems to notice her, and she enters the door to the buttery without challenge. She goes straight through into the kitchen, where Cook is stacking jars of potted meats into a wooden crate. They acknowledge one another with a grim smile each and Isabel walks on, without saying a word, into the long corridor that leads to the Great Hall. With the rugs rolled up and tapestries brought down from the walls the place echoes more than ever.

She is preparing herself to continue into the depths of the house if necessary – to open doors and enter rooms she has hitherto never seen. But Elizabeth is *just there*, as if waiting, her cheeks flushed a bright pink. Dust hangs thickly in the air. A look of shock passes across her face when she sees her friend coming towards her.

'You are *emptying* the place?' says Isabel. 'Are you never coming back?'

'I—'

'Did you intend to say goodbye?'

'*Of course.*'

'God knows what'll happen to us, and you're packing up your tapestries?'

'I'm not taking the tapestries.'

Isabel glances at the bare walls.

'They are to be cleaned while we're away, that is all ... it just seemed ... while the lads were here ...'

Elizabeth takes a step backwards – a tiny step, but a step nonetheless. Isabel stares at her, aghast. She feels unsteady on her feet, overcome with clamouring thoughts and the realisation she is about to cry. She claps a hand to her mouth, furious with herself, but a muffled sob escapes.

Elizabeth clutches her apron, twisting the fabric, her face contorting with anguish.

'*Please*, don't upset yourself. Things seem desperate, but all will be well in the end.'

Isabel throws her hands up.

'Ha! *No doubt* all will be well for you, in the safety of Brampton.'

'Anyone with any sense should be leaving Eyam,' says Elizabeth, quietly.

'Anyone with any *means* ...'

'I cannot help that! My heart is brimming with the thought of who will succumb next to this pestilence. But what do you suggest? What use am I here?'

'You have everything necessary to make medicines. If you stay we can work together against it!'

Elizabeth shakes her head. 'There *is* no working against it.'

'You only say that to excuse yourself.'

'Nineteen dead so far this month – it's ever increasing.'

'So we must find a remedy that works.'

'No doubt Wulfric is trying. And you have labouring women to care for. But I have no purpose here – it is different for me.'

'*It is* different for you – I see that plainly now.'

Her voice cracks and she puts her hands on her hips in an attempt to maintain her composure. She is determined not to cry again, but feels the rising anger and pressing tears – catching at her throat, stinging and pinching the bridge of her nose. She feels a rush of nausea, too, and for a dreadful moment thinks she is about to vomit.

It passes quickly, but in its place, slowly dawning, is the most dreadful thought: *I am sickening with something.* All day she has been troubled by moments of dizziness and nausea.

Her legs feel weak beneath her, and she looks around for something to lean against; there is nothing though, and even Elizabeth is out of reach.

'I thought we were friends,' she says, weakly, feeling her friend's scrutiny as she flounders.

'Are you quite well?' Elizabeth asks, her features contorting into a whole new expression of anxiety.

'I am just upset! I ran here as soon as I heard. And I am tired of worrying what will become of us all. I should have known that you would leave; all the better sorts are leaving. But I thought, despite all this' – she looks around at the grandeur – 'that you thought of me as an equal, a *true* friend.'

'I *do*.'

'But you shut me out to make secret plans – I had to hear it from the gossips in church.'

'I promise, Isabel, I intended to see you.'

'You have Mae's receipt book – I need to take it.'

'Of course. And if there is anything else you wish to take . . . anything that may be helpful?'

'I shall take it all then!'

Elizabeth shoots her a look.

'How will I manage otherwise?' says Isabel. 'Or do you expect me to go grovelling to Wulfric now for tinctures and remedies . . . '

'Is it really such a hardship to go to Wulfric? It is no time for childish squabbles.'

Isabel laughs a singular laugh, like the yap of a fox.

'I have never wasted my time with squabbles, and you know it.'

Elizabeth – flustered – pushes wisps of hair beneath her coif.

'It is not a petty dislike,' continues Isabel. 'I do not trust the man. I do not see what others see in him – I see something else.'

Elizabeth glances around the busy hall.

'You are worried that someone will hear me speaking ill of him,' says Isabel.

'You need to be careful, that is all.'

I know of what she speaks, and Isabel knows also. As a midwife, she has a good reputation, even amongst the better sorts who pay generously for her services. But she walks a narrow path, infringing upon Father's living. She is not licensed to make or dispense medicines. She is a midwife, a woman. She is not a physician; she is not an apothecary. She relies on the turning of blind eyes. It is *Father* who has cause to grumble. And how quickly the tide would turn on her if he did.

'Use the stillroom while I'm gone,' says Elizabeth. 'And all that's in it − so much of it is yours, anyway.'

'You patronise me,' says Isabel. 'We both know it.'

They do not split the bills equally; Elizabeth makes up the ledger, and only ever asks Isabel for a paltry amount.

Isabel sighs, and as she hangs her head and stares at the stone flags beneath her feet she feels another wave of nausea, and the unsettling of the room around her.

'It is not just about everything here,' she says, pressing on as best she can. 'It is more than that.'

'Is it Mae? The two of you hide something from Wulfric, do you not? In the box you took . . . what is it?'

Trust her.

But her mouth won't contemplate such a thing, even if her heart hankers after it. Fleeting thoughts of Mae's buried rags flash in her mind, and then the thought of her own rags − washed and ready to be used again, wrapped neatly within a pocket and nestled in her linen chest in the corner of her bedchamber. When exactly did she use them last? She cannot remember, but certainly more than a month ago.

Thoroughly distracted now by the thought of her stopped courses, she brings her attention to the heavy tenderness of her breasts, her fatigue, her nausea.

'*Tell me*, Isabel.'

'Now is not the time,' she mutters.

And as if she possesses some prescience, there is a shout

across the hall for Elizabeth, to, *come please, right now*. They turn together to look at the housekeeper – her shift sleeves pushed up above her elbows, brow knitted, beckoning Elizabeth as if she were some scullery maid, rather than the lady of the house.

'I'll be with you presently!' Elizabeth calls.

Then she looks back at Isabel, face softening. She takes a step forwards, relenting, closing the space between the two of them, slipping her arm through Isabel's. She steers them across the hall, down the corridor, through the kitchen and into the silence of the stillroom.

The place gleams, peaceably – quite set apart from the turbulence consuming the rest of the house. There is only the sound of their boots on the tiles as Elizabeth draws them into the room, and Isabel surrenders to being swept along. *This* is the person against whom she had hoped to lean. This woman with power, and a voice, in the village; this woman who flees.

'Here,' says Elizabeth, letting go of Isabel and reaching up into a cupboard for Mae's receipt book. 'And I'll have a key brought to you in the next few days. I'll arrange it with the warden. I'll instruct him to grant you access while I'm away.'

'You do not have to, you owe me nothing,' says Isabel, quietly.

'*We are friends*, and I wish to help,' says Elizabeth, reaching out, plucking at Isabel's sleeves with her fingers, as if unsure whether to embrace her or not. They look at one another, and although Isabel does not mean to be petulant and unforgiving, she finds herself looking away.

'I was going to bring you something,' says Elizabeth,

turning, skirting round the table. She opens a cupboard on the far wall, and retrieves something which she brings back to Isabel, holding it out in a closed fist. Isabel offers up her palm, and into it drops an elaborate, silver pomander.

It is weighty, a thing of substance, and Isabel imagines it around her neck, stuffed with spices, and aromatics. She could pack it with herbs to ward off illness, and to protect an unborn child. It is a generous gift, and thoughtful.

'It is beautiful,' she says.

But she cannot quite bring herself to say thank you.

CHAPTER TEN

Leah

I nudged myself between Isabel and Mother, leaning in just as they were – elbows on the table – to pore over Elizabeth's new book: The Queen's Closet Open'd.

'These are the receipts of Queen Mary,' said Mother, slipping an arm around me, pressing her lips to my coif, her other hand resting on the cover of her own tattered receipt book, fingertips tapping. 'Queen Henrietta Maria,' she whispered. 'Just think!'

Mae clambered onto the table, reaching for the new book, tracing her tiny finger beneath the words at the top of the page, sounding out the syllables: Water of Life. She was astonishing for a three-year-old, although it vexed me greatly to acknowledge such a thing. This particular ability – to read words from the page with no tutoring – had been witnessed by Mother's friends before, but still they stopped to wonder at it.

'It is impossible,' said Isabel, looking to Mother.

'I tell her once and she just remembers – whole words, and the letters that go together,' said Mother, as if that explained matters. Her grip on my arm tightened, and she rubbed and patted me there. I knew what she hoped to convey, but pulled away from her anyway, shaking off the warm pressure of her fingers.

'And her sense of smell is extraordinary,' said Isabel, reaching out to stroke the top of Mae's coif-covered head. There followed one of those silences I had observed before between the three women – where they spoke with only their eyes, in some language I had not yet been taught.

'Well, anyway,' said Elizabeth, 'her Water of Life receipt – I have tried it already.'

She jostled John from one hip to the other. He was pulling at his biggin straps, clawing at the little linen cap with desperate fingers.

'It is similar to my mother's, but with the addition of larks, rosa solis and dates, which I did not think provided any improvement. There is a Posset for the Heart-Sick that you should make a note of, it is quite different to anything I've come across. And I know that Johan likes anything with sugar; look here Isabel at her Confection of Three Peppers – white pepper, long pepper, black pepper, thyme, aniseeds, ginger and barbary sugar. I will gift you the sugar.'

'You are too generous,' said Isabel.

'Nonsense. You have looked after all of us so well, and shared so many of your own receipts.'

Elizabeth touched her fingers to the messy bulk of Isabel's receipt book.

'Her Gascoigne Powder too, I think is excellent,' continued Elizabeth. 'It is made with the black tips of crab claws. The snake skins are jellied in the usual way, but she suggests dipping one's fingers into saffron when making them up.'

Elizabeth walked awkwardly – little John balanced on her

pregnant bulge — to a cupboard at the far side of the room, from which she retrieved two small wooden boxes. Walking back, her bright green stockings flashed beneath her petticoats. She slid the boxes across the table: one towards Isabel, the other to Mother.

'For you!' she told them.

Isabel placed her quill onto the table and opened the box. Ten balls of compacted powder — marbled white and yellow — nestled in tissue paper that even I, with my unremarkable abilities, could tell was scented with orange blossom.

CHAPTER ELEVEN

Late Autumn 1665

*I*n the pale dawn light, the unexpected sight of him at the kitchen table makes Mae jump, the contents of her chamber pot sloshing – spilling onto the fabric of her slipped shoes. She is too distracted by his dark silhouette to care now about the mess. She can only stare, transfixed. She realises he is sleeping, his breathing deep and even. And she can just make out his arms folded beneath his head. His face is turned towards her, and if he were to open his eyes she would be the first thing that he would see.

He would hate that – to wake and find her there, to be caught unawares. She thinks about retreating upstairs, slipping her chamber pot back beneath the bed and hiding away until she hears him wake; it would be the safest thing to do. But something keeps her standing there, her gaze caught by the many leaves of paper spread across the table, and the tattered book: *Malleus Maleficarum*. This is the book that draws him down the stairs in the middle of the night, the book that calls to him in his search for certainty.

A candle has burned right down – melted into a puddle of wax as he studied, then slept. And she wonders what it was he was wrangling over. Telling herself he sleeps soundly, she turns and places the chamber pot on the bottom step of the stairs. Quiet as a little mouse, she creeps to the table. She draws breath and holds it in. Bending close to the open pages of the book, she reads: ... *a witch can foretell a death more subtly than a physician ... they may use their powers to cause diseases ... to stir up the winds ... they know more than they should due to the revelations of the spirits.*

Father has underlined: *they know more than they should.*

Mae realises then that what she took for leaves of paper or letters, are, in fact, pamphlets. She reaches for one. The quality of the print is poor, and difficult to read because of it. It tells of a witch trial in Northwold. She picks up another that recounts a trial in Great Yarmouth. As she picks up a third, she sees, beneath it on the table, something else: not another printed page, but Father's distinctive handwriting: untidy, heavily blotted. She bends closer, so she can make out what he has written.

When I saw to what she had given birth ...

She glances at him, checking that he has not stirred, that he sleeps on. She nudges at the scattered pamphlets to discern, beneath them, more of his writing.

... a monstrosity that could only be ...

She feels a creeping recognition, an unsettling of the past: *a monstrosity* flickering there in her memory, an accusation she had half-forgotten. She is confounded by the idea that he keeps a diary. It seems so unlikely; he complains frequently when making up his ledger about his swollen joints, how painful it is to struggle with his quill. And yet, it is, without doubt, Father's own hand on the page in front of her. It is, without doubt, a diary.

Leave it, she tells herself. *Do not risk his wrath.* And yet she cannot resist those few, spare sentences – exposed, bawdy as bare flesh. They are promises and riddles all at once, and how can she turn away from such temptation? She nudges again at the pamphlets, fingers trembling at the severity of her transgression.

. . . I understood what you were asking . . .

She startles as a moth collides with her cheek, dithering there at her face. She bats it away, snatching a look at Father. She turns back to the page.

. . . a sign of your covenant . . . the sky burning red with blood.

Enough, she tells herself. *Leave it alone now.*

She takes a step away, realising, as she does so, that she still has several pamphlets clutched in her hand. As she goes to put them back on the table, on top of his diary, she cannot recall what had been where: which pamphlet had she picked up first? She tries to calculate whether it matters, how likely it is that he will remember. She places them down, spreads them askew. Mouth dry, hands trembling still, she turns away from the dark silhouette of Father. It is only three steps from the table to the bottom of the stairs. And there, she bends for her chamber pot.

She leaves the house with a basket of tinctures slung across her arm and a list of neighbours to call upon. The air is so cold and damp it's as if the clouds have slumped from their place in the heavens. The jars knock one against the other as she walks, and a dart of movement catches her eye above the trees of Eyam Dale: a splinter in the vapid sky. It is a hawk, and she convinces herself that jesses hang from the bird's leg. Then the creature is gone – lost to the wooded valley below.

She pauses, the urgent task of delivering pills and tinctures wresting with her sudden longing to be with Rafe, flying Swift in the forest and forgetting herself. She makes her choice and climbs over the wall into the field, the sheep lifting their faces from the grass as she passes. She pulls her shawl tight against the drifting damp.

As she leaves the field behind and passes through a dense thicket, she hears in the distance – deep in the valley ahead – a singular laugh. She continues on, pausing when she reaches Cucklett Cave. Palm pressed to the ragged stone at the cave's entrance, she feels the dank air drifting from within it. In its depths she has always felt safe – although I never understood how. *It's so dark*, she would say. *As if the world has disappeared.*

The valley is just ahead of her; in three paces the ground plummets. From where she stands – on the edge of a precipice – she can look out across the tops of the trees. Her conscience is tugging her back to the village – to the pressing task of delivering medicines. But with every breath today she feels uneasy, and Rafe, she tells herself, would help her forget that unease. Instantly, she doubts herself; he is partly the cause of her turmoil, after all.

She hears a shriek of laughter from the valley again, and

leaving her basket at the cave's entrance, she descends slowly backwards down the ravine, grasping the familiar rocks that offer wrinkles and creases that fit her fingertips. She slithers in the wet vegetation, digging the toe of her boot into the soft, friable soil.

When she reaches the bottom — trees rising up on every side, the forest floor strewn with fallen leaves — she wipes her hands on her apron. Then she waits, and listens. After a while, she hears the chirrup of conversation and moves towards it. It isn't long before she sees Rafe and his friend, Alice Talbot, standing beneath the Great Beech: the largest tree in the forest. Its lowest branches dip towards the ground before rising up — as if the tree leans forwards, reaching out its ancient arms.

Mae waits, held back by some curiosity. She hears their laughter — hers, then his. They are shifting around the enormous trunk, stepping from one gnarly root to another. After several turns of the tree Alice stops, and twists to face Rafe. She reaches for his hand — the one not hidden in his leather glove — and lifts it to her bodice, pressing it to the soft flesh of her chest. Even at a distance Mae can feel the sudden stillness between them. Alice releases his hand and he withdraws it.

Mae looks to the sky through the canopy of branches, waiting for any sign of Swift. Then she returns her gaze to Alice, who is leaning back, loosening her bodice, unbuttoning her shift, pulling the fabric apart. The words she speaks are just discernible — but only the rise and fall of them, their playfulness.

Mae feels a shift in the pit of her belly.

But then a dart in the corner of her eye distracts her: a glide so smooth and quick she nearly misses it. She whistles without thinking – quick and fierce – raising her fist, understanding the trespass when the hawk adjusts his flight and lands without fuss upon her bare flesh. He sinks his talons into her skin, and she clenches her jaw against the pain, looking to Rafe. He has turned, like his hawk, towards the sound of Mae's call, and for the first time in weeks she feels a rush of pleasure. Enough to make her laugh out loud.

Beyond the cave and the dense thicket, where the trees open out onto the field of sheep, they part company with Alice. Rafe and Mae walk through the centre of the field, back towards the village, whilst Alice skirts the edges of it – disturbing some pigeons that rise with a flustered clap of beating wings. Swift swivels his head towards them – eyes ablaze – to watch their slow, laboured ascent.

Mae sucks the stinging wound on her wrist, licking the blood from her skin.

'You deserve that,' says Rafe.

He says it without looking at her.

She smiles, delighted still, remembering the soft, precise landing, the power of the clenching talons. She laughs again, the joy bubbling up inside of her. It makes no sense – she ought to be fretting about the pills and tinctures that should have been delivered by now. She ought to be ruminating on Father's fractious mood; he detests it when he cannot sleep, and detests it even more when he sleeps by chance. He had seemed unconvinced when she came down so late from her bedchamber asking forgiveness for sleeping in: *I stayed up sewing past midnight*, she lied. *Wasting the candlelight?* had been his reply. He had put his hand to her shoulder, pressing his fingers into the tender spot just beneath her collarbone, and it took all her composure not to pull away from the pain of it.

Rafe stops walking, and Mae turns to look at him.

'That was Alice,' he says. 'I was not . . . I did not . . . '

She looks at him stolidly, realising that she is, in fact, a little angry with him.

'I *care* not,' she says.

He steps towards her, and reaches for her hand, turning it over in his. His fingers feel warm against hers which are tingling with cold. He looks at the soft flesh of her inner wrist where Swift's talons have pierced her skin. He brings that flesh to his mouth, closing his lips around her injuries, pressing his tongue to them.

CHAPTER TWELVE

Wulfric's Diary

March 19th 1650

Florence finds herself with child once more. I can only pray that you will bestow upon me the gift of a boy – to learn the ways of his father.

Leah is causing constant trouble in the household, although Florence is obsessed with her. There is a new carelessness about her that concerns me, as if her calling has been completely forgotten. It taints the whole household at times – all whimsy and laughter.

Isabel Frith is forever bothering us, and only seems to make the matter worse – what am I to make of the woman? Even Reverend Stanley seems to have fallen under her spell – and he is aware of her sinful past. He seems quite prepared to tolerate her superstitions – her amulets, incantations and incense, and her devotions to St Margaret of Antioch. Florence is most pleased with her, and won't hear a word said against the woman. Is it gratitude that ought to fill my heart? My dear wife tells me it is so. But I am full of gratitude to YOU my Lord, and make sure to remind Florence of this; you have spared her the shame of a barren womb.

I have gifted Thomas Stanley five copies of the Geneva Bible, for him to distribute to those most in need of your guidance. I hope to do the same each year. We are willing, Florence and I, to make sacrifices in order to spread your word. Just as Cromwell fills his soldiers' pockets with your scriptures – and look how the war unfolds now in our favour! – I endeavour to fill the hearts of my neighbours with the same: the word of God untainted by the mysticism of Rome.

I see that Florence could keep a little more to prayer throughout the day. It does not pass my notice how she takes to singing all manner of nonsense, when she could as well be lifting our hearts with the purity of hymns. But surely the birth of a child, and the promise of another, will help to sanctify her life a little? Surely through the pain of childbirth she will bear her share of Eve's sin? And through that most exquisite struggle know you, and love you all the greater, and unshackle herself of Eve's influence?

Is it so?

A good midwife encourages the women in her care to look in that direction, imploring them to give themselves up to their own suffering, and to be an example to others. I have heard no such thing from Isabel Frith. Does she offer this guidance in the dark privacy of the birthing chamber? Does she remind women to be grateful for their pain? I am hardly reassured by what I see. It is only for Stanley's sake – because he asks me to stand down on the matter – that I let it lie.

CHAPTER THIRTEEN

Early Winter 1665

The garden is frost-bitten, shrouded in mist.

In the kitchen the cauldron is at a constant boil, and the white-washed walls weep with condensation.

Father spoke in church on Sunday about the early signs: loss of appetite, change of countenance, bitterness of the mouth, a cloying sweetness in the nose. He impressed upon the whole congregation – his eyes moist with pleasure as he spoke from the pulpit, heart fluttering with self-importance – that prayer and preventatives offered the greatest protection. Therapeutics are not to be relied upon. *Do not come to me once you are stricken*, he seemed to be saying. *Come before, or not at all.*

He advised rosemary flowers to be burned upon the fire. For herb broths to be made with bugloss leaves, succorie, and endive. He urged his neighbours to avoid excess and pursue moderation in all things. *Look to the air you breathe, and let it not be foul or corrupt*, he told them. *Eat with care. Pay attention to motion and rest in equal measure. Say your prayers and sleep well. Keep all passions under control.*

But Father fails to practise what he preaches.

He sleeps poorly, and his passions simmer within him, erupting frequently, haphazardly, like pustules on the skin. They burst and blister.

Mae does her best to be a balm to his agitation. She does not attempt to soothe him with words (which would only agitate him further), but with service. She infuses camomile flowers, valerian and verbena, and adds the infusion to his evening mug of ale. She rises early and organises the kitchen. She prepares ingredients for the day ahead. She bakes bread and biscuits before it is even light, and crushes rose petals and lavender so the air they breathe is pure. Tending the fire, she ensures it is neither too hot nor too feeble for their daily preparation of the Great Medicine. This complex elixir is what nearly all the village wants; it is what all the *better sorts* want, at least: it does not come cheap. By the afternoon the air in the cottage hangs thick with rue, and sage, ginger and nutmeg. The mortar is stained yellow from saffron. The Venice Treacle is measured out with care; there will be no more when it is gone; seventy ingredients are used in its preparation and many of them are now hard to obtain, coming as they once did from London.

A few days ago Father had turned to her as they worked together at the kitchen table. She had been tasked with making a Decoction for Inward Decay, and he had left her to it. On his face he'd worn a rare smile; she had flinched when she noticed it. 'This is what you wanted, is it not?' he'd said, gesticulating to the receipt book she was referencing. 'To play at apprentice?'

She had nodded, swallowing, wrong-footed by that smile of his. If she'd been certain he wasn't mocking her she might have told him just how much she wanted it. She might have told him what it feels like when she makes a medicine from start to finish, assessing the exact quantities for herself, *feeling* it in the whole of her body when the balance is right: her bones waking up. She'd have told him, *I would make a worthy apprentice.*

And as if she *had* said it – and as if he shared her joy at the prospect – he had laughed a laugh that was even rarer than his smile.

Throughout the day the village comes knocking. Father keeps all discourse on the doorstep, and drifting through the cottage daily come the same conversations, stale as the air is fresh. Whether green walnuts gathered in June are effective, as everyone says? Whether Gascoigne Powder is worthy of the price? Might they pay him a little now and a little later? They ask about toads and other poisons – how to keep them close to the heart, and for how long? Whether a little arsenic might protect the body by heating it, drying it out, keeping the putrefaction at bay. *Might it?* As if he is an oracle and God whispers directly in his ear.

In this way he conducts his business, passing out packages and small stoppered jars, requesting coins be left on the doorstep.

But by the early evening he slouches in his chair, all angles and bones. He prays aloud and fervently. His long, greying hair falls in front of his face like an oily veil. He swallows large quantities of elderberry and yarrow to induce sweating and cleanse the body from within. To heighten the effect he draws close to the fire – his dark eyes closing, his gaunt face contorting with discomfort. He smells sour, like spoiled milk. And his colour, when she catches a whiff of him, is the brightest white – an empty, desolate, blinding colour that Mae has never grown accustomed to.

As he sweats in his chair by the fire, in the grip of his diaphoretics, thoroughly distracted, she allows her thoughts to meander from leaf to herb, from flower to spice, from one shade of red or blue or yellow to another.

What preventative have they not yet discovered? What therapeutic is waiting to be made?

I could be useful.

Why does he not see that? She understands he wanted a son, and that making do with a daughter causes him great frustration. But a daughter is all he has, and if he paid attention he might see she could be helpful to him. Not just as a pair of hands that chops and pulverises and measures under instruction, not just as a helpmate trained to follow a receipt and understand its uses, but as an assistant permitted to contemplate the task, the problem, the challenge at hand and offer suggestions.

We must try urgently for new remedies.

Does he not see it? How does he not see it, when the fact of it nudges at her, incessant as lice? They should be looking for something new, something *that works*. They should, because they can. The burden is heavy. But it is also as enticing as the light that glimmers on the river at the end of the day. It dances, lifting her heart.

What if, it asks. *What if?*

If God provides, she reasons, then somewhere there is a cure for this pestilence that stalks them. The Doctrine of Signatures tells them it is so. Somewhere is a plant or combination of plants that will provide a cure. Some process will draw out that cure – whether it be steeping, distilling or infusing. Some method will administer it – poultice or plaster or pill. It may be a simple remedy, or a compound. She does not yet have the answers. But she knows they are there, waiting to be rooted out.

As Father perspires in his chair, Mae muses on a variety of sought-after ingredients that she does not have access to: rarities that cost twenty, thirty, forty pounds an ounce. The pestilence is ruinous, a furious God; it seems reasonable the solution will be rare and expensive. *Let us offer Gold. Let us slay the unicorn.*

But no. The plague may be God's work, but it is also the basest of ailments. It is mould. It is rot. It is not crushed pearls she should be contemplating. To fight it, perhaps she should match it like for like, with herbs that bring forth in her mind the same dark shade of green that the plague brings forth.

Angelica and chervil.

The short, thick, blackish root of devil's-bit, boiled in wine.

Dove's foot and juice of foxglove.

Alert with the implication of this new line of thought – the possibility of matching a remedy's colour with the colour of the ailment itself – she puts down her mending and rises from her chair. Leaving Father by the fire, she goes through into the pantry. She reaches for bunches of dried herbs, and stoppered jars. She bruises leaves between her fingers and brings them to her nose. She pours one decoction after another onto her bone spoon and lifts it to her lips.

She samples preventatives, and curatives. She smells, and she tastes. And another realisation dawns, something she is surprised not to have noticed before.

She takes a quick look into the kitchen at Father – his face slick with sweat, his eyes closed. His breathing is slow and even, and she guesses that he sleeps. She nips past him, through into the parlour. She fetches ink, paper, quill. On her way back, she imagines him pleased with her, and wonders what it will take. *Would* he be pleased if she conjured a therapeutic that actually worked – if she created something to give the village hope?

Back in the pantry she clears a space on one of the shelves, lays down her paper and quill. Then she starts again – lifting jars to her nose. She needs to be certain that her earlier realisation is sound. And, as she continues, little by little, she realises that it *is*. For several years she has known – despite Father being loath to confess it – there are therapeutics that work, and those that don't. What she has failed to notice before now, though, is that the colour-alchemy of every remedy she would swear by is magnificent: a skin-tingling, fulsome, resplendent blend of colours. The emerald green of St John's wort and Peruvian bark (for melancholy), the black-brown-gold of milkweed and figwort (for warts), the burnt orange and copper of willow bark and tormentil (for pain of all kinds). *Eye water, emollient gargle, saline draught, infusion of linseed, diuretic julep.* So pleasing is each burst of colour, so *right*, that they make the bridge of her nose ache.

Could she define what makes the colours so pleasing? Why they work so well together? As she tries to imagine explaining it, she can't.

She takes up her quill, thinking of the plague, and makes a list of possible combinations. Substances to heat and dry. Poisons to prepare the body for the corruption that comes. She arranges them into groups on the page, imagining each combination and doing her best to intuit its scent-colour.

She records her predictions carefully, so they are legible. She fetches a second sheet of paper and fills that too.

Eventually she has to withdraw – to pull herself back, to quieten her thoughts. She checks on Father and finds him sleeping still. She pours him a draught of ale, adding his camomile infusion. Leaving it out on the table, so it is there when he wakes, she collects her sewing and (with her notes tucked beneath her arm) makes her way to bed.

The night has settled into itself by the time she hears Father on the stairs. The cold, white light of the moon is draped like lace about her bedchamber. She listens to the scuffle of his slipped shoes, to the clunk of his bedchamber door, to the fainter sounds of him preparing himself for sleep. After that, she listens to the silence being broken by the brush of moth wings on the wall.

Once the church bell has rung for midnight, then for one o'clock, her courage rises. She slips from her bed and returns with her notes to the kitchen. She lights a candle from the embers in the fire, perches on the edge of her chair and contemplates her earlier hypothesis. There is the rush and rustle of the wind at the casements, the night-time bone-creaking of the house.

She takes her candle with her into the pantry and brings ingredients slowly, quietly, methodically, back to the kitchen table. She ponders. She fetches the mortar, gripping it tightly, the pestle nudging back and forth as she walks. She stokes up the fire, and adds a faggot. Her heart pounds with the trespass – with fear, and excitement.

Consulting her previous notes, she groups herbs, spices, flowers and powders into little piles upon the table. She rubs them between her fingers. She chops and grinds. She wipes her hands on a damp cloth, and cleans her knife. She bends, inhales and tastes. She searches for a combination of ingredients which – when brought together, colours swirling – will glister in her mind like gunpowder.

She does not find that combination, but she fills another three pieces of paper with her observations. When she pauses, weary and contemplating bed, she begins to worry that Father will notice the missing paper. He might accuse her of stealing – it wouldn't be the first time. But as she looks down at them it is suddenly not the pieces of paper that matter so much as the words written on them. *Then* what would he accuse her of? He would, she knows, be furious, and offended by her attempts to create a new medicine. She had never considered confiding her idea to him, and looking down at her record of failed recipes and the list of possibilities to attempt next time, she knows she must see it through to the very end and be sure of the virtue of any new receipt before he has even the faintest knowledge of it. Then there is the prospect he might accept it from her. Presented as an accomplished fact she stands a chance of impressing him – of proving him wrong. As she stares at the inky page, she is unsettled that *that* is what she really wants. She has never felt it so clearly before. *Does* she want his admiration? Or does she only want to punish him?

She pulls on her boots, takes the key from the nail by the door and lets herself out into the darkness. The moon is nearly full, and she waits – the bitter wind whipping at the bones of her face – just long enough for the blackthorn tree at the end of the garden to assert itself in the gloom.

Clutching her notes, she steps carefully down the icy path. At the end of the garden, beneath the tree, the great wall rising up around her like a fortress, she bends for the spade. She puts the pieces of paper between her teeth, clenching them firmly, and digs the frozen ground as slowly and quietly as she can, so when the spade finally clatters against the buried box it is a sound too feeble to trouble her. She crouches, scrabbling in the soil. Opening the lid, blind in the darkness, she presses her notes amongst the hidden rags. As she does so she thinks of Father's diary, and how keen they are to hide from one another. She has looked several times over the last few weeks for his scrawled, leather-bound thoughts; searching the parlour in the dead of night, looking at the back of drawers and on the top of dusty cupboards.

Teeth chattering, she scrapes the earth back into the hole, pressing it down with the heel of her boot, covering the area with some mulched, icy leaves.

She glances towards the house, looking for movement or a candle now lit in Father's chamber. The sky in the east is lightening, blotting the stars, and if Father is down in the kitchen he will surely ask her, *why in the Lord's name have you been out in the garden? And how is it that you see in the dark like the devil?*

CHAPTER FOURTEEN

Leah

*M*ae's forehead was forever ruined with bruises. It was entirely her own doing; she refused to keep her pudding cap on – tugging it loose however carefully Mother tied the straps beneath her chin. As if by a quirk of fate she was also a climber – out of the crib before Mother was awake (throwing herself to the boards, unperturbed by the promise of injury). All throughout the day she heaved herself up onto the table or stools, or – worse – onto the pantry shelves, furious at the tangle of nursery gown and leading strings, and the awkward angle of the shelving.

One afternoon I found Mae on the third shelf in the pantry, cascading the contents of a jar into the folds of her grubby gown and down onto the floor. The husks of the spiny fruit, long dead, were colourless as bone. Within them, and spilling round about, were tiny black seeds. I picked up a dry husk, and turned it over in my hand – unperturbed, unimpressed.

But behind me, Mother cried out in alarm.

She prised open Mae's fists and checked the folds of her nursery gown, then snatched up both child and jar and took them to Father.

'Thornapple!' she said.

'It was on the third shelf.'

'But Wulfric, you know how she is! You must get a cupboard made for the poisons. Something she cannot get to, something with a lock and key!'

It was unusual to hear Mother speak to Father in this way.

He took the jar from her, passed it to me, and steered me into the pantry.

'Pick them up. Then wash your hands.'

He bent and scooped up several seeds from the floor. They stuck to the tips of his fingers, and he held them in front of my face. They looked like fleas, and I imagined them jumping away from me, making the task of collecting them quite impossible.

CHAPTER FIFTEEN

Winter 1666

The sound of voices from inside brings Mae to a stand-still halfway down the path. The thought of another person in their home unsettles her. Some calamity must surely have occurred; even the better sorts are kept on the doorstep these days, despite the bitter February snowstorms. The only exception is Thomas Stanley, but she cannot imagine the banished rector entering the village in broad daylight. And besides, the voice she can hear has the light, tumbling quality of someone much younger. And it gabbles nervously, which stirs her unease even further. She cannot imagine what has provoked this breaching of Father's unbendable rules, and she kicks snow quickly from her boots, anticipating as best she can the crisis awaiting. One thing she has learned these last few months is that every visitor means desperation of some sort; the village refrains in ever greater numbers from coming to Father with minor complaints.

Opening the door into the small lobby, she divests herself of her cloak. She unlaces her boots and reaches for her slipped shoes. Her face feels pinched by the cold, and wet from the falling snow. She presses her palms to her cheeks, then wipes them hurriedly.

She enters the kitchen and is confronted with a young man she recognises from the village – older than herself, cap in hand; he wears a clean, good quality shirt beneath his waistcoat. She tries to recall his name, and realises she has never known it. As the two men exchange glances, looking pleased with themselves, a terrible suspicion enters her mind, takes shape, then drops into place like a coffin into the ground. It settles there, weighty and final.

Father claps a hand to the young man's shoulder and she knows what he is about to say.

'Meet Sam, my apprentice.'

She cannot hide the depth of her disappointment as she looks between the two of them, her eyes settling eventually on this new face, as peachy-pink as Father's is grey.

'Sam *Chapman*,' says the boy, with a quick, downward nod.

'Pleased to meet you,' she says, forcing the words from her mouth.

His presence is the scratchiest wool against her skin, and she prickles. No matter her cold face, a fiery heat is burning within her and her disappointment is roiling now with her anger. How can he do this when she has been so dutiful and hardworking? What more could she have given him? Even her deception has been motivated by her desire to give *more*. To *be* more.

Tears sting in her eyes and she pinches herself to keep

them from overflowing. She will *not* cry in front of them. Her mind buzzes, hardly hearing Father as he talks through the manner in which they will, from now on, carve up each day. She tries to calm herself but is furious, not only that Father has cast her aside so easily and so soon, but that she failed to see it coming. How blind she has been! Too busy with notions of new medicines. Too obsessed with her own plans to consider *his*.

Father looks delighted with himself, laying down the law to his apprentice and pulling the matting from beneath her feet all at the same time. She is surprised by just how bereft she feels. This turn of events should not, in truth, be so shocking. His judgement and dismissiveness are, after all, so familiar. She hides from him because she cannot show herself. She keeps her hopes buried in a box at the bottom of the garden. He has never once said to her: *tell me what you know.*

This week, Father explains, Mae will provide Sam with the rudiments of his education: the differences between decoctions, tinctures and infusions. How to pick and dry herbs correctly. How to chop. How to grind. What might constitute *coarse* and *fine*. Some guidance as to the contents of the several hundred jars that line the pantry shelves. This, he presumes, is the extent of her knowledge.

The following day Father is speaking from his chair by the fire as Mae demonstrates to Sam how to press simples and compounds into pills. She has already, under Father's exaggerated instruction and Sam's equally exaggerated watchful eye, measured out the ground ingredients – milk thistle, aconite, golden seal, buckthorn bark — before combining them with gum arabic. She points now to the correct spatula for him to bring from its hook on the wall and shows him how to smear the thick, dry paste into the brass mould. She takes his freckled hands and presses them upon the wooden paddle.

'Do not rock, press it evenly.'

He nods enthusiastically, smiling at her with his eyes as well as his mouth. It is quite overwhelming being so close to him. He is all amber and gold, like the sun's rays at the end of the day. She feels nauseated by the sticky heat of his hands beneath hers, stifled by the bulk of him: this cheery boy in the body of a man. He constantly wants to pass things, fetch things, hold things. Fidgety as a fledgling. His pale eyelashes flutter, catching the light. His auburn hair — spattered with ground liquorice root — falls in front of his eyes.

Mae eases the rolls of paste from the mould and, taking a sharpened knife, she cuts the pills smoothly, briskly, perfectly angled, holding her breath. She straightens and passes the knife to Sam so he can try the precise rhythm for himself. He takes the blade and begins to cut. The part of her that settles, satisfied, at a thing done *just so* wishes him to master his lessons with ease; there is nothing more gratifying than freshly cut pills lining the table in a warm kitchen. But the other part of her — the part of her that resents this earnest, ignorant boy — wishes for his fingers to be thumbs, and for his brain to be forever befuddled with blood, phlegm, yellow bile and black. With mouse-ear and mugwort, moneywort and moonwort. With liverwort, spleenwort, toothwort and lungwort. With where to find these herbs, and if it be root, stem, leaf or flower he must take. Whether from a specimen in sun or shadow, at dawn or dusk.

'No,' she says, instructing him. 'A little thinner.'

She is leaning on the table, shift sleeves rolled to her elbows as she watches him cut the pills. He stands to his full height and takes a breath, grinning at her, bending again, trying once more.

'Better,' she says, nodding, waiting for him to finish the lot.

It isn't Mae that Sam looks to, though, when he is finished, satisfied with his efforts; it is Wulfric. Father obliges, coming to the large table in the centre of the kitchen. He nods approvingly, giving Sam a smile. And Sam looks to him with a face full of pride. Mae turns away, her disappointment no less heavy than it was yesterday.

At that very moment, full of his own bitterness, Rafe scurries the perimeter of the apothecary's garden wall – half running, following the curve of stone, the wind gusting against his tear-stained face. The wall is too high to be climbed over, but there is a fox run beneath it, in the furthest corner near the blackthorn tree. It has always been his way of coming to the house without announcing himself at the front door.

Father has never once heard the flicker of grit at the kitchen casement: the *tck* of stone against glass. Mae is surprised, though, when Sam's young ears do not hear it either. Not the first time it happens, nor several moments later when it happens again. Nor the third time, when Rafe gets impatient. As if there is no tiny piece of stone at all. No sound to be heard. As if Rafe's signal seeps through from another place to her alone. In the same manner that Swift comes to her in the forest – appearing on her wrist from nowhere.

She cannot go to Rafe immediately. But some twenty minutes later, when there is a lull in Sam's lesson, she goes outside to see to the hens. And that is where she finds him, in his usual spot behind the henhouse. He stamps his feet, his hat pulled low over his brow.

She sees that something is wrong. 'What is it? What's *happened*?'

'Not the pestilence,' he says straightaway, and her tightened muscles relax a little. She notices his eyes are tear-blurred and puffy.

'Then *what*?'

He looks upwards into the grey sky and shakes his head.

'I don't have long,' says Mae, glancing towards the house. 'I'm sorry.'

'They want to send me away. They broached it this morning.'

'Send you away *where*?'

'To Sheffield. To be apprenticed to a watchmaker there.'

Mae wants to put her arms around him, to bury her face in his lavender-scented hair. She twists her apron in her hands and the silence between them takes on a shape of its own. She cannot think of a thing to say. *Everybody leaves*, she thinks. *Why does everybody leave?*

'I tried to tell them I don't want to go, but Johan says it makes sense – that I have better opportunities if I go to a proper workshop for my training. Better than if I stay with him.'

You are my only friend, she wants to say. *My only real friend.*

'I *truly* don't want to go,' he says.

'But you *do* want to be a watchmaker.'

She sounds so pragmatic, as if she does not care so much one way or the other. And she wonders why she does not tell him that she too, *truly*, does not want him to go. *Tell them no!*

'Have you agreed to it?' she asks.

He shrugs.

'It will take some time to arrange,' he says.

Mae stares at him, thinking reluctantly of all that unfolds in the kitchen behind her. She cannot dally too long. *I also have bad news to share*, she thinks. *There is a boy who knows nothing in my kitchen, messing with my things.* But she cannot tell Rafe that now; she does not have the time. It seems likely that surely any moment Father will open the kitchen door for her, will shout for her irritably, catching sight of Rafe if he is not quick enough. She is fretting about all this when Rafe leans forward and plants a kiss on her mouth. His lips do not linger against hers, and before she has a chance to feel them there the moment is gone. He plucked that kiss from her. He snatched it. And she is dumb-founded that this thing she has thought so much about is no longer a moment to be dreamed about, but to be remembered: that brush of soft, dry lips. Such a fleeting thing. She puts her fingers to her mouth as if she might find something of him left behind: evidence of what occurred.

Then she looks at him, and he returns her gaze, easily, as if reading her thoughts and examining them thoroughly.

'I don't want you to go either,' she says, just to be clear – just in case he *cannot* read her thoughts.

And he smiles a small, quiet smile. As if that is all he needed from her.

Later that afternoon, once the pills have dried, Father tells them to fetch the necessary jars. Mae takes Sam to the pantry, and shows him where the empties are kept. He can reach the higher shelves without the need for the steps and she points to three jars for him to pass down. He passes them one by one and then pauses.

'What's in here?' he asks, pointing to the locked cabinet on the wall.

'Water hemlock, thornapple, spurge laurel, bella donna,' she says. 'The key is the one that Father keeps around his neck. It is the poison cabinet.'

She waits for him to ask more, but he says nothing further. *The palm of Christ* and *naked lady*. He will be told at some point about these poisons. *Henbane* and *meadow saffron*. It will be Father, no doubt, that shares with him their properties. Sam will be told how a drop or two of thornapple tincture will settle limbs that spasm. How a pinch of dried mandrake will relieve an agony in the gut. A poultice of palm of Christ will speed the healing of wounds in the most astonishing way. And a clumsily administered additional drop, or too generous a pinch, will bring death to the door.

CHAPTER SIXTEEN

Wulfric's Diary

November 18th 1650

It was surely your anger that brought the
storm. What am I to make of it all? Two days of
labouring, and nothing but a poor dead boy to
show for it. You see everything, Lord, so in heav-
en's name guide me. I only hope to piece things
together. Hailstones as big as walnuts! And the
storm raged throughout her labour to the very
end – two days and one interminable night. If
only that had been the end of it. Until the day I
die never will I forget the sight of Isabel Frith
with my poor dead boy, tainting his innocent
flesh with her sickly mysticism, whispering
some ritual over his body when it should have
been a baptism. What could I do but take the
child straight to Stanley? But it was all too late.

I see now that all was wrong from the very beginning. Was the storm raging then? I think not, for I would remember that. But it raged once the house was full of gossips. They were laughing! I can hardly countenance it! Perhaps the wind you sent was a mercy as much as a warning – it distracted me from the sound of their voices. And later it covered the sound of Florence's cries. But each time the wind abated, what I heard from the birthing chamber was nothing like salvation; it was struggle.

I am full of sorrow that I failed to advise Florence correctly – to remind her to turn to you throughout her labour – dismissed as I was by Isabel Frith. What folly persuaded me simply to obey? I should have stayed with Florence and focused her mind on how to best give herself to you.

And now she has lost her mind. I fear for her soul when I hear her gibberish. She fails to recognise her own daughter, and I am full of fright.

If the mind is the gateway to you – to your goodness – then I can only conclude that Florence is lost. Will she ever recover? Isabel assures me that she will – that sometimes after giving birth a woman loses her senses. But I trust her not. Stanley was shocked when I described matters to him. I have asked him, and the women too, to keep the details to themselves. I cannot bear to think of Florence being spoken of in the village. She has been so well regarded, but if this foul news were to spread – gaining substance along the way – there would be no coming back from it.

We await the doctor – a good man that I trust, although I hardly know what to tell him. She sleeps when I give her milk of the poppy, but when she wakes she asks for Leah – always asking. But as soon as I take the child to her Florence screams and cries, sending her away, insisting she is not our daughter at all! I fear she is quite mad. My poor lost Florence.

CHAPTER SEVENTEEN

Spring 1666

The tip of Johan's nose feels cold when he places his palm against it, and he pulls the blankets up to his face, shifting down into the warmth of the bed. He reaches out towards Isabel, groping gently for her hand. He stares into the darkness, thinking about the letter that lies on the floor, just inches away. He reads it all over again in his mind, imagining the words enunciated by Jacques himself, as if his friend were there in the bedchamber, interrupting the silence of the night.

Katarina has returned from the dead!

He had never met Rafe's mother; she was gone already when he first met Jacques at The Mermaid, in Lothbury, London. His friend, Tom Loomes, had introduced them and they had retired together to a coffee shop to smoke and drink and discuss the latest quarrels within The Clockmaker's Guild. Whilst Tom, and his brother-in-law,

John Fromanteel, talked big of the latest outrage, the sorry sight of Rafe nearly broke Johan's heart. Making no fuss, demanding nothing from the men surrounding him, the small child had repeatedly brushed tears from his cheeks. Johan and Jacques had tried to cheer the boy with tobacco, and sips of coffee, but nothing could raise a smile. *His mother has passed*, was all Jacques said, and it would be some time before Johan was to learn that Katarina was Jacques' sister, and that her *passing* was more conjecture than fact; Katarina had merely disappeared, but Jacques had thought it simpler for the child to think her dead. And this was surely her fate – she had, after all, been devoted to the boy.

After an hour or so of staring into the darkness, the line between the shutters at the window shows a glimpse of light, and the keenest of birds begin their morning chorus. Isabel shifts, turning towards him. He squeezes her hand and she threads their fingers together.

'Isabel.'

'Johaaan.'

There is a slow, treacly warning in her voice, as if she knows the words that totter on his tongue. Her desire to stay in the foggy comfort of half-sleep provokes him, and he pushes back the blankets, reaching for his tinder box from the floor. He goes to the window and opens the shutters on the half-promise of a little daylight. Prising up the lid of the box, he feels for the tatters of charred cloth and pulls at them, loosening the scraggy threads into something of a tangled nest, pressing the sharpened flint into it. In the gloom, he gropes for the cold steel, wraps his fingers around its smooth curve and strikes repeatedly at the stone.

'*Mmnnhh!*' Isabel complains.

'But I cannot sleep! My thoughts are a jumble.'

'Come back to bed, Johan.'

A spark catches, threads of charred linen fizzing in the darkness. Johan lowers the tinder into the box and blows upon it, coaxing a tentative flame, taking a splinter of wood and holding it to the heat. It takes, and he lights his candle. Slipping back into bed he reaches for the letter from the floor and positions the papers against his blanket-covered knees, holding a light to them.

'My dear friends,' mutters Isabel, eyes still closed. 'I write with the most astonishing news, which I am sure you will hardly believe. I hardly believe it myself and yet the evidence is right before my own eyes; a sorry sight if the truth be told, but nonetheless surely a gift from God in these times of trouble.'

Johan looks down at his wife.

'Would it please you for me to continue?' she asks.

'Do not tease me; I am quite justified.'

'But you have read the letter more than twenty times – we need not consult it again. Talk if you must! But do not vex me with spelling it out.'

Johan sighs, running a hand over his beard, looking down at the letter.

'I will have to go,' he says, getting to the very point of things.

'You cannot!'

Isabel pushes herself to sitting.

'If she is as sick as Jacques says, and medicines as scarce, then there is not a moment to lose,' says Johan.

'This is no time to leave your family, Johan. It moves through the village, house by house. We need to plan what we're to do before the summer comes.'

'But we're resolved on that, we are to stay.'

'And perhaps we are wrong. The Sheldons have left. Elizabeth is safe in Brampton. The Mompessons have sent their children to stay with friends in Yorkshire. Perhaps we should be doing similarly.'

'Where would they go? My *brother*? We've exchanged but two letters in the last ten years.'

'Fulwood is not so far. James would have them if he understood how bad things were,' says Isabel.

'We can be sure of no such thing. You know how it is between us. He is a stranger to the children, and what would he make of Rafe? I do not imagine he would countenance taking a foreign child into his household.'

'Then we should speak to cousin Fran. It's far enough away to know they would be safe, but close enough to visit.'

'It is hardly fair to ask – with six of her own and recently widowed.'

'She would be glad to help!'

'We should stay together. I don't know why I feel it, but I do.'

'And yet you speak of disappearing.'

'I will be gone a short while. A visit, nothing more.'

Isabel shakes her head. 'It is tempting fate for you to go. All is well if we are together; we are blessed in that regard, and you know it.'

She is speaking of their luck in matters of life and death; every child born to them has lived to thrive. It is a rare woman that can boast of such a thing, and at times she is burdened by the sorrow of her own good fortune – especially when she thinks of Mother, and myself so soon in the ground after her.

'You are my charm,' Isabel says. 'What if the baby comes when you are away?'

She thinks of how it has been before, and how she should like it to be the same again – the gossiping women gathering about her, Johan bringing candles, and warm spiced ale into which he will have whisked the freshest of eggs. He will have prepared their bedchamber for her lying in, sealing the gap between the shutters with wax. And when he hears his child's first cries he will take the shirt from his back and bring it to them. Together they will slip the baby into it, feet first, swaddling it tightly to keep the spirits away.

'The baby will not come for weeks yet, maybe six or seven,' says Johan.

'Feel the vigour of this child, and tell me that again.'

She pulls his hand towards her undulating belly, pressing it firmly against their squirming child.

Johan takes a long, divided breath; much of what he loves resides within these walls, but not everything, not everyone. Isabel knows this – has always known it.

'Things may not be as bad as we fear,' he says, moving his hand across the expanse of her stomach. 'There has not been a single death for three weeks now – I believe it may have passed.'

'Isaac Thornley is ill with all the signs, Johan. It has not passed at all. It rests, nothing more. It bides its time till the summer – as soon as the heat returns it will rage against us.'

Johan thinks about Jacques, and Katarina, his desire to

go to them – to be helpful, and loyal, and do what any true friend would do.

'It is a miracle that Katarina has returned,' he says. 'But all these years Jacques held strong his belief that she might. You and I thought him deluded, and he has proved us wrong. I *must* go to them with the medicines they need.'

'Please don't choose them over me,' Isabel says, quietly.

He looks her in the eye.

'I do not choose them over you. I am *here*. Both of us know the bargain we made, and how the heavens have smiled upon us because of it. I chose *you*. I chose all *this*.'

Johan feels the emotion at his throat and swallows it down.

'I have never prevented you from going to London,' Isabel says, eventually. 'When can you say that I have?'

Johan sighs a deep sigh, looking at his wife by the candlelight. She has never been the scolding sort, nor one to demand a thing that is not demandable. She sees how it is: Johan looks to her, and always, at the very same time, he looks away from her. Not just towards London and Jacques, and everything that matters there, but towards the other worlds he glimpses through his telescopes, his maps and books. And through his wrangling with time as well – the measuring out of it with clocks and stars and tides. He breathes in unison with his family and is glad of it. But these other things, they take his breath away.

'Katarina is Rafe's mother,' Johan says. 'We have to do what we can.'

'But the rector says London is coming back to life. The better sorts are returning. The markets are trading, the streets are busier by the day. So surely the physicians

have returned? And the apothecaries? It perplexes me that
Jacques cannot find the medicines he needs. He asks a great
deal from you in the name of friendship.'

'You know his main reason for writing and it was not for
the medicines.'

'And how can he ask for such a thing – to relinquish our
boy just like that? Does he not consider our feelings in the
matter – that we have come to care for the child?'

'Rafe will soon be indentured to a watchmaker,' Johan
says. 'He will be leaving us in any case.'

'It is hardly the same thing!'

She pulls back the covers, steps out of bed and reaches
beneath it for the chamber pot.

'I'm sure Jacques knows we love the boy. But his mother
has returned, Isabel. It is not possible to keep him here with
his mother returned.'

'But now is not the time; it is not safe for Rafe to go to
her while she lies in her sickbed.'

'But Rafe *must* go if Katarina rallies.'

Johan says these words deliberately, slowly, so that one of
them has said them.

'Yes,' says Isabel, pushing the chamber pot back beneath
the bed, rearranging her night clothes. '*If* she rallies, we'll
discuss it then.'

'And *I* must away to London in the meantime, and take
the medicines they need.'

Isabel does not respond.

'I must do what I can for Rafe's mother. We must have a
clear conscience in this matter, Isabel – we must not serve
ourselves.'

'Do you suggest I wish her ill? How can you? Although, where has she been? And who did she think would raise her child in her absence?'

Johan holds his hand out towards his wife. She ignores it, standing there beside the bed, wondering whether to slip back inside or make a start on the day.

'Come here, my love,' he says, pulling back the blankets.

But she turns away, bending for her clothes, removing her night coif.

Isabel looks through the congregation to the head that protrudes above all the others — in the front row, of course. She cannot see Mae, but knows she will be there, and that Father's hand will be resting on her shoulder, proprietorial fingers pressing through her cloak. Isabel feels the weight of that hand, and knows, just as I do, that with every day that passes the urgency to do something grows more pressing. She racks her brains, and hefts the possibility that Mae understands her predicament — she has always been quiet, and hard to judge because of it. But there is spirit in the girl too, she reasons, and such a quantity of wit.

Isabel looks along the pew to Rafe, thinking about Jacques' letter, and her confusion of feelings on the matter. *Of course* she wishes to keep Rafe close; he is more than just their ward — he is more like a son, and he is Jacques' flesh and blood. She understands what that means to Johan, and she feels it too; Rafe is the child that connects them all. It is natural to resist relinquishing him to London — to a woman they know so little about. But there is another reason for her resistance, and that reason is Mae. In her friendship with Rafe, Isabel sees something fruitful – some possibility that may provide the answer to her anxieties. They are old enough now, if she could find a way to broach the subject, to wrest the girl away for long enough and explain her plan – spinning sense from carefully chosen sentences. She has muttered these words of persuasion quietly to herself in the garden, and on the way to Bakewell for the market, and staring out of her bedchamber window, preparing herself to say them for real. But to who? Not to Johan! There was a time when she tried to share her anxiety that all is not straightforward with Wulfric – that a sickness eats away at him, and his home is no home at all, certainly no place for a girl.

But Johan had put her *ramblings* down to grief, and her pregnancy with Edward – she had ailed all the way through. He had been patient, but later on – as she persisted with her accusations – his patience had given way. *You cannot start rumours such as this. I like the man no more than you, but what you speak of is repulsive and I command you to hold your tongue.* It was the first time that Johan had commanded her to do anything, and it surprised them both.

He caused her to doubt herself, which has only meant more work for me. She waxes and wanes with the moon. There are times still that she knows, *really* knows. But there are times, too, when she doubts. She listens to her husband; why wouldn't she? He persuades her with his logic and the evidence he has seen with his eyes and heard with his ears. And from that place she loses all sight of the truth.

Johan herds his children out the church, keeping half an eye on the back of Father's head, keen to have a few words here in the open air, to save himself a visit to the house – that sparse, cold parlour with little more than two stools and a table, and those blasted books that make the world a tiny, vengeful place. The apothecary kitchen is a different matter, of course – what a joy *that* room would be to explore. He would be only too happy to wander the shelves, selecting jars and lifting lids, asking Mae question after question as he rifles through their cupboards. But he is always refused access to Father's place of work – offered instead a stool beside the empty hearth in the parlour.

Johan waits for his neighbours who, reassured by their Reverend, now seek instruction from their apothecary. Just a few yards from the church doors, they gather round him as Father holds his prayer book to his chest, and dispenses his advice for free. Johan watches the grateful, upturned faces – the nods of appreciation, the sincerest of smiles. These people love the man. He glances around for Isabel, knowing how it pains her for either of them to ask Wulfric for medicines. She had been perturbed when the key for Bradshaw Hall had not arrived as Elizabeth said it would. Then desperate, when she discovered the warden had succumbed to the plague. And furious when his wife refused to give Isabel either the key she had been promised or Elizabeth's address in Brampton.

When it is finally Johan's turn to step forward, the two of them play a game of geniality in amongst the graves. Father asks after the health of the children who, by now, have dispersed into the spring sunshine. Johan looks beyond Father, to Mae, who is picking coltsfoot flowers from between the headstones: posies of yellow, bright against the brown of her cloak. He feels a sense of relief when he looks at her these days – knowing that soon she will be old enough to marry, and to fly then from that cold, sparse parlour. He might not share Isabel's worries about Wulfric's blackened heart and perverse intentions. But he does see that Wulfric is the kind of father that diminishes his children, preferring them timid and subjugated. Johan wishes for Mae to be free as fervently as his wife wishes for it.

'I have been called away urgently to London,' says Johan. 'To a sick friend in need of medicine for the most debilitating fever, and persistent pains in the head, right *here*.' Johan presses two fingers to the place just above his ear. 'On both sides, and most unrelenting.'

Father's eyes are flitting around the churchyard, nodding at people as they pass.

'Violent dreams?'

'She sleeps fitfully.'

'A mother?'

The question takes Johan by surprise and he hesitates before nodding, hoping that what he thinks, all of a sudden, is not somehow discernible. In the background, behind Father, Rafe has joined Mae, both of them now collecting the spindly stems. Perhaps Father senses Johan's divided attention for he turns and watches the young people together.

'Mae!'

She looks up, and Father beckons her with a small tug of his head. She comes to them, Rafe following. Isabel appears too, Frances by her side.

'What will you do with those?' Johan asks Mae.

She looks down at the flowers in her hands, then she looks to Father.

'I will make a juice from some of them, and dry the rest,' says Father. 'They are good for a hot cough, wheezing or shortness of breath. Dried, they can be added to tobacco and taken into the lungs for the same benefits. Distilled and mixed with elderflower they will bring a fever down.'

'But, what *else*?' asks Isabel, snatching a look at Father, before reaching for Frances' coif fastenings. Frances bats her mother's hands away, re-tying the fastenings herself. Isabel pauses, then answers her own question with, 'The same infusion you might prescribe for a cough can be soaked into cloth and applied to a woman's privy areas after birth – to relieve soreness and burning.'

Mae looks up at Father anxiously, noticing that he clenches his jaw in irritation.

'Come tomorrow,' Father says to Johan. 'Everything will be ready after breakfast.' He turns away and Mae follows, squeezing both hands into fists, ignoring the soft stems she crushes in amongst her fingers. She clenches her jaw, just as he does. And when they are home and she has an excuse for it she pulls the pestle and mortar into the centre of the table and pounds those weeping stems until they are nothing but liquid.

CHAPTER EIGHTEEN

Leah

The folded linen, the colour of teeth, held all his curves of bone and half-moon nails. It held his smears of black hair and the empty space where his spirit would have lived. It held everything he was, and all that was missing. Father took the linen from the house, with not a glance at Mother. The words that rose in my throat, then slipped away: but we never saw his eyes.

Isabel brought water, and washed Mother's legs. She brought clouts and cleaned away the blood on the floor. She used a clean cloth for Mother's face and re-lit the herbs, filling the air with the scent of sage and chasing off the cloying sweetness of Mother's travail. But for all the washing and rinsing, and for all the sage, when Isabel moved past me I could still smell the thyme oil on her hands.

Mother did not seem to need me. I stood by the open casements, watching Isabel clear away all signs of the last two days. By the time she had finished, Mother looked as if she was settled in bed for nothing more than a good night of sleep. Her damp hair had *dried, and Isabel had brushed it out and tied it up. The three of us were silent, and still. Every hour the church bell rang out – bright as the silver frost and clear as the starry sky.*

I woke in the morning after a dream of dragons, to find my breath of fire was real after all – I lay in bed blowing smoke from my fearless mouth, making of myself a powerful beast. My dragon heart lifted from its bell tower, just a singular launch into an endless, cloudless sky, and I pushed away the sheets and coverlets, swinging my legs out of the warmth of an imagined fire-nest, and into the chill of the bedchamber. I saw the few steps from my own chamber to hers before I took them; I saw her smile, and felt sure that Father was making a caudle for her down in the kitchen: whisking oatmeal, eggs and cream together, adding them to wine and saffron. I imagined Mother sharing her caudle with me – spooning the warm sweetness into my mouth. I imagined all this before I even reached her chamber door – which was flung wide just as it had been the night before, and the casements too. The air was shifting right through the house, and I shivered. I wondered whether to say that I'd felt him leaving – that I was sure he had gone, so we could close the casements now to keep the winter out. But clearer than that knowing, was another knowing: this was not the time for words. Father was pacing and praying. I tried to discern the prayer he had chosen as if it would tell me something, but his words were tumbling too fast.

Mother looked past me, even as I moved right in front of her. But then she began to see me – I saw it happening, her eyes focusing. I reached out to her and she snatched her arm away.

'Who are you?' she whispered, almost too quietly to hear. Father had not heard, or he did not care, for he continued to pace, muttering his prayers.

'Who ARE you?'

Now he heard. He stopped his pacing and turned to us.

'Mama?'

*She was pulling the coverlets up to her chin, shuffling backwards
to get away from me.*

'It's me, Mama. It's Leah.'

She was shaking her head, eyes wide with terror.

'You're not my daughter!'

CHAPTER NINETEEN

Spring 1666

*E*lizabeth Bradshaw may have fled with her children to Brampton, but she returns from the county of York in the half-light of Isabel's dreams. They work together in the stillroom, lighting braziers and stoking furnaces and laying wet rags over curved, hot copper. They strip dry leaves from brittle stems, and wrap twine around bunches of mint and marjoram. They wade through drifts of snake skins and piles of bones and pelt, pouring waters – distilled, perfected – into shapely bottles. And they forge keys in the furnace – thick, heavy keys. *I'm sorry about the blasted warden*, Elizabeth says, with a roll of her eyes. And they push candied plums into one another's mouths.

The dreams are so real that Isabel feels the disappointment each time she wakes. Elizabeth is still in Brampton. There is no blasted key, and no address. There are seven cold hearths in Bradshaw Hall, and a pantry emptied of perishables. There is a well-stocked stillroom, shut away behind so many locked doors. She imagines it all in darkness – no sunlight bouncing off the glass funnels and pewter stills. She conjures all the shapes as shadows. And she thinks of Mae's receipt book that she left behind in a moment of forgetfulness. She imagines it on the table where Elizabeth placed it; lost now in that abandoned house.

From the warmth of her bed, with her eyes closed, she drifts repeatedly to the stillroom. She reaches for a multitude of herbs and flowers, powders and pastes – hyssop, thyme, angelica and aniseed. Violet flowers, rosebuds, camomile and thistle. Chervil, cowslips, tansy and wormwood. And when she opens her eyes she contemplates the spring weather so late to arrive and the bleakness of the frozen forest floor. She remembers the precious, expensive ingredients they sent away for, waited patiently for – things they used sparingly, seeking permission from one another. Isabel fantasises about her friend's return, but what good does it do? And in the meantime, she can only grit her teeth when she visits Father for the medicines she needs for the labouring women of the parish.

After breakfast she goes to Johan, watching him from the doorway for a moment or two, bent over the upturned face of a clock, turning a tiny screw.

'I'll go for the medicines. I want to see Mae,' she says. 'Something is not right, I am sure of it.'

Johan leans back in his chair, reaching for his pipe.

'Imagine living with Wulfric,' he says. 'If that man were *my* father, nothing would ever be right.'

Isabel steps into the parlour, going to the table to stand before him, wanting to spill her words into his lap and have him scrabble to catch hold of them. She is tired of worrying about this all alone.

'You love her, just as I do.'

Johan nods, looking up into her face.

'And you have said it, nothing would ever be right living with that man. Nothing *is* right, Johan.'

Johan reaches out for her hand, and she grapples with where to begin.

'He is . . . such a despiser of women.'

Johan shakes his head a little. It is a tiny movement, hardly noticeable, but Isabel understands from it that he will not catch her words at all; he will let them drop like dry soil through his fingers. She tries to warn herself off, to say nothing further. But she cannot help herself.

'Remember how he was after Florence died? The things he said? Not only about her, but about me.'

She is careful with her words, afraid of antagonising him.

Johan waves the hand that holds his pipe.

'The man was grieving.'

'It's more than that – there's a darkness there, and Mae feels it too, I'm sure of it. I truly believe she's no fonder of him than I am. What does *that* tell you?'

Johan lets go of her hand and reaches for his tobacco, opening the box.

'Please, spare us both this conversation,' he says.

'The man is a brute, hiding behind that God of his.'

'Can you not content yourself with disdain? Do we have to demean ourselves with name calling and accusations?'

'I've accused him of nothing.'

'And yet I know where you go with this.'

'So discuss it with me! You are the only person with whom I can talk this through.'

'I do not wish to talk it through. Since Florence died, Wulfric has been nothing but genial. I am the first to confess I do not care for the man. But this obsession you have with him – it has gone too far.'

'It is not *my* obsession we should concern ourselves with. You've heard how he talks of witches, how he accused *me* after Florence died. Such an accusation, and yet you forgive him for it. Why? You've seen the books in his parlour.'

'All manner of books languish on our collective shelves!'

'You were not there when his sons were born. You did not see how he looked at me afterwards. How he looked at Florence.'

'He was *grieving*. And what a shock, for Florence to give birth to a child so unusual. Any man would have been full of horror.'

'It wasn't horror, Johan – it was something else.'

'Something *else*?'

Isabel knows from his tone that she would be wise to leave off from speaking further. He pulls at the tangle of tobacco, stuffing some into his pipe, putting the stem between his lips.

'I do not like her there with him,' she says. 'I cannot put it any other way than that. He is not what a father should be. He is a brute, and full of perversity.'

'You cannot say such a thing!' Johan throws up his hands. 'He's had more than his share of bad luck, and we have all the good fortune. All things considered we're blessed to be well-regarded in this village.'

He looks up into her face with a knowing expression, eyebrows raised, reminding them both of the past and how close Isabel had come to ruin as a girl of sixteen.

'You have worked tirelessly to prove yourself,' he says. The clay knocks against Johan's teeth as he shifts his pipe from one side of his mouth to the other. 'So do not give people a reason to doubt you now. Do not give them an excuse to remember. For this is what you do if you start a rumour such as this. They will question you as keenly as they question him. They will rake things up, and query your judgement. You know they will. Two decades does nothing to diminish the memories of the village gossips.'

'I do not intend to speak of it more widely. I only wish to discuss it with my husband. My beloved husband who chooses flight to London to escape the trouble that is about to find us!'

The wretched betrayal of tears sting at her eyes, and she senses Johan softening. He puts his pipe down, unlit, onto the table, and stands to embrace her. Pulling her against him, wrapping his arms about her, standing to the side of her large, taut belly, he presses his mouth against her head, kissing her repeatedly.

'You upset yourself,' he says, eventually. 'The baby coming . . . it reminds you. That is all this is. You haven't talked this way for years, and now it all comes back.'

Isabel sighs and keeps her head rested against Johan's shirt, waiting for her tears and frustration to subside.

*

Isabel takes a clay jar and drops a coin inside; a coin dated 1651, the same year as Mae's birth. She dribbles a little oil to cover the coin, adds a sprig of lavender for love, and two drops of sandalwood, for protection. She presses the wax stopper into the top and slips the jar into the leather pouch that hangs from her belt.

The sun is flaring behind scattered clouds, and it feels as if spring might finally be on its way. It is a relief for the cold weather to be relenting a little, despite their collective fears of what the warmth will bring.

Isabel makes sure to be quiet. She pushes open the small gate, the timber soft and smooth from all the years of coming and going: loved ones of the dying, wittering hypochondriacs, travelling tradespeople, neighbours and their visitors. They come for their medicines, tobacco, coffee and herbs. They came once upon a time for comfort too, from Florence – her gentle hand upon theirs. Still they hope for something of the sort, although they ought to know better by now.

Isabel enters and silently shuts the gate behind her. She casts her eyes across the ground, searching for the perfect spot of soil in amongst the herbs – somewhere near the path that she can get to easily. There she crouches, shielding her hands from view with her cloak. She takes a spoon from her pouch and digs a hole, presses the clay jar into the ground and covers it with soil. Then she makes a show of tying her boot, before standing and walking to the door.

From the pantry, Mae hears the knocking.

'See who it is!' shouts Father. He is explaining to Sam about the humoral system, and the two of them are sitting at the kitchen table looking at a diagram of the human body.

Mae goes through to the lobby, pulling the door closed behind her to keep the warmth of the kitchen in. The key hangs from its nail and, taking it, she slips it into the lock, turning it easily, the ironwork of the door handle cold in her palm.

Isabel is backlit by the sun, her eyes the bright blue of forget-me-nots.

'Mae.'

'I cannot ask you in.'

'You explained last time.'

Mae searches for something to say, wrong-footed by her swirling emotions. She remembers Rafe's news about the watchmaker in Sheffield, and cannot help the nip of bitterness she feels towards Isabel. Her resentment, though, has been building since the loss of her receipt book – forgotten and left behind in Bradshaw Hall. Since the broken promise of a key. Since, too, the tin box and the instruction to bury her rags, which is yet to be explained to her. *You* don't have to live with him, she has wanted to say. *It is all very well for you to antagonise him in the churchyard with blenching talk of a woman's privy area. It is* I *that must return home with him. It is* I *that must withstand his terrible humours.*

'Your things are ready,' she says curtly, and turns to go for them, but Isabel grabs her arm.

'What troubles you?' she asks.

Mae shakes her head, trying to look Isabel in the eye.

'I should fetch your things,' she says. 'Father—'

'First, explain to me,' says Isabel, letting her go, stepping back a little, shaking her long silver hair down her back. 'What would your mother make of you now, hardly able to look me in the eye, flinching from me?'

'I do not flinch!'

'Something is not right – tell me what it is.'

Mae offers Isabel a stolid stare.

'What troubles you so?' says Isabel.

Mae has thought about this at great length just lately and an answer has not been easy to find. She had hoped a willingness from Father to see her as worthy of an education might have filled the emptiness she drags around with her. It had seemed that an apprenticeship might have shone a light into the darkness. But then Sam came, and snuffed out that light, leaving her to dwell on what Father has planned for her. He has, after all, never mentioned the possibility of marriage and she supposes he'll always want a helpmate in the house with him: a woman to do woman's work.

'I just—'

The door to the kitchen opens and Isabel arranges a polite smile upon her face. In that moment, feeling as if something has been lost, Mae regrets not having been more honest and straightforward.

Father must have heard Isabel's voice, for he holds her jars of pills and tinctures in his hands. Isabel holds out her basket at arm's length and he places the things into it. In return, Isabel holds out some coins, but he gestures for her to give them to Mae.

'Peculiar business,' he says, puffing his chest. 'Johan travelling to London when most men with any wit are fleeing it.'

'He goes to a friend in need, because he is a good man.'

Isabel looks Father in the eye.

'But *London?*' says Father.

It is the first time Mae has heard this news – that Johan is going away.

'Why London?' she asks, looking from Isabel to Father and back to Isabel, swallowing the unease that bobs in her throat at the thought of Eyam without Johan in it.

'He goes to Jacques, Rafe's uncle. The city is much changed and medicines are scarce.' She rearranges her cloak around her shoulders.

'Surely you heard the rector's sermon?' says Father. 'That we should stay and endure together what God has chosen for us? Our neighbours search for all manner of excuses to flee. But those who love God will stay, finding refuge and salvation in prayer.'

Isabel watches Father as he speaks, her chin lifted so she can look him square in the face.

'Johan goes to help a friend,' she says. 'I'm sure God will look kindly upon such an act.'

'You dare to suppose?'

'And you *do not*? Forever meddling, and sitting in judgement, as if you know better than the rest of us. How do you think God judges you, Wulfric? How is it that you think to rise above your neighbours? Good men and women getting on with their lives?'

'So full of venom, are you not? Where is God's love in you?'

'Oh! The hypocrisy!' she says, turning and walking away, leaving Father to slam the door behind her. Mae can hardly force her limbs to move, to be somehow nonchalant – to follow Father back into the kitchen. She busies herself with bottling pills, imagining Johan on a coach to London – a small, manageable chest his only luggage. She thinks, too, of the sparrowhawk, circling the skies above the stage coach and the cantering horses.

CHAPTER TWENTY

Wulfric's Diary

December 16th 1650

I had hoped once churched that Florence would seem like Florence again, so I find myself disappointed. We have left the worst behind and I am thankful, but there is some part of her that has not returned to me.

This last month has been the greatest test of my life.

I pray for forgiveness if her churching should have come sooner. It had been impossible though for her to leave the house for some weeks after the birth. She was not fit to be seen, and certainly not fit to receive the Lord's Supper.

One comfort is that she has finally taken Leah to her heart once more. Can I dare to hope that this particular affliction has passed?

What in heaven's name came over her – to see Leah as something other than her own flesh and blood? What trickery was that? Give me the blessing of patience, for I sometimes look at her face and hardly recognise the woman I married. She asks for Isabel repeatedly, and I can hardly refuse the woman entry when she comes, but I must confess to the darkest doubt. She is so well liked, but with no substance – no piousness or virtue – to explain such popularity. I find myself questioning whether there is some evil at work. She is a lover of magic and superstition. Still now she wishes to burn sage all through the house – as if we were papists or pagans! She is quite vexed that I will not allow such a thing. And I am visited by the cruellest of nightmares. I see my son flying through the air, naked and cold, with a hag stone tied about his neck.

As if all this was not enough, I lately find myself unable to do my duty as a Christian husband when my wife requests it. She asks for another child – convinced that the boy who was lost to us is not yet truly lost, that his poor, unsanctified soul is waiting for another chance of salvation. It seems ungodly to entertain the idea, but I confess to finding the thought a comfort. Might you be keeping safe our son's soul? Is it an insult to even suggest such a thing? Perhaps I have my answer already – perhaps the mystery of my body's reluctance when it comes to chamber-work is precisely your guidance? Never before have I experienced such lack – as if my yard has been taken from me altogether. Florence tells me that the matter is most urgent – there is a look in her face that I do not like, and a fierceness about her that I find most unappealing.

CHAPTER TWENTY-ONE

Spring 1666

Johan begins his journey to Doncaster as the sun is rising. The day is mild, with a stillness about it. His jacket is folded in his saddlebag and there, he fancies, it will stay all day. His mare knows the way she goes and he holds the reins lightly in one hand and pats her hot neck with his other. He tries to think he is as content as she to be riding out so early, and makes the most of the spark of gladness within himself – the familiar kind that excites his spirits every time he makes his way to Jacques.

But despite that spark, there is a knotted morsel of his heart that won't allow his nerves to settle. It is the part that listens to the wisdom of his wife – the part that knows she at times intuits what he cannot. Never before has she asked him not to leave. Never before has she come to get the horse from the field with him, unwilling to let the matter drop. He had been vexed that she felt the need to go with him into the moonless night and had tried to persuade her to stay in the house. But she had determined to make her point, and succeeded in doing so several times over. Once they reached the horse's field, however, she resorted to silence – watching wordlessly as he threw the saddle across the mare's great bulk, reached for the bridle and tightened the buckles. It was not until he was ready to mount the horse that she finally spoke to him.

'When you return, things will be much changed.'

He had shaken his head, attempting a smile. But, as if a blood-red ruby of fear had passed from her mouth and into his as they kissed, from the moment he dug his heels into the mare's sides to get her going, and all the time they climbed slowly out of the village along Water Lane, past the slaughterhouse and water troughs, there had been a subtle vigilance stirring within him: *what if she is right?*

Not only has he Isabel's warnings to concern himself with, but the fact he is travelling so light – ignoring Jacques' request to bring Rafe to the miracle of his mother's sickbed. What will his friend make of that? Each time he contemplates the matter, hefting the disappointment of both wife and friend, he realises with a thick knotting of his stomach that in all likelihood he will dismay them equally.

For his own sake he wishes he *were* travelling with Rafe – he has always enjoyed their journeys to London to visit Jacques, liking especially their quiet discourse and how it meanders in an altogether new kind of way when they are on the road together. How their conversations (about the Moroccan markets of Safi, Agadir and Marrakesh, about the Battle of Alcazar, or Kepler's invention of a telescope with two convex lenses, or the moons around Jupiter, and the orbit of Mars and how it is not circular at all but elliptical) ease the tedium of so many days travelling. And how his young travelling companion is not afraid of the stinking, belching chaos of London in the way that Johan is sometimes afraid of it. And how, when they visit Tom Loomes' workshop at the sign of the mermaid, Rafe asks only the most astute of questions – impressing Tom. And how Jacques is impressed then, too. Johan likes it most when they are proud together – as if, between the two of them, they have done a good thing. As if this child, in those moments when it is just the three of them, is somehow *their* child.

So what shall he settle on for the day? Gladness, or knotty regret? Johan concludes there is nothing to be gained by dwelling on the conflicting requests of Isabel and Jacques. He will offer whatever help he can in London – this is what he has decided upon. *The matter is settled*, he tells himself. He will pray for Katarina's recovery, and he will pray for everyone he leaves behind in Eyam. He reassures himself that the baby will wait for his return – he feels it in his bones. And that his family will be safe. That Rafe will be safe. And Mae, too. He loves his wife; she is a wise woman. But she's not right about everything.

However, whatever he tells himself, that blood-red ruby of fear that lodged itself deep inside keeps pulling him back to heft his worries, even as he tries to keep his mind occupied throughout his day in the saddle with a small selection of fascinations: the recent discovery of a great red spot on Jupiter (the cause of such a thing and what it might signal), the comet of 1665 (how it is said that it made its way across the sky so languidly, so solemnly, as if foretelling what has now come to pass), and the pages of Hooke's *Micrographia* (all the finely drawn details of fleas and lice and gnats).

He stops to eat his eggs in the dappled shade of a curmudgeonly oak, letting his mare have a good long drink and cool her hooves in the stream. She tempts him in when she refuses to budge and he removes his waistcoat, rolling his shirt sleeves up above his elbows. He crouches, upstream from his horse, and splashes the cool water across his face and neck, cupping it in his hands and taking it into his mouth. He doesn't remove his boots, although considers it, and they stand there in the stream together, man and beast, mouths dripping.

'C'mon,' he says eventually, grasping the bridle and giving her a persuasive tug, so she makes her way behind him, out of the little brook, up the incline and back onto the road.

'Time to be gone,' he mutters, lifting himself into the saddle, giving her an encouraging kick – as gentle as he can get away with.

It is late afternoon by the time they reach The Old Angel at Doncaster. The place throngs with coachmen and horses, and as he steps inside, Johan experiences a brief anxiety that the inn will be full.

'There is always a place to lay your head,' says Mrs Morton, the landlady. 'As long as you do not mind sharing it, there's still a bed for the taking.'

He reserves it, along with stabling and fodder for the two weeks he will be away. His belly growls, reminding him it is late in the day, but he postpones the pleasure of eating something hot because the letter he must write to Jacques is playing on his mind. He arranges himself a place on the stage coach that will take him to London, buys a draught of ale, sits at a table in the corner, and watches Mrs Morton as she deals with her customers. She possesses a much-talked-about comeliness and runs a generous ledger; quite happy to let her customers chalk up their latest borrowings for themselves. There is always banter amongst the merry about her sunny disposition, and her generosity. But they are drunk, whilst she is sober and misses not a jot. It astonishes me how blinded we are by a comely smile from a woman, or a little authority from a man.

Johan dips his nib into the black ink and plays around with the words in his head, determined to create some parity between the good news and bad: *I am coming with medicines, but not with Rafe.* He plans it all out in his mind before committing his words to paper. He finds a candle, seals the letter and arranges the posting.

After some rabbit stew and bread he retires early, keen for the day to be over. He feels he has hardly laid his head upon the pillow before they wake him at dawn.

It takes four days from Doncaster to Islington: from one Angel to another. Four days of early mornings and draughts of ale, of stowing luggage in the basket at the back, and climbing atop the black, leather-clad coach to crouch – clinging to the wooden handholds – exposed to the vagaries of the weather. Four days of discourse about the state of the roads, the state of politics, the state of the weather and the famine of 1661. Four days of iron-rimmed wheels on uneven roads, of shaken bones and teeth. Four days of staging posts and turnpikes, of changing horses and tipping coachmen.

The Bell Inn, the Razor and Hen, the Eagle and Child, the Shovel and Boat. The company of strangers. The jingling of brass work on harnesses. Four days of hedges, trees, flowers and songbirds. Streams and flooded ditches. Skittish horses held by battling carters so the coach can pass. Four days of English weather in English towns and villages: a torrential downpour in Barnby Moor, a mizzling in Newark, the warmth of the sun in Stamford and Stilton. Four nights of beef shin or rabbit, of ale and brandy. Of falling into cards with strangers, of staying at it long after the candles are lit, and sharing rooms with them afterwards – the beds lined up, six to a chamber. Four days worrying for Isabel, and four nights longing for Jacques; plenty of time to have that old conundrum grip at his weary heart – tears soaking his pillow in the darkness, and the shame of weeping like a child washing over him in the short moments before he is rescued by sleep.

From Hatfield, nearing London, Johan feels the bumps in the road a little less. The ache in his hands ceases to be so bothersome. It no longer concerns him that it rains for three hours without relenting, all over again soaking his nearly dry clothing, right through to his drawers. He hardly hears the one-eyed coachman's rabid talk about the dire roads. He is happy the draughts they take at Barnet and Highgate are brief, supped quickly. And by the time they set off again, on the very last stage, his heart is bumping along with the jaunty coach, his child-like excitement turning every minute into an hour – as if St John's Street, the Red Bull Theatre and the Angel Inn will simply never be reached.

It is late in the afternoon when the coach arrives in

Islington, held up behind a flock of bleating sheep – a hundred or more, spanning the width of the road, destined for the abattoir tomorrow after a night in the fields at the inn.

Johan is unsure whether the letter he sent on Monday evening in Doncaster will have made its way safely – whether Jacques will be there to meet him. But he spots his friend from afar, standing beneath the inn's sign: *The Angel of Annunciation*. As the coach arrives in the yard, Johan lifts a hand of acknowledgement – a meagre gesture that fails to even hint at the state of his agitation. Jacques wears a burgundy waistcoat with ruby-red buttons, and Johan smiles at the sight of him – all carnation cherry and barberry sauce. He is a vision to behold and for a moment the arresting sight of the coaching yard – the jostling sheep, the sweating horses, the raucous crowd around two shrieking, fighting cocks – seems to evaporate.

CHAPTER TWENTY-TWO

Leah

'The roses are red, but their scent is gold,' said Mae, pressing her face close to the blooms. She looked to me, then quickly to Mother.

'Gold?' said Mother, crouching next to Mae.

'Why is a scent-colour not the same as the colour-colour?'

'You see a colour with a scent?' asked Mother. I heard the excitement in her voice. I was working with my hornbook, struggling still to recognise any word of the Lord's Prayer if I did not permit myself to recite the whole thing through. I gritted my teeth against Mae's chattering explanation, endeavouring to give the infuriating marks in front of me – those messy inky-worms – my full attention.

'My precious child,' Mother said, distracting me with her gushing. She was clutching Mae's face between her cupped hands. I thought there should have been fear in her voice, but there was none. Nor was there consternation; there was only wonder. I wanted to *say, you should be afraid! You should punish her! Your changeling child is an imp!*

'Tell me the other scent-colours,' Mother said, keeping her voice low. I seized upon it.

'Let us tell Father!' I said. 'Is it a special power she has?'

Mother flashed me a look, tapping her finger on the wooden frame of my hornbook.

'Concentrate on your lesson,' she said. 'Speak the prayer aloud, and follow with your finger.'

CHAPTER TWENTY-THREE

Spring 1666

ae's scalp burns with the fury of being dragged across the kitchen by a handful of hair, and I cannot help but think of all the times I subjected her to the same pain and humiliation. Her mind is straightaway shuffling reasons like a deck of cards, trying to fathom what it is she has done. Father drags her outside and up the cinder path, striding out with long legs. She stumbles after him, bent over, doing her best to keep up – past the plum tree and the chopped trunk of the long-dead beech, past the elder, the pot marigold, bitter cress and garlic mustard. Past the stone trough.

Beneath the blackthorn tree she understands; her buried box has been unearthed, spewing its contents across the ground. The wind plays with a rag end, tossing it limply.

She stands at full height now, there at his side, but he still clenches her hair in his fist.

'Do you smell that?' Father asks.

She nods.

'And do you know what it is – that stench?'

Although she looks down at the ground she knows how he has arranged his face; his disgust is so familiar, and he wears it so easily. She knows exactly what the stench is; she wants to tell him that a fox cub lies on the other side of the wall – it is alive with maggots, its eyes long gone.

The smell is rotting flesh. But she knows it is not the right answer.

'It is the smell of deceit,' he says, tightening his grip.

She feels singular hairs giving up, coming away from her scalp.

'No sooner a woman than the lies begin.'

He reaches out his foot, lifting a rag with the toe of his boot, as if the rag is still dirty with blood. As if she has not scrubbed it and boiled it. And the shame she feels is like a murky river running right through her. She notices he holds several sheets of crumpled paper in his other hand – her notes.

He lets go of her hair and gives her a shove in the lower back. Her foot catches on the uneven ground and she falls, splitting her knee on the edge of the protruding box. There is a gash, and blood, and crumbs of soil clinging to the broken skin. It stings when she pushes herself to her feet, and the breeze feels cold against it.

'Why would you do this?' he says, proffering the pieces of paper in her face. 'What possessed you?'

She searches for the right words – words that might calm him.

'I wanted to help.'

'*Like this?*'

'I—'

'Do you understand what *this is*? These visions you have?'
She shakes her head. 'Not visions,' she says. 'They—'

'You do not have to tell me. You think I do not know?
You think *you* might educate *me*? Your mother was just
the same.'

It feels unwise to admit knowledge of Mother's scent-
colours, so she says nothing. She lets her face fall as best she
can into some suggestion of ignorance.

'Forgive me,' she says, the words reluctant, sticking in her
dry mouth.

'Why did you not tell me about your courses? What do
you hide from me?'

She flinches, perplexed by the question; it is obvious what
she hides. How can she possibly defend herself? She lifts her
head and forces herself to look at him directly, hoping there
might be some morsel of love left in his heart for her.

Please, she thinks.

'I hoped to surprise you with a new therapeutic. I thought
you might be impressed.'

'How could I be impressed? You speak such rot! To use
black magic in my house, tainting what I do. Creating
medicine is a Godly endeavour – have you learned nothing? What of God, child? This is the truth of the matter,
is it not? You fail to carry God in your heart, and so what
of your soul?' – he breaks off momentarily, running his
hands through his hair, shaking his head, looking up to the
heavens – '*What of your soul*, I ask you?'

Mae shakes her head also, her stomach churning.

'Burn them,' he says, pushing the pieces of paper at her. 'And burn those too.' He nods at the rags sprawled across the soil.

Grateful to move away from him, to have been given something to do, she lifts the pieces of linen from the tin box, shaking them free of mud. She bunches them together in her hands, as if she can hide them from his sight.

'In the kitchen?' she asks, quietly, voice breaking.

'Of course not – light a fire here.'

He picks strands of her hair from between his fingers while she fetches a shovel of embers from the hearth. She blows on the hot coals, and feeds her notes to the tentative flames. The fire crackles greedily. Then she adds the rags – they fizz and splutter, too damp to burn well.

'I *am* sorry,' she says.

He is silent for a moment. Then he bends, easing himself to his knees in front of her, gesturing for her to kneel also. He takes hold of her arms, softly, then runs his fingers down the fabric of her shift, stroking her gently. His face is so close to hers that she can smell his breath. He licks his lips and his face forms an expression that is half sadness, half relief.

'I can help you,' he says, looking at her straight.

She tries a smile of encouragement, doing all she can to look sincere and grateful.

He holds her gaze, and it is like being flayed.

'Would you *like* me to help you?'

Slowly, she nods. And he joins her in nodding, so it feels as if they are in agreement, although she has no idea what she is agreeing to.

'You do wish to be free of this darkness, do you not? You do understand that you must reject it?'

Again, she nods, doing her best to look him in the eye.

He looks tired, sad, and she feels the stirring of pity within her. But more than anything she feels revulsion; she would like him to release her – to remove his fingers and overgrown nails from her smock.

Eventually, he does. And he pushes himself to his feet. He motions for her to stand also and then guides her to the corner of the garden, to the fox run beneath the wall. He tells her to fill it in before she comes back inside.

She takes the shovel and gets straight to it, aware of him watching, leaning back against the great stone wall that encloses their garden; it is twice the height of Mae, built by Marshall's father decades ago. It is untroubled by the wind that hurtles down the valley from west to east, and keeps the chill from those plants too frail for night frosts in June and hail in July.

'Be quick about it,' he says, before walking back to the house, rubbing his knuckles: one hand then the other.

She cleans the mud from her boots at the door with a tough-bristled brush. She is holding back, uncertain what awaits her now – her fingers fumbling as she lavishes the soles of her boots with the kind of attention usually reserved for the measuring of compounds. When she can delay the moment no longer she steps into the kitchen. Sam glances at her, then looks quickly away.

She braces herself, scalp prickling.

She does not see the blow, coming as it does from behind.

She does not feel it either. She hears the crack of something against her skull. Sees pulsing, moon-white light. The table breaks her fall, splits her lip. She feels his well-shod foot kicking at her stomach, stealing her breath. Tastes salt in her mouth, vomit in her throat. Her body struggles to right itself, scrabbling desperately for that simple rhythm of inhalation and exhalation. But there are only airless spasms, and the flutter of wings at her face.

Do not fight it.

As she falls in and out of consciousness, I urge her away from this place. I whisper as persuasively and sooth-ingly as I can.

Fly, fly away.

And, as if she hears me, she keeps her eyes closed and does not struggle. She lets herself drift. It takes great strength to soften her body and let his blows fall upon her, one after the other: to be what he wants her to be. Sometimes, when there are no alternatives, it is better to pretend – to collude with his righteousness.

Do not be seen to lift yourself above him.

She flies high above the forest canopy, up and up into the blue. And much later, when she returns, the kitchen floor is cold beneath her cheek. There is pain in her nose and lips. There is a deep, dark ache in her abdomen. Her face is wet and sticky. She wants to cry, but holds back the tears. Sam's boots are in her line of vision – he stands motionless in the corner of the room awaiting instruction. Because he is a stranger here, and is yet to learn how things work.

She gropes for some sense of Father's whereabouts. The kitchen feels peaceful, so she knows he is elsewhere. And as she lies on the floor, unmoving, listening, she hears the steady tread of his boots pacing overhead. She pushes herself to sitting. Turns slowly to kneeling. Presses hands and feet to the stone flags and unfolds herself to standing.

Sam looks at her, aghast. She tries to tell him that all is well – that it is not as bad as it looks – but her mouth has forgotten how to form the sounds. Her throat creaks dryly, frightening her. She tries to swallow, but everything is sticking together. And when she reaches for a mug of ale that has been left on the table, her hand is shaking too violently to lift it. Stiffly, she walks through into the pantry. Looking up, she casts her gaze over the multitude of drying herbs that hang from the beams, their stalks bound by pieces of twine. She reaches for some herb robert, snapping the brittle stems with trembling fingers.

With the herb robert still clutched in her hands, she sits at the tiny casement in her chamber, looking down onto the street that runs through the middle of the village. Her thoughts drift to Mother, her body aching for her. All memories of her are faded, like fabric washed through too many times, and she reaches down the side of her bed for a sprig of lavender tied with a ribbon. She squeezes it, letting the pungent oil stain her fingertips, inhaling the scent of it. Father wouldn't know that this is how she keeps us close – forced to find us in the subtlest places since he burned our things to *cleanse the household of the foul miasma*. She lets the pale pink scent wash over her, suffusing her with Mother's colour. And she touches her split lip with the ribbon that ties the lavender. It is the ribbon that once tied my hair.

The blood has dried, tightening her face so it feels strange to move her mouth or lift her brow. When she runs her fingers across it, the skin around her eyes feels puckered and smooth all at the same time, and she scrapes away a few congealed lumps. Slowly, she comes away from the window. The floorboards feel strangely solid beneath her feet. At her bedchamber door, having opened it a tiny crack, she listens to Father and Sam conversing in the kitchen – about some stone required to cover the filled fox run. Father is telling Sam to take his message to Marshall, and to press upon him that the job is most urgent.

At her basin she soaks a cloth, pressing it down into the water, watching as it rises to the surface. She wrings it out and brings the coolness of it to her hot face. She presses the linen with tentative fingertips over the swollen, unfamiliar contours. The water softens the dried blood, and slowly she cleans her wounds; gentle with herself in the way Mother would be gentle if she were here. She chews the herb robert – her mouth so dry it is hard to work up a good mush from the leaves. She lies against the bolsters on her bed and spreads the chewed herb across all the parts of her face that feel sore, swollen and weeping.

Sleeping, she dreams of Johan, of trying to reach him.

She is woken by a thumping that resonates through the structure of the house and into the architecture of her dreams. Startled, she is up on her feet at her bedchamber door, sloughing off her sleep, picking pieces of dried poultice from her face with one wince after another. Her heart beats hard in her chest, slowing only when she hears Marshall

Howe in the kitchen – the dull vibration of his conversation with Father drifting up from the floor below. Everything slows, and she runs her fingertips across her face, checking for any last pieces of dried herb.

Sunshine is falling into the room, leaving watery pools of light across the floor. Emboldened by the thought of Marshall here in the house, she decides that she will go downstairs and behave as if it were any other afternoon. She will ignore the swelling around her eye that has half-blinded her. Perhaps she will even get on with soaking some comfrey, or making a sow-thistle cordial.

She opens her bedchamber door and goes out into the small hallway, letting her eyes adjust to the gloom, feeling for the wall with her fingertips, and feeling for the steps with the end of her boots. She can see almost nothing through her damaged eye, and she is careful as she descends the stairs: one, two, three, keeping to the left; four, five, six, straight down the middle; avoid the second to last altogether. It has become a habit to walk as silently as possible around her home.

Marshall Howe takes up more space in the kitchen than is somehow feasible, blocking the light from the small window, filling the room with his earthy odour. He belongs *out there*, Mae thinks, noticing that his eyes dart back and forth to the green of the garden beyond the door. But, despite the discomfort that he wears about himself like an extra layer of clothing, she wishes him to stay right where he is; she likes that Father is diminished by his presence – scrawny beside Marshall's bulk, required to look up into Marshall's face, and to stand in his shadow.

Marshall has brought the stone that Father requested, and holds a great slab of it in his arms – the tendons in his neck as taut as harp strings. He looks at Mae briefly, then straight back to Father, meeting him eye to eye. Father is explaining about the fox and how it tramples the delicate herbs that are hard to come by out in the woods or in the common garden – herbs that Father has taken great care to cultivate. And then, of course, there are the hens to consider. Marshall listens, replying with the smallest of sounds as if he can hardly spare the syllables, his body trembling now with the effort of holding such a weight of stone.

When eventually he is released outside, he finds the spot that Father has described. He drops the slab, looking down at it, taking off his hat and giving his bald head a good scratch. Father and Sam have returned to work in the pantry, organising jars. Mae stays in the sunshine, watching Marshall. He crouches, and leans his weight against the edge of the stone, shoving it closer to the wall. He stands, turns, walks towards her down the cinder path, rolling his shirt sleeves as high as he can get them. When he is two paces away he looks at her, holding her gaze – noticing. She reads in his face a little seed of sorrow, and a familiar awkwardness. She knows he will likely never mention her injuries; he will not enquire when they see each other next, out on the street, or deep in the forest. But he has seen them today, and although it fails to show upon her face she is full of gratitude.

'All done,' he says.

Father appears at the kitchen door with a drink of ale for himself and Marshall. Then he passes a mug to Mae.

'For you,' he says.

She smells the complexity of the decoction before it touches her lips – coltsfoot, rose, burnet, betony. Perhaps comfrey roots? Perhaps something else?

Marshall stands on the backdoor step, blocking out the evening sun, drinking thirstily. He pushes his wide-brimmed black hat off his face a little, and Mae knows he is about to speak, although he takes a while to get around to it.

'Ann and Jonathan Thornley are down with it,' he says eventually, looking into his drink. 'And Isaac is a sorry state – great black lumps all over.'

Mae imagines the stuffy rooms and festering flesh.

'Isaac will make a good death of it,' says Father. 'The family faces their fate with humility.' He wears a look of approval on his face. 'May they each be an example before the others.'

Does Father think of me? If he does I fail to catch him at it, although I wonder how he cannot. Weak with the coughing epidemic, how easily I took his medicine – like a baby bird opening my throat. And later how I thrashed about, haunted and confused. There was nothing good about it. No redeeming myself in the eyes of God. No preparation, humble prayer or blissful surrender. I gritted my teeth and bit my lips bloody.

But then, I always was difficult.

'And the Mowers' youngsters have a fever,' says Marshall, leaning against the door frame. He's peering at the sole of his shoe, which is peeling away from the leather – in need of a nail or two. 'I may as well dig graves from morning till night.'

It is the most Mae has ever heard him speak, and, by the way he empties his mug and passes it to her, it seems as if his words are now spent. He has shared everything he cares to share. He rearranges his hat, and nods to Father. And after he leaves – ducking down beneath the doorframe – the house feels empty.

For seven nights Father keeps her awake and upon her knees in his bedchamber. The prayers dance off her tongue in the beginning. *Whatever is true, whatever is pure, a Christian death, without sin, without shame.* She clasps her hands in front of her, wringing her fingers and pressing her palms together, eyes shut tight. *I confess to you, Oh almighty God.* She keeps it up as the church bell keeps tally on the time, the words falling from her mouth – *hedge up my way with thorns, that I may find no path for following vanity.* And she dreams not of slumber, but only of besting him, praying longer and more fiercely than he can manage himself.

By the time the sun rises each morning her mind is good for nothing but scrubbing floors and kneading dough; jobs that are best done half-asleep anyway. And when she knows that Father has taken himself away for a sly little rest, she sleeps also wherever she finds herself – resting her head on a step, a shelf, or table top. Her slumber, stolen in snatches, is all velvet and feather, warm as fresh bread, sweet as honey. And Sam shifts around her, careful not to clatter his things, nudging her gently when Father rouses himself overhead.

CHAPTER TWENTY-FOUR

Wulfric's Diary

November 14th 1651

I endeavour to be grateful for the blessing of a new child in the house. After all the trouble with Florence, and my own body's reluctance, it is something of a miracle that we find ourselves where we are: another girl that Florence fusses over constantly. She is a tiny thing – a little mouse, Florence says. But she bellows like a beast, and refuses to feed. Leah has seen the back of my hand a great deal – calling the child a changeling! Where has she heard such a thing? Leah refuses to touch her at all, and Florence refuses to put her down.

As if it were not fraught enough already, Isabel insists – despite knowing it is quite out of the question – that the child is in need of a wet nurse. It is infuriating that she puts the notion in Florence's mind, instead of directing her properly. At my request Stanley dedicated his sermon to the matter on Sunday – wet nursing is a divine betrayal!

I have been forced to take my hand to Florence to quell her repeated request for a nurse for Mae. She is a sickly thing – a just punishment, no doubt, for our hope that a new child might be a vessel for a lost soul. It was not our place to ask for such a thing from you. And this sickly infant is my daily reminder.

I have implored Florence to see her trials and tribulations as an opportunity to sanctify her soul, but there is resistance within her. She denies it, of course – and what can be done with a sinner completely in ignorance of her own sin?

Did her episode of madness alter her in some permanent way? Or was the weakness always there? Was it something she hid from me deliberately? The more I have opened myself to the possibility, the more memories return that I have previously dismissed. When we first lay together she said the scent of my body was the colour purple – that I was the colour of a royal prince. I must have laughed it off at the time, thinking her words were just a kind of flattery. But I know now that they were no such thing. She has revealed this peculiarity on a number of occasions, although I know she tries to hide it. What am I to make of it?

How would you have me guide my family, Lord? What else can I do, but that which I attend to on a daily basis? The study of your scriptures. Prayer and contemplation. The strictest observance of the Sabbath and the perpetual preparation for the gift of your supper every Sunday. I look for any opportunity to spread your word, and encourage those that are as mute as fish on the subject of salvation to take you into their hearts. We rest now as a nation under the guidance of our Lord Protector – not just a pious man, but a commander of great strength. These are successes – so why does it seem at times as if all is lost, even in my own home? Is it because I am surrounded by weak, unsanctified women? Is this a man's lot? To be lost in his own Garden of Eden? Beset on all sides by weakness and sin?

CHAPTER TWENTY-FIVE

Late Spring 1666

*J*ohan is the last to alight the coach and he slithers artfully from the curved roof – nonchalant, but secretly keen to impress his friend. The two men reach out for one another, shaking hands, squeezing their affections through fingers and palms. Jacques turns his attention to Johan's beard, grasping it playfully between finger and thumb, pulling at it as if he wishes to remove it right there and then.

'It does not suit you,' he says, his voice low and sonorous. 'This orange moss of yours, these streaks of white like pigeon shit, you make an old man of yourself!'

Johan laughs and swipes Jacques' hand away, and the two men – equal in height and stature and, although they do not know it, equal in the pace of their beating hearts – clap one another upon the back. Greetings over, they take a step backwards, away from one another, coming back to the mayhem around them: dogs chasing sheep, cocks fighting, men jeering. Their smiles fade as they remember simultaneously the task at hand.

'I am most sorry about Rafe,' Johan says, shaking his head and looking into Jacques' dark brown eyes. 'Isabel refused to bend at all on the matter.'

'She asks for him still,' says Jacques. 'And what can I tell her? She knows as well as I do that she gets worse by the day, not better.'

'She worsens?'

'She has eaten nothing all week. She takes a little water if I press it to her lips on a cloth. She is not long for this world, Johan. Not long at all.'

'Then we must hasten – let us find a coach.'

Jacques shakes his head.

'Let us walk – it is not so far. It does me good to be away from those rooms for a short time – to be here, where the air is a little fresher. My neighbour is with her.'

'Has Katarina spoken about what happened to her, of where she has been all this time?'

'Just that she was held against her will. She would give me no details beyond that. She only wanted to hear about Rafe. And now she sleeps.'

Johan turns away to receive his bag from a fellow passenger who has been leaning down into the large basket at the back of the coach, extracting luggage a piece at a time. Taking it, he bids farewell to his fellow passengers. Jacques holds his hand out for the bag, insisting on the burden when Johan tries to shrug away the offer.

'You will be weary,' Jacques says, grasping the bag and

throwing it over his shoulder. They push through the flock of sheep, sidestepping piles of luggage and skirting round the queuing coaches. A yapping dog barks at their heels and Johan kicks it away. The cocks by now are dead, held limply in a casual hand, and Johan imagines a maid steeping them in the pot overnight with dried plums and a little Malaga sack, if such luxury can be afforded.

They leave the coaching yard and walk south along St John's Street, away from Islington, towards Clerkenwell. The road teems with vendors selling mackerel, flounders, cheese, and fruit. There are coaches heading into town and carters returning from Smithfield Market. Johan and Jacques fall into a stride that is brisk, Jacques setting the pace – clearly keener to be home than he was willing to admit.

There is so much to discuss, but no words of significance pass between the two of them, and soon Jacques is ahead as they walk in single file; keeping to the narrow grass verge to avoid the rutted, muddy road to their right, and the ditch to the left. Jacques turns to Johan when their progress is thwarted by a knot of coaches and carts.

'These roads are worse by the week,' he says, irascibly, teasing fingers through his thick curls of black hair.

Once the carts have negotiated the best way around one another the two men begin to walk again, and it is not long before they pass the scattered graves and small white church on the hill that Jacques likes so much, and the once-peaceful fields of St Mary's Nunnery – now busy with half-constructed houses and halls.

'All work is halted,' says Jacques, nodding across to the

timber-framed skeletons. He stops and turns. 'It is the same all over the city; the wage-payers fled once the pestilence came, and they leave the workers destitute.'

It is the gentlest of illustrations. But in Jacques' face Johan perceives the burden of these last months. There is certainly something changed about his friend – some alteration in his features that Johan hopes to fathom during their few days together. Perhaps when the sun sets, and they see each other only by the dim candlelight. Perhaps after a few mugs of rum or brandy. If Jacques can find the words. If he cares to.

So much has changed since Johan was last here, and Isabel's words flicker like a flame in amongst his thoughts, making him think of Eyam, and how change has been rolling through the place like a heavy fog. He feels strangely untethered all of a sudden, and so very far from home.

Things will be much changed.

He throws off her words as best he can, but immediately they settle upon him again. He wishes to talk, to distract himself, but Jacques and he are back to silence.

Soon they are alongside the gated vineyards of St John's Priory – its stone wall flanked with stalls offering bread and corn, faggots and coal, brushes and earthenware. Vendors and hawkers shout to Jacques and Johan as they pass. A boy swings a cockerel by its legs – the bird beating its wings and straining to right itself. Carts and coaches pull over onto the grass verge to make space for one another, and a fight breaks out between two men.

Johan's insides tighten at the deep roar from one of them as he loses his footing and slides to the ground in the mud.

Johan looks to Jacques who keeps up his stride. Jacques is unconcerned that two men might make a bloody mess of their faces or – as Johan fears – involve passers-by in the spectacle. His friend is quite at ease with the tumult of London – the noisome stench of the city, the racket of never-ending altercations, the lowing and squealing of animals on their way to meat, the pestering of those who have something to sell; here now a brace of rabbits on offer, proffered right beneath Johan's nose. He politely declines, rejecting too the hawker's remonstrations – *fresh from the field this very afternoon! Delicious in the pot with a little sage! Two for the price of one as it is late in the day!*

Jacques ignores everything around him, keeping up his stride, leaving Johan behind. As Johan catches his friend, he wants to slow their pace and ask Jacques to reminisce – the time they scaled the priory wall one summer and slipped between the vines and filled their mouths with musty, bitter grapes, warm from the sun. Their fingers had been stained from the over-ripe fruits that had split upon their skin, incriminating them. *Do you think about that day?* he wants to ask, remembering them stopping afterwards at every alehouse on Turnbull Street, and then at a cookshop just as it was shutting up for the night, grateful for the last of the roasted mutton. They had eaten their meat and bread out on the street, with a little mustard and salt, hungrily and merrily.

But now is not the time for musing. Jacques' shoulders are hunched, and he continues to stride out at a pace, causing Johan to think that he frets about his sister. Or Isabel – and her stubborn refusal to relinquish his nephew.

On a happier day they would find their way to Jacques' tenement at a leisurely pace, wandering St John's Square, marvelling at the architecture of the new flat-fronted houses, brick built with gutters and drains – the homes of knights, baronets and men of ability. They might take a detour down New Prison Walk to ogle Clerkenwell's second gaol – imagining the hot, stinking belly of that great beast. Today, though, they pass these landmarks without comment, turning right onto Clerkenwell Green in silence, the stench of the river Fleet drifting towards them on the breeze. It starts to rain, giving them even greater cause to hurry on. They pass the substantial mansions with ten hearths a piece. They pass the smaller, narrow-fronted timber houses that belong to the clerks and administrators of the city. They pass the coffee shops and the smart eating house on the corner.

Bearing left onto Turnbull Street, they follow it down, leaving the better sorts behind. The smell of the Fleet mixes with the reek of cess pits in cellars. Terraces of houses rise up on both sides, edging in with every storey so the roofs are almost touching; blocking out the daylight, pouring rain from their overhanging jetties into the centre of the road. People hurry along the very edges of the street as the rain gets heavier, twisting their bodies towards the blackened stone of the houses, away from the hooves and coach wheels that send flying the filthy water from stinking puddles.

They take a left off the main road, away from the cobbles and into a muddy alleyway that twists through a labyrinthine maze of tenements. All corners of the buildings and outhouses have been converted into useful dwellings – however tiny the rooms, however decrepit. Rats scurry ahead of them, over crates and behind barrels. Johan notices the many doors marked with a painted cross and the words, *Lord have mercy upon us*. They step over rotting vegetables, desiccated fish heads, dead mice, dead kittens.

The door to Jacques' building hangs off its hinges. They enter the dark lobby, foul water pooling beneath their boots as they wait for their eyes to adjust. They take the narrow stairs up the three flights to the attic – Jacques drawing his friend's attention to each rotten step as they get to it.

Johan is always grateful to arrive at the locked door to Jacques' garret; reassured each time by the sturdy wood, and the heavy clunk of ironwork in good order. It may be no small matter to put a lock upon one's door in a place like this – it gives a certain impression, and draws attention to that which might be better kept hidden. But nonetheless Johan is grateful that Jacques, in the end, agreed to lock away his little corner of Turnbull Street.

I make something of myself in the eyes of others with this lock and key, he had grumbled in the beginning, Johan having persuaded him to bring in the carpenter and locksmith. *I was a child in this place. These are my people.*

But Johan had scoffed at the notion, pointing out the strangers who had arrived that very week. *The place is full of newcomers all the while*, had been his retort. *They know you not and notice you anyway*. Johan had been referring to Jacques' foreign looks that, even here in London, turned a head or two. *You do not pass unnoticed and half your neighbours are strangers – put a lock on your door!*

The garret is a single room in the eaves; spacious but snug, festooned with coloured drapes and strips of tapestry, rush matting and squares of lined linen to cover the windows at night. Several shelves are strewn with trinkets, pieces of coloured glass and amulets. The place is lit by beeswax candles that fill the room with the smell of honey, and bring to mind the slow, oozing golden thought of it. Strewing herbs are scattered across the floor – lavender, mint and meadowsweet – and release their fragrance as Johan steps across them, crushing their dry stems. He thinks of Mae, and how she has always helped Isabel with the making and repairing of their matting – bringing wormwood and camomile to weave between the rushes.

A woman that Johan has never met rises from a stool to greet them, telling Jacques that Katarina hasn't stirred. Jacques thanks her for her trouble as she takes her leave.

The bed has been pulled away from the wall and positioned in front of the hearth. Coal embers burn in the grate and Jacques builds up the fire before lifting an extra chair across the room, from table to bed. They sit across from one another, not speaking, watching the rise and fall of Katarina's coverlets as she sleeps against a mound of bolsters and pillows. Johan assesses the familiar stranger; her face is turned towards him and he sees in it Rafe's strong nose and high cheekbones. Her full lips are unfamiliar, but it is Jacques' hair spread across the pillow – that thick mass of tight curls. Across her cheeks, tiny black freckles are scattered just as they are scattered across the cheeks of her brother and son – the boy that is nearly a man, much changed from when she saw him last.

She will, Johan knows, have conjured pictures of Rafe over time. Imagining him taller. Wondering, no doubt, by just how much. Thinking him thinner too, with something to say for himself. And Johan is right. Katarina has imagined all these things. But no imagined image has ever blotted the small child preserved in her thoughts: soft, wide-eyed, and so careful with his words, as if they were precious as pearls.

'There are tinctures,' Johan says. 'We can give them as she sleeps.'

Jacques nods, and Johan fetches his bag from the other side of the room, shadows dancing across the walls. His stomach growls, but there is no sign of food in the place, and it is not the time to ask. His slipped shoes sit atop his other things and he realises how uncomfortable his feet are in his boots. It is days since his feet have enjoyed the comfort of slippers. He bends, unlacing the leather, releasing his feet, sighing with the simple pleasure of it. Further inside his bag, the bottles of pills and tinctures are wrapped in a piece of cloth — skilfully folded by Isabel so none of the bottles are touching. The whole thing has been bound with ribbons, just tightly enough. Despite all her protestations, she made this little parcel for him the night before he left and, here now, he unwraps it carefully. The earthenware bottles crunch against one another in his hand. He returns to the bed, lays them down. Taking one, he eases out the wax stopper and looks to Jacques.

'Lift her a little.'

Jacques slips an arm beneath his sister's shoulders, easing her off the pillows, letting her head fall backwards. She whimpers, and Jacques kisses her forehead.

'Johan has come, Katarina,' he says, kissing her again. 'Johan has come.'

They drizzle a little of each tincture between her lips, then settle her into her pillows, and themselves into their chairs.

'You were right to stay,' says Johan, looking across at Jacques. It is a concession. His friend's decision to continue living in the squalor of Turnbull Street, *lest she return*, is a subject they have discoursed on a great deal over the years. Johan has often accused Jacques of being stubborn and foolhardy – staying in this place when he could, these days, have his pick of accommodation in the city. Perhaps not a mansion with ten hearths, but certainly a house fronting the street. And certainly on another street.

Looking at Katarina's features, pinched with discomfort even as she sleeps, Johan skirts around the knowledge he imagined her dead all these years – was certain of it. Jacques' belief that *perhaps she lives* had seemed so fanciful. Now it is prowess itself – a fearless lion and valiant knight. Johan's doubt, on the other hand – there is no pluck in that, no valour.

'How could you have known she would return?' Johan asks him.

Jacques shakes his head. 'I did not *know* anything. It was possible, that was all.'

'And there was I, so convinced of her death,' Johan says, miserable at the thought that somehow he single-handedly brought her to the very brink of it.

Please live, he thinks, reaching out for her hand. *Please live*.

They drink brandy, and drip water from a cloth into Katarina's mouth. They give her more tincture and mop her burning brow. And as the candles burn out one by one they finish the brandy, and Jacques speaks of her voice, like

that of a songbird, and how their father made her sing for
the sailors before they set off for Seville and Cadiz. She had
been afraid of those big men – with their rough hands and
rough voices. Those men that liked to have her sit upon their
knee. But she sang for them anyway, because her father told
her to. And Katarina loved her father more than any other
person in the world, even when he lost everything they had
to the rum and cards.

I see her move before they do – a twitch that starts in
her chest, then pulls at the muscles of her neck. There is
a solitary candle still burning in the furthest corner of the
room, drenching the three of them in shadow, encouraging
Johan's eyelids to droop, his head to nod.

Another twitch.

And this time they notice. They are silent – alert – as they
wait to see what the tiny movements mean.

Jacques puts a flattened palm upon the coverlet.

'Katarina,' he says.

Another twitch. Then stillness.

They look across at one another – the contours of their
features forming demon faces in the dark.

'This happened before,' says Jacques.

Before Johan can ask, *what happened before*, the movements build from twitch to tremor. From tremor to a
violent shaking.

Jacques is on his feet, holding Katarina's head and
chest against her pillows. He motions wildly, vaguely, to
Katarina's now flailing limbs.

'Her arms! Her legs!'

Her limbs have freed themselves from the coverlets and

Johan subdues as best he can the storm of skin and bone and cloth. Her body's appetite for such a commotion is astonishing; it lasts an eternity. After which they light more candles and wipe the blood from around her lips.

It is a long time before either of them speak.

'She has made it home, from heaven knows where, to this!'

Jacques rises from his stool and kicks it away across the room. As Johan takes a step towards him, Jacques halts him two paces away with a raised palm.

'Calm me not with your witless words!'

Johan takes a breath and tries not to be offended.

'I do not wish to hear you tell me one more time that this is not my doing.'

'How can it be?' says Johan. 'What have you done but stay right here, hoping for her return?'

'You say it exact! What have I done?'

'What else *was* to be done? In what manner could you have looked for her any more than you did?'

'Do not speak to me of excuses! All the time you look to ways that you can wriggle free. Do not include me in such pitifulness.'

Jacques paces, hands clenched. Johan stands by the bed, by the hearth, stuffing tobacco into his pipe, lifting a candle to light it.

'You think me weak,' he says, pulling the hot smoke into his lungs. He says the words quietly, almost to himself, as if toying with them for the first time instead of the hundredth. He says the words as if they are not a question at all and he hardly expects an answer from his friend. As if he hardly needs one.

'And so you are!' says Jacques.

The words jounce around the room in the silence that follows.

He thinks me weak.

It hardly helps that a thickness forms in Johan's throat, making him think he might be about to cry. He pulls on his pipe, concentrating on the taste of it, the smoothness of the clay between his lips.

'I only want to get things right,' he says.

Jacques laughs, steadying himself with a hand against the wall. He lets his head hang as he continues to chuckle, rubbing the back of his neck. His hair is pulled back and held with a black ribbon, invisible in amongst his curls. He lifts his head and with two strides he is there – his face in Johan's, their breath mixing hotly. He reaches round and grasps the back of Johan's neck, pressing his fingers into the firm muscle there. He gives a short shake of Johan's head.

'Do not speak to me of *right*.'

'Then what would you have me do?'

'What does it matter now? It is all in the past and nothing is to be done.'

Johan tries to fool himself that they speak of Rafe – and Johan's failure to bring him to London. But he knows that truly they speak of other matters. They speak of old decisions, long since passed. Jacques' hand is hot through the fabric of Johan's shirt, and the squeeze of his fingers is not quite affable enough; his grip just a little too tight. Johan twists away from him, but Jacques catches his arm, keeping him close. There is a rustle in the bed and they turn, waiting motionless for a beat or two – a perfect stillness. Then they drop beside her, holding parts of her beneath the coverlets as the tiny movements build to something wild and strong. This time they are ready, and restrain her without the briefest glance between the two of them. Jacques must have been holding his breath because by the time she has quietened he is gasping, heaving the warm air into his lungs. He rests his forehead on the linen bed covers, his hands clasped together behind his head.

Johan pulls his stool close to the bed and cups Katarina's hand beneath his own. Her skin is rough, her fingers slender – delicate beneath the calluses and bitten nails. It is not only her nose and cheekbones and freckles she has given to her son, but those tiny, tapering fingers that Rafe puts to good use – cutting leather into strips and squares, wetting and stretching and coaxing the stiffness from them, and later stitching the softened pieces into a tiny intricate hood, or a pair of jesses.

'Your son is a fine young man, Katarina. A young man I would be proud to call my own. He reads on all manner of subjects – in Latin and French. He is quick to learn, and keen to assist with any work required of him.'

Jacques lifts his head, casting his eyes across Johan's face.

'We have discussed an indenture for him with a watchmaker in Sheffield,' says Johan. 'But a better plan is now for him to return to London, if I can arrange with Tom Loomes an apprenticeship. Tom is a maker of watches and clocks and other instruments, and has quite the reputation. It would be a most favourable indenture if I can arrange such a thing for him. And he has your hands, Katarina; they are small, the fingers delicate – he would prove himself quite skilled, I am sure of it.'

She must have bitten her tongue again, for a dark ring of blood has dried around her lips. He thinks to ask Jacques for the cloth so he can clean it away, but before he can do so the tremoring begins. They lean across her, bearing down, using their weight to pin her to the bed.

This is the end, he thinks. *This is the end.*

But nothing ends. The night goes on in the same manner, broken only by Katarina's fits. It is long after the sun has risen that peace descends – Katarina breathing softly, her body still.

Johan pulls Jacques from his stool to the pile of blankets he has stretched across the floor. They lie beside one another in the soft light of the early morning and Johan makes a fist of Jacques' hair. He imagines Frances lighting the fire at home. He thinks of Isabel, full of child and worry. And he thinks of his youngest boys, irreverent and oblivious.

He presses his lips against Jacques' shoulder, grazing his teeth against the linen, releasing the buttons of his shirt. He finds his friend's collarbone with his fingertips, and the firm, smooth undulations of his chest. He finds his mouth, and his tongue.

And he wrestles Jacques' body into feeling something.

CHAPTER TWENTY-SIX

Leah

From the doorway of the parlour I caught a glimpse of dark hair at the pale flesh of Isabel's briefly exposed breast. Her shawl must have slipped just as I opened the door, and she snatched at it, pulling it back across the infant's head, smoothing it there. We held one another's gaze and I saw it in her eyes – she knew she had not been quick enough; despite requiring a breath or two to make sense of what I had seen, the oddity would not be disguised now.

I looked accusingly at Mother. She stood by the hearth, the fire burning behind her layers of petticoats. A swaddled infant – not her own – lay with its face in the dips and curves of her collarbone and neck, and she patted at the still, rounded lump of sleeping child. I entered the parlour and closed the door behind me.

I knew what this was. But now it was hidden from view I wanted to see it again. Careful in the placing of my stockinged feet (avoiding the gaps between the floorboards) I stepped towards

Isabel. When I was stood right there in front of her I could smell the lavender water on her hair. Reaching my fingers to the edge of the thick shawl, I peeled it back and revealed the deception up close. Mae's mouth worked a steady rhythm, milk dribbling into the scraggy wrinkles of her neck. Her eyes were shut, and every swallow was met with a brief sigh of pleasure.

'But Father said no,' I said, turning to Mother, who continued patting at Frances.

'Leah?' Isabel said, grasping my forearm.

Her bright blue eyes looked deep into mine.

'Your sister will die if I do not feed her. Your mother has not the milk she needs.'

'Father says it is a sin.'

'And I say it is not. I say it is a sin to let a child die when she can just as easily live.'

'She does not feed because she is a changeling.'

I did not intend for my words to sound as sulky as they did.

Isabel's hand slipped down the long sleeve of my nursery gown and her fingers took hold of mine. I tried to pull away, but only half-heartedly, and she held on to me, bringing my hand to her lips so she could kiss it.

'Your sister is not a changeling, Leah. If she was we'd have taken her to the forest to sort out the muddle before now, would we not? She is restless because she is hungry. Here together now' – she gestured around the room with my hand still in hers – 'this is women's business. And you may be small yet, but you will grow to be a woman one day. Your father does not need to know about this. Do you understand what I'm telling you?'

I was not sure that I did, not entirely, but I found myself nodding.

'You care for your sister, do you not?' she asked.

I stared into the keen clarity of Isabel's eyes, lost in them as I weighed the truth and whether to speak it: I did not much care for my sister; she was an unrelenting storm in the household, and I longed for the peace and quiet that comes when a storm has passed.

CHAPTER TWENTY-SEVEN

Late Spring 1666

*M*ae opens her eyes after a night of disturbed sleep, clammy with the thought of leaving. The feeling reminds her of waking when she was younger to find she had wet the bed: the dismay of it; the disappointment as she crept towards full consciousness.

From beneath her blankets she grapples with this new idea, shaping it this way and that like a handful of pastry.

How can she possibly leave?

The idea seems preposterous, and yet now it is present in her mind it also seems inevitable. It has a life of its own. It nudges and nips at her.

I have sat upon her chest all night, the moon casting shadows around the bedchamber. I have whispered into her ears and fluttered my warnings as she slept.

You must go.

I cannot, though, take full credit; I seized the moment,

nothing more. She had conjured the idea of herself in London with Johan and I caught her at it. It had been barely a thought at all – little more than a tremor at the back of her mind as she drifted from consciousness into sleep. And she had disguised herself deep inside that thought; she wasn't *with* Johan at all, she was flying above him, hollow-boned and hungry.

It is Johan she thinks of now – a twisted thread of hope. She brings him to mind dismantling a telescope, reassembling a clock, reading an article that reimagines the world. Might he be willing to reimagine *their* world?

Can you find me a place in London? Will you help me?

But what would she tell him in order to explain herself? A multitude of men beat their daughters, and a multitude of children detest their fathers. How could she describe the shadows that lurk? How could she get him to see that which she cannot yet see clearly for herself? And even if she could create some clarity, she would be asking Johan to risk a great deal; she cannot take flight to London simply because she chooses to; she can go nowhere without Father's permission. She asks Johan not simply for a kindness, but to commit a crime: to abscond with something that does not belong to him.

It is Monday: wash day. She wonders how her bruised body will stand it. She pushes herself to sitting, her muscles tight and sore. Leaning over to peer out of the casement she checks the weather, hoping for rain. At the sight of a blue sky – the sun caught playfully in tangles of cloud – she sighs, unable to reconcile the blithe day with how she feels. Pushing back the covers, forcing herself upright, she eases her legs across the edge of the bed.

This is what it must be like to be old – her body a complaint.

She notices the marks down the front of her nightclothes, shiny and dusty all at once as if a moth has scrabbled against her as she slept. She brushes at the powdery stains with her fingers and looks at the moths gathered in the eaves – scores of them, some of them the size of her palm. She has no idea where they come from, how they find their way into the house. She is forever cupping them and releasing them outside. But they make their way back to dust her in the darkness, to brush her cheeks with the tips of their wings as she sleeps.

After breakfast and prayers and her daily tincture she collects the linen Father has left for her in the upstairs hallway. She is not permitted in his bedchamber. He strips his own bed and cleans his own floor. He demeans himself with housework rather than allow her in that room.

With the linen and soap in her basket she leaves the house, conscious of her injuries, her shame like a cloak. She thinks of the troughs on Water Lane and how busy they will be with the day so sunny, how thick the air will be with lamenting. So she heads for Hall Hill trough instead. The water flows weakly there, but it will be a small price to pay for the blessings of silence and solitude.

To her left, in the sheep field, the sun cuts through the low-lying mist with blades of yellow light. In the distance High Cliffe rises, craggily, looking down over the village. She thinks again of running away, trying to imagine herself in some other place. What would she be, away from here? Without Rafe, and Isabel? Without Johan? What would she be without a pantry of tinctures, infusions and herbs – without the purpose they offer? She pauses, unsettled, and a seed pod falls like a charm, like a spell from the elms overhead. She plucks the dry, brittle seed from her basket of washing and holds it between her fingers. Then she lets it drop, resting her hand on the wall that encloses the field, watching the lambs on new, nimble legs: as skittish as her heart at the thought of leaving.

Somehow leaving.

She thinks of those who have recently fled from Eyam – leaving their comforts to set up home in the hillside beneath the rocks on the outskirts of the village. Perhaps she could do the same – but somewhere further away where no one would look for her. She tries to imagine surviving: setting traps for small animals, eating from the forest. She thinks of crones and cunning folk. Of loneliness. She thinks of wagging tongues and tittle tattle. She thinks of poverty.

By the time she arrives at the water trough she is nauseous with pain, tired from thinking. She wets her mouth with running water and slumps on a rock, waiting. When she has the energy to move again she stands, bends, lifts linen from her basket. She wets her soap, rubs it against the cloth. She scrubs and dunks and heaves.

Her body trembles with the effort of it all.

Her fingers are numb in the water despite the sun beating down. Her skin stings with sweat, her injuries awakening: a hundred needles pricking at her face.

She pauses when she hears the clack of hobnails in the distance. She looks warily down the lane, anxious at the thought of any kind of interaction, of having to answer questions and pull sentences together. But then she sees it is Rafe, come to find her. She stands, water dripping from her fingertips, waiting for him to notice her face, wondering how close he will be before he does.

He falters when he sees it, slowing, shoulders slumping. Then he stops altogether, several paces away.

'What has he done to you?'

She motions with a hand, a flourish, theatrical. And he shakes his head, his face crumpling with anger. He comes to her then, touching her arm, pinching the fabric of her shift between his fingers, letting his gaze move across her injuries. It is not the first time he has seen her like this.

'Why did he do it?' he says.

'Because I'm wicked, deceitful and disobedient.'

She says this only half facetiously, thinking of God and how exactly he might be judging her. Perhaps she should not be thinking of fleeing at all. Perhaps the darkness she senses is, in fact, *her* darkness, not Father's. The sin: her own sin. Perhaps, after all, she *does* need his help; Father's help to sanctify her soul, not Johan's help to run away from it all.

'What did you *do*?'

And there it is from Rafe, also. What did *she* do?

'I hid things from him.'

'*Why?* When you know what he can be like?'

Because Isabel told me to.

But she does not say this.

She shakes her head, unable to explain to Rafe about her notes and her colour-scents; fearful he will think of them as visions as Father has, or leap to the idea of oracles and conjuration as Johan did. Afraid he will think of witchcraft.

And she is too embarrassed to speak of her courses and rags. About the fox cub, dead and rotting. About the stench beyond the wall that Father believed was *her* stench.

'I need to get away,' she says.

He looks at her guardedly.

'I can't stay in that house with him.'

Rafe reaches for the other end of a bedsheet, bunching it and holding it steady so Mae can twist the linen – letting the water pour into the grass between them.

'You're afraid of him,' he says.

'Of course I'm afraid of him. *You* would be afraid of him.'

They spread the linen out across the rocks.

'You *will* get away,' Rafe says. And she knows what he means – that one day she will marry, live in another house with another man. He says it with confidence and reassurance in his voice, like a mother kissing a cut knee.

She shakes her head. 'I will not wait for that.'

He frowns, watching her.

'I mean to leave soon, Rafe – as soon as I can.'

She thinks of going *now*. How delicious it would be to leave his bedsheets wet across the stones and run all the way to Bakewell. *But then what?* She does not know.

Rafe shakes his head, concern creeping across his face. *Now you understand.*

'I've been thinking I could go to London, with Johan.'

She is trying the idea, like a new piece of clothing, pulling it on, smoothing it down. Holding it out now for Rafe to try.

'London? Why on earth London?'

She looks down at her puckered hands, red from the cold water. She thinks of Johan knowing the way, and how the city works — how to take a wherry across the river, how to navigate the thronging crowds that Rafe assures her are a hundred times greater than the crowds in Bakewell on market day.

'It is far away and full of possibility. And the plague is abating there,' she says.

Rafe searches her face, and she feels him plucking meaning from the cuts and bruises.

'I understand why, but, Mae, you cannot *just go*.'

She prickles at the thought he does not think her capable. That he thinks he understands.

'What choice do I have? It is not just the beatings.'

'Then what is it?'

She thinks of how Father watches her these days — his gaze a liquid he pours over her. His craving has seeped into every room of the house, into every crack of every board, into the thrashed straw of the thatch and the feathers of her pillow. She feels it wherever she is, no matter his physical presence. It follows her everywhere, dragging itself along behind her. She can hardly breathe when she sits across from him, mending in the evening by the hearth. How can she explain all that?

Rafe waits for her to say something.

'I cannot explain it fully. I only know I need to get away, and it does not matter where. If not London, then perhaps Chester, or York. I could find work.'

Rafe shakes his head.

'It's not so simple, and you know it. There is no town in the kingdom that welcomes foreigners wandering about, making themselves familiar and looking for work – especially girls. A day taunted in the stocks would be the least of your worries. It is not safe for you just to go.'

'It feels safer than staying.'

Perhaps in his heart he knows it is true, for he glances around himself with the look of a person who is suddenly lost.

'It won't be for ever,' she says.

'Will it not?' he says coldly, his disappointment obvious. She wants to tell him that *she* is disappointed also; disappointed in him. She scowls.

'What do you expect me to say?' he asks, helping her wring out another bedsheet.

The water pours between them as they say nothing.

'I need to go for Swift,' says Rafe eventually, after they have spread the bedsheet in the sunshine. 'I told the rector I would fly him this morning and it's getting late.'

'I'll come with you, then,' she says, and he shrugs his agreement.

As they pass through the church gates Mae's gaze flits from one new grave to another – the mounds of soil like molehills, or clusters of dark buboes. They had fallen back to silence as they walked, not a word between them the whole way. Soon they will be at the mews and Mae feels a rush of urgency. She cannot let Rafe go for Swift just yet; as soon as the bird fidgets and rouses on his wrist he will be lost to her. She wants his agreement; she *needs* it. She needs, more than anything, to return home not only with her clean linen but with the start of a plan: fresh, sun-dried, folded neatly.

'Come inside for a moment?' she says, motioning to the church doors.

He nods, and they steer to the right where the path forks.

They push open the heavy door, and the dank smell rushes into her nostrils. The church is empty, its desolation and celebration hanging together in the stagnant air.

She glances up at the singular stained-glass window. The colours – purple, blue, jade and maroon – bringing to mind the Buxton Fayre: the brightly dressed actors and tumblers, the sword swallowers and fire-eaters. Her mind drifts from conjurers, wrestlers, gamblers and cardsharps to the spectacle of monkeys on ropes pushing babies in wheelbarrows, to the *commedia dell'arte*: Scaramouch, Pantaloon and Punch.

Any soul can get lost at the fayre. Does she think it for herself or do I suggest it?

All that fire and smoke. Trumpeters trumpeting, drummers drumming.

A place all of its own. Welcoming of strangers with something to offer.

She lets the thought settle, looking around the church in the same way she always does when it is empty – looking upwards, as if seeing it for the first time, marvelling at the size of it. As if she is Jonah in the whale, a ribcage curved above her.

'There are one hundred and nine arches,' she says, twisting her head to look at Rafe.

Every door is an arch, every window, the end of every pew, the panelling behind the altar and the space between the great pillars. Rafe looks from one arch to another while Mae bends, unlacing her boots and pulling them from her feet. Hurriedly, she pulls her stockings down and Rafe looks back to her, confusion and concern flashing across his face.

'What are you *doing*?' he says, his voice a whisper.

'This here.'

She crouches, touching a pattern on the floor with her fingertips. Between the pews runs a path from the back of the church to the front: a lattice of ironwork set into stone. The metal is raised, smooth as bone, cold to the touch. The pattern repeats so evenly, so pleasingly, leading a congregation from door to altar.

' . . . to feel it . . . beneath your feet . . . ' she says, holding a boot in each hand, stepping onto the geometric ironwork. It is even colder, even smoother than under her palms.

'Try it.'

Rafe does as he is told, and unties his laces. They walk barefoot the length of the church from the great stone font to the front pew. When they get there Mae pauses, contained for a moment in this place of neat, narrow arches; all around her they are cut into stone, carved from wood, filled with glass: doorways that refuse to open.

She sighs, and bends, pulls on her stockings and slips a foot into its boot, threading and tying the laces. Rafe grasps her other boot and holds it behind his back. She stands, meeting his gaze.

'Give it to me.'

He backs away from her, smiling, and for a moment she forgets everything; remembering other things, forgotten things: the brief brush of his lips against hers.

She holds out her hand, then swipes for the boot. He is too quick, and laughs at her, turning, retracing his steps, barefoot again over the cold ironwork, back to his own boots and stockings scattered around the font.

Mae watches him, but does not follow. She wishes she were more in the mood for his game.

'I need a kindness,' she says, too quietly for him to hear.

A plan has been taking shape in her mind since the colours of the stained glass sparked that memory of fire and smoke. The fayre is on its way to Buxton, like a gift to her. She will go to meet it. She will run from this village as a boy – in breeches and a waistcoat.

She walks quickly, one boot off, one boot on – a subtle limp that makes her think of Marshall Howe. By the time she reaches Rafe he is stood there in his stockings. He kicks her boot towards her, puts his hands on his hips.

'Let me come with you,' he says.

She shakes her head.

'You cannot go alone,' he insists.

'And you cannot come with me – it would break their hearts. They love you. They do not deserve such a thing.'

'So you would just *leave*?'

He looks at her as if it is the worst thing she could possibly do.

'I have no choice.'

'You *do*!'

The words echo back, rejected by the walls. Rafe reaches out and grasps her arm, holding on to her, and too tightly. She snatches her arm away, glaring at him. He makes to grab her again and she pushes him away. He stumbles, toppling, falling backwards against the font, banging his head.

'Ow!' he says, accusingly, scowling at her, leaping up so

they are facing one another, poised and unsure. She taps her fingertips to her breastbone, searching for the right thing to say and the right way to say it.

'I could go to Buxton Fayre, and take medicines, rare supplies, things of use. They'll take me with them, I'm sure of it.'

I could be useful.

'It would be safer than London,' she says.

He looks at her as if it is a plan worth considering.

'I would go in disguise as a boy.'

He says nothing, looking down at the floor, resignation settling over him like whispered prayers.

'I would need breeches and a waistcoat ... other things ... '

Her journey is coming together in her mind, and already it seems possible now he no longer argues against it.

'I can get you the things you need,' he says.

Relief floods through her.

'It comes the second week of June,' she says.

'I know, I'll get them together in time.'

When he looks her in the eye she sees that he is about to cry. She drops her boot to the floor and moves towards him, encircling him with her arms, resting her sore, aching face against his shoulder.

I love you, she thinks.

It is awful, now she thinks properly of leaving him. But her mind is made up. She lifts her head and looks into his eyes, brushing away a tear from his cheek. She presses her mouth against his, wondering whether her cut lip will feel unpleasant to him, whether he will be repulsed by it. He responds first with his mouth, kissing her back. Then he places his hands to her body, holding her sides, stroking her there.

She opens her mouth, and leans her body into his. She presses all her soreness against him so he is holding it, absolving it. She falls into the taste of him, into the smell of him, into the buttery yellow colour of him. She falls so fast and fully that she does not feel her lip split open. She does not taste the blood passing from her mouth to his. She does not hear the sound of the church doors opening, heavy against the stone flags. And she does not hear the soft tread of Father's boots in God's house.

CHAPTER TWENTY-EIGHT

Wulfric's Diary

September 16th 1658

I would have called him Oliver, if he had lived. But like Cromwell, my son is dead. Another dead boy! What sin lurks, that I do not see? Two daughters, both thriving – even the little scrap that refused her mother's breast has seen seven years of health and vitality. What magic has them flourishing, year after year, and my sons perishing?

I would have called him Oliver, in anticipation of his courage. But now I can only grieve for the life he will never know. And what a life it could have been. He might have been a leader of armies like his namesake. Or served you in another way – as a minister, or physician perhaps. My son looked ready for a good life – he was a good size, strong looking, with a full head of hair. And yet he was taken before he drew a single breath. Tell me how I have displeased you – there must be an answer to this riddle.

At least this time Isabel had the good grace to send for Stanley, and a proper blessing was given.

January 21st 1660

There is little joy in the news, but Florence finds herself with child once more. I hardly dare to hope for a healthy son, but Stanley reminds me to be strong, and to have faith. Of course I have faith in you! It is only that I wonder what other powers might be at work. Not just because of the girls that live and the boys that die. But because of other matters.

The angel says to Tobias, that the devil begets power over those that devote themselves to lust. And I think back to the early years of our marriage with great sorrow. Just as Adam allowed himself to be gulled into sin, so too did I. The lust that Florence brought to our marriage bed has surely tainted us both. In those moments of earthly pleasure we not only displeased you, but surely let the devil take advantage! Still now I am so often thwarted in my Godly duty as a husband. There is no pleasure in it anymore – although that hardly concerns me. It is the possibility of witchcraft that torments me – that a witch possesses easily the power to take away a husband's fruitfulness. I have read of men having their yard stolen away completely so they are as flat as a woman between their legs. There is a multitude of testimonies along such lines! And if the member is not taken entirely then it is rendered soft as dough.

When I devote my life to you, Lord, why am I afflicted so? It is astonishing that Florence finds herself with child at all.

CHAPTER TWENTY-NINE

Late Spring 1666

ast week Marshall dug a grave a day, and the village filled it. So far this week those numbers have doubled. The tailor's house where it all began lies in the middle of the village. The plague has spread from house to house, east and west. It continues to make its way like a curious visitor – unperturbed by bolted doors, the burning of gunpowder, the strewing of herbs, the dousing of aromatics and perfumes. The children play no more in the streets, but it seeks them instead in their parlours and kitchens. It seeks them in their beds.

Mae has been locked away, kept to the house and to women's work. She is not to help with Sam's education, and she is not to leave the cottage unless accompanied by Father. The house key that has hitherto always hung on the rusty nail next to the door now hangs around Father's neck; he keeps it tucked away out of sight, patting at it all through the day.

The cottage has become a fortress and Father her shadow. She hears him standing outside her bedchamber door at all hours of day and night. It seems as if he is forever on the stairs at the same time as she. And he requires her each mealtime to sit and eat with him whether she is hungry or not. He does not speak to her unless he has to, and after every meal he selects her decoction or tincture in silence. He lets his gaze drift across her, saying nothing. And when it seems that he cannot help himself, he froths up on the subject of *witches and their visions, women transforming into animals of their choosing,* or *stealing the yard,* or *moving through the night as far and easily as the wind.* He likens it to a pestilence – visible, yet invisible. He tells Sam that with the right kind of microscope, serpents can be seen in the breath of witches – just as they can be seen in the breath of those beleaguered by the plague. Such microscopes are hard to come by, which is a great pity.

When there are jobs in the garden out the back then he takes her to them and watches over her as if she might, without him there, tumble away on the wind. She tends to new shoots and dead wood, and notices, as the days go by, how the path that the fox took through the garden is disappearing – grass unfurling, stems straightening. She wonders about that fox, imagining it standing there that first night after she had filled in its hole with soil. Did it start digging, scraping all over again at the loose, friable earth, only to find that slab of stone in its way? Or did it not bother with digging? Did it lift its muzzle, tasting the night air, discerning another way?

After he has brought her back into the house, they put

their cloaks in the lobby. In that small space, bending, they untie their laces and remove their boots. The house key might dangle momentarily from Father's wrist, or be placed on the floor as he fumbles with slipped shoes. But before they return to the kitchen, he always pulls the twine over his head, tucking the key back beneath his shirt, patting it there. She tells herself that she can have that key and be away – that a moment will come when he will forget himself; when he will fail to hang it about his throat, and will hang it instead on the rusty nail by the door. Because new habits are quick to perish.

It is not yet light, and she lies in bed listening to the quiet sounds of Father dressing. She wonders whether he sleeps with the house key around his neck – whether it grazes his skin there as he tosses and turns – or whether he places it beneath his bolsters and pillows, risking whatever he knows might happen if she were to get her hands upon it. She hears his door opening, after which there is a long pause. A quiet step across the stairwell, and he is outside her bedchamber door. Deliberately, she keeps breathing, slow and steady. She guesses at his thoughts, juggling with them. He withdraws, stairs creaking beneath him. He will feel his way through the gloom of the night-time kitchen, unlock the front door and slip away into the sleeping village. He goes to church alone these days, before dawn.

She hears the front door closing, and waits for him to lock it before she allows herself to move. She pulls on her stockings and shift, leaving her shoes beneath her bed so she can move quietly around the house in her stockinged feet. She takes her candle and slips down the stairs to the fire, pokes a stick into the ashes, disturbing them cautiously. There is a tiny ember and she holds a match to it, urging it to take. It does, and she brings that little flicker of orange to the blackened wick. Her candle burning, she stands.

Shadows dance on the walls and she takes a deep breath. She tries the door that goes from the kitchen out into the garden, and finds it locked. She walks quickly to the front door and tries that too. When it resists her she rattles it, as if by just wanting a thing she can make it happen – as if she possesses the kind of power that Father is so afraid of. She imagines transforming into a beetle right there – slipping beneath the door, leaving her shift and stockings in a little pile in the lobby.

She looks around the sparse parlour. Apart from Father's leather bag, a shelf of books, two stools and a small table in the far corner, it is empty. The hearth is brushed clean, and Mae cannot remember when they lit it last. Her eyes settle on his books and she goes to them, running a fingertip down the spine of each in turn: Dr Dee's *Relation of his Actions with Spirits*; Thomas Ady's *A Treatise Concerning the Nature of Witches & Witchcraft*; Ludwig Lavater's *Of Walking Ghosts*. She need not open them; she knows what they contain – what they might convince her of.

She pulls back the shutters, running her hand across the small panes of glass, pressing and knocking at their solidity with the soft heel of her palm. She goes to the kitchen, to the window that looks out onto the street, and finds, as she investigates, that it is in as good a condition as the one in the parlour. She has never looked at her home in this way before: searching for weakness.

Holding her candle aloft she turns about the room, casting a critical gaze across the shelves, the food safe, the fireside chairs and large table – the pans, cauldrons, skillets and kettle. The toasting fork glints in the candle-light and she pauses, thinking a string of evil thoughts. Unsure of herself, she looks away to the shelf stacked with saucers, trenchers, platters and porringers. And the shelf above, with its ceramic pots of dried insects, viper skins, bones and pelt.

She climbs the stairs, the wood creaking. She stops at his door, knowing she is about to open it, that she is about to step inside – hardly believing she has the audacity. She can feel a breeze coming from within, trickling cold across her toes. Her quickening breath sets the candle guttering, bringing the walls alive all over again with dancing shadows. She lifts the latch and lets the door swing open in front of her, looking around the bedchamber from the doorway – taking in the bed, and the little table next to it with its basin and jug. She walks towards them, puts her candle on the table and folds back the covers, lifting the pillows and bolsters to look beneath them for a spare key that she is sure no longer exists. She replaces them just as they were – the coverlet rucked on the far side, the nearest bolster higher than its bedfellow.

She goes to the window; it is open, and smaller than she remembers. She reaches her hand to that space where the inky night is coming in. Leaning through the window she looks left to the lightening sky – a faint glow in the east. She pulls back, suddenly fearful of being seen. Grasping the handle she tries to open the window fully, but the hinges are rusty and they resist her nudging. She twists her shoulders, leaning towards the open space again, trying to imagine squeezing through, fancying it might be possible. *But what then?* She would surely break her bones jumping to the ground?

Leaning once more out of the window, she looks down, calculating the leap and the chances of landing lightly – of making herself somehow weightless. She sighs, coming back into the chamber. Looking to Father's bed – sturdy, with a heavy frame – she imagines tying to his bedpost the corner of his linen sheet, tying his coverlet to that, fetching her own bed linen too for the task. Her mind plays with thoughts of Petrosinella, trapped in her tower, letting down her long rope of hair.

It would have to be dark, and he would have to be out of the house. *This time of the morning then*, as he prays in church and the rest of the village sleeps. But still she will need breeches, and a waistcoat. Still she will need money and food and items from the pantry shelves. *Rafe has promised to help*, she thinks. But she has no way now of checking their arrangements. She has no way to be certain he has gathered the things he promised.

Looking around the bedchamber again, her eyes fall on the oak chest in the corner. Once it had been full of Mother's petticoats and bodices, shifts and spare coifs. But they are long gone, burned with everything else.

She goes to the chest and lifts the lid, looking into it. Her mind stitches together the possibility of Father having some old clothing she might be able to steal for herself. *Might he?* Could she adjust something of his – something old and unused that he might not miss? Could she cut and sew in snatched moments?

She places the candle on the floor and kneels, reaching into the chest. She puts aside his spare shirt, the breeches he wears to church on Sundays, a pair of drawers and a coverlet. She lifts out several layers of linen, then sits back on her ankles to listen to the aching of the cottage – the cracking of old joists; reassuring herself that *that* is all she can hear.

She lifts out an old tattered shirt of his and there beneath it is a book. As she stares at that book she realises what it is: his leatherbound diary. Dropping the shirt in her lap, she grabs the diary greedily, bringing it close to the candle, opening it. There is no hesitation in her fingers as they turn one page after another, although I notice they have begun to tremble – and so they should. Not because Father might discover her; he prays still, at this very moment, in the darkness of the church. But as she gobbles page after page there approaches something far worse than Father himself.

It is not immediately clear, the horror that awaits. It is thinly disguised, after all, behind the veil of Father's self-deception. He does not state it as plainly as he could have stated it; he dresses the whole thing up with angels and feathers and blood turned to liquid gold. And for a moment the words make no sense to her, as if she has skipped across them too quickly and her mind has played a trick on her – rearranging letters and syllables for its own amusement.

It cannot be true.

She is tired, and the candlelight feeble. Certain that she has made a mistake, she brings her gaze to the top of the page and starts again ... *a monstrosity that could only be the work of the devil . . . as she drank the thornapple tea I felt you moving within me . . .*

The inky words come alive on the page – they are tiny beetles, scurrying for her hands, and she slams the diary shut. Stomach churning, the chamber fading in and out of focus, she does not move. *Cannot* move.

Then slowly she kneels, and puts the diary back where she found it. As she does so she sees at the bottom of the chest some items which for a moment she presumes he has overlooked. For the merest flicker she believes they belong to Mother or me – a shift, or nightgown perhaps? But before her fingertips have stretched as far as that new, good-quality linen, edged with embroidery, she hears a muffled sound from somewhere in the house. She snatches her fingers away, her heart hammering. Hands trembling, she folds everything hurriedly, doing her best to reconstruct it all just as it was.

Lowering the lid of the chest, she looks quickly about the place. Checking she leaves no trace, she tiptoes away, closing the door behind her.

In her own chamber she does her best to collect herself. She looks out of the casement to the night being chased away. She dresses, leaving her breasts unbound, thrusting the long strip of linen beneath her pillows.

CHAPTER THIRTY

Leah

I had known, heart sinking, what he pointed to. My fingers groped at my collar and, sure enough, the amulet was pro-truding there, betraying me. I attempted to stuff it back beneath my smock, but Father gesticulated, indicating I was to remove it and give it to him. I obeyed, picking at the tightly knotted twine.

'It belongs to Mae,' I said, quickly, scattering shards of truth. I had stolen the necklace from her some weeks ago and worn it secretly ever since. 'Isabel gave it to her.'

The knot unravelled and I passed the mole's foot to Father. There was no weight to it at all – just a sharp, dry scratchiness.

'And yet you are the one wearing it.'

'I was hiding it from her, that is all. It was never mine.'

Father hit me on the side of the head, across the ear, and tears sprang straight to my eyes. He waited, as if calculating, before hitting me again. When he hit me for the third time the words tumbled from my mouth as if they had come unstuck.

'Mother wears an eagle stone that Isabel gave to her.' I felt no shame – in that moment, at least – spilling their names from my mouth. 'And Isabel nursed Mae when she was an infant.'

I stared up into his face, waiting for him to hit me again.

'They all have their secrets, but it's only ever me that gets into trouble.'

I ran in the direction of the stairs, but Mother was there. Her eyes found mine, and they said, 'How could you?' But still her hand was kind as she grasped my arm and steered me back into the kitchen.

'Does the child speak the truth?' said Father.

Mother said nothing, but I felt her fingers fretting at my shoulder.

'Does she?' he said.

'Nine years have passed, Wulfric. Please. What does it matter that another woman nursed our child all that time ago, other than we are blessed to have her living? Mae is the brightest—' Mother paused, closing her eyes briefly. 'She would have died if Isabel had not helped us. You should be grateful.'

He hit her then, too. A slap across the face; not hard enough to make her stumble.

'I forbid you to see Isabel,' he said. 'I will find a new midwife for you. Now, give me the eagle stone.'

Mother shook her head, and Father slapped her again.

Mother brought a hand to her reddening cheek.

Despite the fury I sometimes felt towards her, I wanted him to stop. I wanted to stand right in front of Mother's pregnant bulge so he could not get to her.

'Wulfric,' she said, voice wavering, 'I have worn the stone all through this pregnancy. I cannot cease to wear it now, for such a thing . . .'

'Give me the stone!'

Mother shook her head again, backing away.

'It is my protection . . . ' she said.

'GOD is your protection.'

'You want a son, do you not . . . ?'

He started pulling at the collar of her smock, grappling with the buttons.

'It is tied to her left arm,' I said.

When he had done away with her layers of linen, he pulled unsuccessfully at the knotted twine, then turned to me.

'Pass me a knife, Leah.'

'You'll regret this, Wulfric,' Mother said, straightening herself in front of him, lifting her face to his. 'I swear, you'll rue this day.'

'Are you cursing me, woman?'

She thrashed her arm until he lost his grip upon her.

'Damn you, fool of a man! You WILL rue this day.'

And full of fear, I turned away to fetch a knife.

CHAPTER THIRTY-ONE

Early Summer 1666

When Sam arrives he is as sparky as ever – cheeks flushed, beads of perspiration across his nose. He had been subdued for a few days after Father found Mae's things and beat the light out of her. But then he had returned – like the sun rising – to his old brightness.

''Tis warm outside,' he says, wiping his forehead with the back of his hand. He looks from Father to Mae, and back to Father. They are eating by the fire, and Sam – who looks as if he is bursting with news of some kind – fidgets with his shirt sleeves, rolling and re-rolling them, knowing that Father does not like to be disturbed with discourse whilst eating. Mae nibbles the edges of her bread, watching Sam, wondering what he could be so eager to share with them. More death, perhaps? But he seems too animated for that.

Father folds a slice of bread, tears a portion of it and

pushes it into his mouth. He chews, lips parted. Mae's hunger drains away as she watches him. When at last Father finishes, he reaches for his ale, swigging it, before holding out his saucer to Mae.

Sam takes this as his sign and says, 'They've called a meeting of the village. The rector and Thomas Stanley.'

Father picks crumbs from his waistcoat, plucking them with some effort between thumb and forefinger, passing them between wet lips.

'Six o'clock at the delf, he said.'

At the delf. Sam looks to Mae when he gets no response from Father, and she nods at him, attempting a smile – something that might convey curiosity, and gratitude for bringing the news; wondering briefly whether that is what shows on her face.

'They're saying the whole village is to go. Anyone who does not ail with it must attend the meeting.'

When Father has eaten all the crumbs from his clothes he leans forward, resting his elbows on his knees, clasping his hands in front of him. He looks into the fire rather than to Sam. Mae senses him calculating, and wonders what his decision will be.

She thinks how old he looks with his face so hollow, and so many jutting bones. He has no time for celebrations, so she forgets his exact age. Forty-six? Forty-seven? Hunching in front of the fire, rubbing at his troublesome hands, he looks ancient. And Mae knows now as well as I do how he has made an old man of himself – every swollen joint, each loosening tooth. A louse in his hair catches Mae's eye, and she watches it scurry down a single strand that falls in front of his face. She presumes he will see it, *right there*, but he is lost in the flames, and the creature dangles unnoticed.

Will Father take her with him to the village meeting, or will she be left behind? She weighs the two possibilities and realises she does not care what he decides; either way, it is an opportunity, and she feels a turning of something within. She thinks of Rafe and whether he might already have gathered the things she asked for. She will need a little money for certain. She will need breeches. She will need to steal a multitude of things from Father's shelves.

'We shall eat early then,' says Father, looking to Mae.

'I have bread to make, and a rabbit to skin,' she says, getting up with their saucers and mugs. She wipes them carefully with a cloth and sets them back on the shelf.

Sam stands at the table, fidgeting, turning the pestle in its empty mortar, waiting for Father's instructions for the day. His fair hair falls in front of his face and he pushes it back. He fiddles with his sleeves, while Mae fetches flour and yeasty ale and makes a great sticky pile of it at the end of the table, kneading the dough with the heels of her hands.

Father has fallen into a routine of practical tasks in the morning, and lessons of theory in the afternoons. He seems confounded about where to put himself in the presence of Sam's enthusiasm which, even now, still shines like a copper dish in the sunlight. Mostly, Father chooses to flow against the tide of Sam's zeal, as if it is a thing to be wrested from him. If Sam finds a thing exciting, Father will make it dull. When he takes to a thing easily, Father will strive to make it complicated, leaving his apprentice less sure at the end of the day than at the beginning. It is as if he cannot help himself.

On the rare occasion that Father leaves the cottage, Mae coaxes Sam through the lessons that confound him: the Doctrine of Signatures, or the complexity of balancing humours. *One disease,* she reminds him, *left unchecked, will lead to another.* She tells him that *balance is everything.* That the old are cold and dry – that ginger, garlic or cloves might bring them a little warmth. That children overheat with the slightest provocation, so orange, vinegar or cucumber might be the answer, or else a little time spent in the cooling moonlight.

She knows he is grateful for her help – he wants to prove himself a competent apprentice. But he worries about accepting her assistance too. He is a boy that prefers to follow orders, and his master's orders were clear: keep her inside and keep her to housework.

Mae does not let herself dwell on Sam's worries, and enjoys the snatches of time working whenever she steals them. As she deciphers Father's untidy notes for Sam, explaining how to make a herbal water for the King's Evil from white archangel flowers, sweet fennel seeds and aniseed, and a quarter of an ounce of sassafras cut small and mixed with rose essence, she briefly feels every part of her settling. The alchemy of ingredients skilfully mixed, balanced *just right*, gives vigour to the tentative notion she could survive if she were to leave. More than survive. That there is a place *out there* where she belongs: some place beyond the village boundary where she would be safe. Where she could be useful.

But then she remembers all that is ahead of her. And she wonders if the churning she feels is sickness or a warning, or something growing within her: some demon that Father has taught her to fear. *What if he is right?* At times she knows the maleficence belongs to him, and him alone. But at other times, she is not so sure.

Her shame is her shadow, and it follows her everywhere.

After she has finished with the dough, she scrubs the table and wipes flour from the stone flags with a wet clout. She fetches a rabbit from the thrall in the pantry. Its feet are soft and hard all at once in her hand, and its body swings, head lolling, as she takes it to the damp table. She lays it down. Its gutted stomach gapes, rimmed with bloody, matted fur. But its innards are perfectly smooth – all bruise and sinew. She sharpens her knife and lays it aside. Tugging skin from flesh, she prises her thumbs between the two, working her way around the rabbit's body beneath its coat of fur, separating it from itself, feeling the bumpy ridge of its backbone with her fingertips. She withdraws her hands, chops off its head with a cleaver, and with a tug or two peels its skin clean away. It lies there on the table, as raw and naked as a newborn.

The villagers gather in the clearing at Cucklett Delf, encircled by trees – held by so many ancient arms, meadow grass beneath their feet. The better sorts and the destitute are all present together, but not quite milling – their fear measured out in the yards kept between themselves and others. Family groups huddle together. The dusty-white lead miners and their families. Richard Talbot, black from his smithy. And the Hancocks down from their farm at the top of Riley Lane. Half the woman she was six months ago, Jane Hawksworth stands all by herself, cloak twisted about her shoulders despite the warmth of the evening. And Mae thinks she understands that kind of chill – the relentless cold that comes when everyone you love is taken.

She looks about herself, desperate for some sight of Rafe and Isabel, wondering whether Johan might be home by now. Father's hand grips her elbow, his fingers digging into the soft flesh of her arm. His nails are hard and sharp, and she wants to push him away. She wants to shout, turning heads, *away, you terrible man!* She wishes, if it would do any good, to cause a scene that would never be forgotten.

She feels the temptation to run. But she knows she must do it right if she is to have a chance of making it work; she must wait for the fayre.

Eyes darting from person to person, she sees Rafe through the crowd, taller somehow. She wishes for him to turn to her, to see her there, to be reminded. She wants him to give her a sign – some nod, or tug of the head. Something to indicate that all is well, that he has not forgotten their agreement and the items he promised.

But no sooner has she seen him than he is gone, lost in the gathering together of the village. She and Father do not walk about the place as lots of others seem to be doing. They stand, and wait. And eventually, William Mompesson clambers onto the jagged rocks that look down into the grassy amphitheatre in the trees. He reaches for Thomas Stanley's hand, pulling him up to join him on the rocky, elevated ledge. They look out across their congregation, waiting for a silence that does not come. Shouts and questions fill the air, above an undercurrent of endless murmuring. Stanley rings a bell, shaking the thing above his head until there is a chance of being heard.

'Let us pray!' Mompesson tells them, quite sure that this is the place to start. And quietness descends at last, rippling through the crowd, finding everyone eventually.

'Guide us, Lord, in all the changes and varieties of the world, that we may have evenness and tranquillity of spirit, that we may not grumble in adversity, but in serene faith surrender our souls to your most divine will, through Jesus Christ our Lord.'

Within a few seconds of him finishing, the murmuring of voices starts up again, spreading through the crowd so that Mompesson's words, when he begins once more to address them, cannot be heard. This leads to an even greater racket, of shouts to, *Be quiet! Pipe down! Stay your tongues!*

Thomas Stanley brings order with his bell again, then rolls his deep voice across the open space in front of him.

'My friends,' he says, 'it is time to listen.'

'We share a common purpose in gathering this evening,' says Mompesson, calling out across the crowd. 'And we share a common faith.'

He glances at Stanley, as if the two men have agreed upon some new fellowship. Mae wonders what Father will make of *that*. The loss of Thomas Stanley as the village rector when he refused the Book of Common Prayer is still, several years later, an outrage Father finds energy to speak about at great length. And there are plenty of neighbours quite willing to indulge him. That the two rectors stand together, here now before the village, must surely be exciting great curiosity.

'There is not one soul among us who has not yet been touched, in some way, by this terrible plight. Every one of us is fearful. But we must comfort ourselves with God. We grieve those lost already, but consider this – the loss is only ours. Our sorrow is their gain, which should sustain our drooping spirits. They rest now in the house of Our Lord.'

There are quiet murmurings at this. Father's grip has loosened on Mae's elbow, and she imagines slipping from his grasp.

'We can look to the principles of the Church of England to inform our piety and devotion to one another. In our faith we will find the humility and modesty we need. There is goodness within this village – so many of you live with charity in your hearts, and value nothing so dearly that you would fail to give it away if your neighbour found themselves in need of it.'

There is a general nodding of heads, and glancing around at one another as if to reassure themselves that *yes*, they would indeed give what they had if another found themselves in need of it.

'Those with the means have flown already from this place of death. Bradshaw Hall stands empty, and we find ourselves without a squire with this pestilence spreading amongst us. We are faced with a grave choice, dear friends, and it is for this reason that Thomas and I have gathered the village.'

'Get to it, man!' shouts a voice, followed by a stream of admonishments.

'We can choose to continue as we are, and risk this

pestilence spreading to our neighbouring towns and villages. Imagine it in Bakewell, or Buxton. Imagine it in Sheffield! For make no mistake, it will reach them all before too long if we continue travelling to and fro.'

The crowd erupts into so many different conversations. Stanley furiously rings his bell.

'The grief it would bring to these towns would be beyond anything that even we could imagine,' says Mompesson. 'Already we are not welcome in these places. We are forced at Bakewell to trade across the stream at Stockingcote. And I hear that Sheffield has erected posts to prevent strangers entering the city, for fear of us taking this terrible disease into their streets and houses. They fear us, and who can blame them?'

Jeers and objections fill the evening air. Stanley rings his bell and quiet returns, as if all of them have learned the rhythm of this meeting by now.

'Thomas and I have discoursed on this at great length. It is not lightly that we stand before you with three suggestions.'

A pensive hush settles over them; it seems that even the infants stop their whining for the news that is coming.

'Firstly, there will be no funerals or burials within the grounds of the church.'

Cries of dismay ripple through the crowd.

'Marshall Howe cannot dig night and day to meet the demand. Our dear departed cannot lie for days on end. From now on, we will bury our dead in whatever place we think most suitable, and as quickly as possible. My time, and Thomas's, and the time of my dear wife, Catherine, will be better spent administering to the bereaved and dying – comforting those who need us most.'

The village unites in thought. Which little corner of the garden will do? Which part of the orchard or meadow, or the field where the cow grazes? The idea that in death they will be denied the comfort of consecrated ground – lowered instead into the wet clay onto which the sheep blithely shit and piss – seems to stun the village into silence.

Father lets his hand drop from Mae's elbow.

When she looks around herself she sees that family groups are embracing one another. The village is gathered, but somehow it has also broken apart, hearts clustering where they feel most safe.

'Secondly, we are to lock the church, and hold our services here,' Mompesson says, sweeping his arms in gentle circles. 'This space is like a natural church, perfect for a congregation – as if God intended it for just this purpose.'

The villagers look about themselves, nodding vaguely, as if it does not matter that the church doors are now closed to them. But it matters to Mae. If the church is no longer open for prayers, then Father will no longer leave the house in the early morning darkness, and *she* will find no opportunity – as the village sleeps – to tether a rope of linen to his bed and squeeze herself through the tiny window that lets the inky night come in.

'We must gather no more in the church,' Mompesson continues. 'Or any other building where the miasma can float about, trapped in the stuffy air between us, tainting ever greater numbers. Out here the wind can clean the air, and we can offer our prayers to God just as well.'

There is no objection to this, and Mompesson glances briefly at Stanley who gives a firm little nod of the head.

Mompesson assembles himself, adjusting his hat and fiddling with the white frills of his collar. He bows his head, clasping his hands in front of his long black robes. Finally, he looks to the waiting crowd.

'We are also here to implore each and every one of you to surrender yourselves to the mercy of God. To trust in him, and demonstrate your love for him. Just as Jesus Christ suffered death on the cross so that the world could know redemption, so too we have an opportunity, through our sacrifice, to save the lives of others. By staying here together and establishing a quarantine, permitting no soul to enter our village, or to leave, we can ensure that this terrible disease stays here with us.'

Mae looks into Father's face, which is flushed – eyes moist, lips pressed together. How he loves an opportunity to demonstrate his fearless piety. All around him, though, objections are flying through the air. *We'll starve! We'll die! Impossible!* But somehow, between the two of them, Mompesson and Stanley talk the village down. They speak again of sacrifice and faith and redemption. They speak of charity. And they speak of love.

The voices of dissent peter out as assurances are given that arrangements have been made with other villages. Food and other necessities will be brought from Fulwood, Bubnell, Foolow and Stoney Middleton. They will be left at either the top well, or the stone circle at Wet Withens. The Earl of Devonshire has promised that supplies will be brought weekly to just south of the village. Special requests and letters for posting can be left at the boundary stone.

When it is all decided – after Mompesson asks the

village if they are agreed, to show their hands if they are — Thomas Stanley calls on Father *to advise us all on the best medicine.* As Father steps forward, he grasps Mae's arm so she is forced to navigate with him around the huddled groups of stricken families. All eyes are upon them, and as they reach the fearless crowd at the front it somehow makes space for them.

Here, pressed together, are the villagers who do not care how the pestilence finds its way from one person to another. Here are those who believe prayer will protect them. Or a tussie-mussie pressed to the mouth, or an amulet around the neck. They are thronging, a thick seam of leaden faces, and they part for Father like the scriptures say the Red Sea parted for the Israelites. Suddenly, though, there is a surge of bodies around them, and in that blessed jostling Mae loosens herself from Father's grip. She sees Marshall, a little distance away to the right, and presses back against the heaving of the crowd, relief flooding her as Father disappears ahead and she is lost from him. She pushes through the mass of linen and buttons, breeches and petticoats, rancid breath and smoke, salt and lye soap.

She pulls on Marshall's shirt sleeve, breathing in his earthy, clay smell.

'Can you see Isabel?' she asks, looking up into his face. He hardly pauses, unquestioning, scanning the delf and the hundreds of shifting bodies. It takes him almost half a minute, but then he nods, turning back to Mae, using his thumb to indicate somewhere behind them. He bends and tells her in a rough whisper, 'Head straight for the cluster of oaks. She is between here and there.'

There is a wind picking up, blustering about the place. Father is doing his best to be heard above it, straining to cast his voice out into the crowd as he tells them all how the eruptions on the skin should not be left – they must be cut, and seared with a hot iron, or made to suppurate with a cupping glass. His voice is hardly up to the job – it is thin and reedy, splitting over *glass* and *skin*. Out here, she notices how brittle he is. She thinks of ginger tea, of garlic soup, of warm, spiced ale. But he would rather talk of dried toads, and she turns away from the sound of his voice.

He must have seen her first, for with a sudden start Rafe is there in front of her, his face full of all sorts of worry, looking strangely unfamiliar. He smells different, his colours darker, but she does not dwell on that.

'He keeps you shut away, does he not?'

She nods, the memory of Father finding them together in church rushing over her, swilling around her. She is still not sure what was worse – the look on Father's face or Rafe's.

'Has he beaten you again?'

She wishes he had; it is worse that he has not, that her punishment is yet to come.

She shakes her head.

'Your face looks better,' he says.

Mae's fingers trace the cuts around her eyes, and above her lip. They have almost healed, and she had forgotten about them.

'What of the things we spoke about?' she says. 'How can I get them from you if I have a chance to leave?'

She wants to tell him what she has discovered since they saw each other last, although blood pulses fiercely at her throat, urging her to be quick. She opens her mouth to speak — to tell him of the monstrous thing that Father did — but finds she cannot. Rafe might see things differently if she tells him — he might see *her* differently. If she was to say *Father thinks me evil*, then Rafe might surely *imagine* her as evil. If she was to say *he thought Mother a witch*, then would he not ask himself, *was she?* Just as she asks herself that question if she dwells on the matter too long.

'I found his diary,' she says, whispering.

Rafe stares at her, scrutinising her face.

'He—'

The words form in her throat, but refuse to come from her mouth as if her lips and tongue want no part of it.

'He—'

She *knows* the truth, but as she tries to speak, it sounds like a lie. *He poisoned Mother because of the dead baby boys. Because of the colours she saw. He calls her witch.* These are the things she wishes to say. *And he murdered Leah too.* But the words do not make it through her shame. *Her* shame — which makes no sense at all.

If I could have my two-penn'orth now, I would. *My* tongue would not be shy in my mouth.

'He has always been so clever with the poisons,' she says.

It is a start, and the boy is bright, so perhaps it is enough. She thinks of the embroidered shift and coif that she found beneath his diary, and the winding sheet she discovered when she went back the following morning to look again.

'I am not safe there with him anymore.'

Rafe holds her gaze, and Mae watches him inhaling what she is trying to tell him. From the pooling of his dark eyes, and the waspish flicker of his brow, she knows her words are seeping into him, unsettling everything. Slowly, he turns his gaze to Father, who is addressing the crowd.

'And no one would believe it of him, so what can I do?' she says. 'If I don't do something he'll have me in the ground along with Mother and Leah, and himself a beacon of pity.'

Rafe presses his palms to his eye sockets, then drums them against his temples, knocking something into himself, or knocking something out.

'We must tell Isabel,' he says, making it sound so simple.

She shakes her head.

'No one would listen to you and Isabel over Father, and he would make the most of any conflict with her, believe me. It is not safe for her to accuse him, and you must not speak to her about it, Rafe – not with Johan gone.'

'But—'

'We do not have time now to talk it through!'

'So, you must go! Go now! Go tonight!'

She considers it again, but she cannot leave as a girl. She has fought this from all sides but it holds its shape.

'I need to cut my hair, and dress as a boy. I need to take things of value with me to stand a chance. It is the only way to get away safely.'

'I can get you all the things you asked for,' he says, looking strangely vacant, as if he is not sure that he can at all. 'They are all at home,' he reassures her.

'How do I get them from you?'

'I could go for them now.'

She takes his arms, squaring up to him.

'There is no time for that. Listen to me. Leave them at the back of Cucklett Cave, up on the ledge. Will you do that?'

He nods.

'And you need to get the Talbot boys to make me a key for the front door. They *like* you, swear them to secrecy so you do not get into trouble. And when you have it throw it over our wall at the very back, where the fox run used to be. Just ... *as soon as you can.*'

She tells herself it does not matter that the church doors will be locked from now on. If she has a key then she can leave in the darkness when the time is right – at a moment of her very own choosing. She likes it much better than the idea of squeezing out the window on a rope of linen while Father is at church.

'And what about all this?' Rafe says vaguely, looking around them.

'What *about* all this?'

'No one in, no one out.'

She shakes her head, sorrowful, uncertain.

Rafe's eyes are wide and watering.

'You are truly my only friend,' she says. 'The only person who can help me. And I am so sorry. I do not wish to cause you any trouble ... '

It is the first time she has given much thought to this. That after she goes he will be left behind. That Father or Isabel might suspect him of knowing something. Or, even worse, of having assisted her. She knows that she will need money, but does not press him on that matter; she cannot bring herself to make a thief of him.

'I need to go,' she says, throat thickening with emotion.

It is time to lose herself in the crowd all over again, so she is there when Father finishes speaking. She must not arouse his suspicions. She must create the illusion of obedience, and gift him a sense of superiority: make him think that *he* is the one with the best laid plans.

Rafe presses a hand to his head.

'Rafe..?'

'It hurts,' he says.

She reaches for his hands, and finds them cold as stone. Something shifts, her stomach dropping. She touches her fingers to his forehead which is hot with fever. The heat is pouring from his body and she feels it now at the bare flesh of her throat.

As she stands there, face to face with him, his hot breath spreading across her skin, she can smell it on him too; a rank pond-green swirling with his butter yellow.

CHAPTER THIRTY-TWO

Wulfric's Diary

August 8th 1660

Never before have I known such peace. You
have lit the way, and sent your angels to wrap
their feathers about me. You knew my anguish
when I saw to what she had given birth – a monstrosity that could only be the work of the devil,
and yet Florence saw beauty in its deformity.
Beauty! It was when she uttered such blas-
phemy that I knew what must be done – what
you were asking of me. Just as the thought came
to me, the house filled with the strangest light –
pink as roses – and I felt quite calm. Then when
you drew me to the casements I saw sign of your
covenant – a sky burning red with blood.

It was truly a wonder that I felt no doubt.
No doubt at all! As if you had spoken directly,

assuring me that all would be well. As she drank the thornapple tea I felt you moving within me, and never before have I known such ecstasy. It was a pleasure to rule all earthly pleasures – surging through my veins as if my blood was liquid gold. In those hours as she slipped away, you gave me a glimpse of heaven. A promise of what is to come. The sign that I have hoped for all my life – to know that I am saved. I am truly your servant, and will labour ceaselessly in your name. I see it plain, and I see your wisdom in it. What good am I to you, if my name is tainted by association with a witch? And how else can we fight this threat but directly? What good is the Constable or the Sheriff, when they have not seen what I have seen? What good is a court that lets witches go free? What good is a judge, when with just a glance a woman can have him beneath her spell?

CHAPTER THIRTY-THREE

Early Summer 1666

When Johan opens his eyes he thinks it is Katarina's ghost he looks upon standing at the small casement. She is staring across the maze of tenements, her face empty of all expression and no hint of corporeal body beneath her shift. It seems entirely plausible it is her spirit there – so impassive and still. He does not dare to blink – he hardly dare breathe – for fear that if he does she will disappear. That he will turn and find her dead upon the bed, and will have to break the news to Jacques. And he has not the stomach for that sorrow.

He tussles with the thought of what a coward he is. At every turn, the world seems intent on demonstrating that he has no valour; that he runs from every battle, even when the cause is worthy.

'Katarina?' he says, pushing himself up onto his elbow, reaching out an arm to Jacques, shaking the slumbering curve of him. He pushes back the bedsheets and stands. Kicking Jacques awake, he nods towards the casement. She looks more ethereal by the moment, as the bright sun blazes through the small window, silhouetting her.

Jacques leaps to his feet, springing towards her, faltering and holding back. Johan glances at the bed as if, even now, he expects to find her lying there.

'Katarina,' whispers Jacques.

Johan hears the joy and the hesitation in his friend's voice. Jacques has kept his sister alive in his own mind all these years, and he has shared her with Johan, bringing her to life so brightly it is as if Johan has known her all this time too. Not as well as he knows his beloved wife. Not as well as his children, or Mae. But as well as if she were a dear cousin that lives just beyond the parish boundary; a dear cousin of whom he has fond memories. And this wraith at the window is not how they remember her.

The men look to one another.

'Katarina,' says Jacques, again. And slowly, so slowly, she turns her head to look at him. Except she does not truly look at him; she rests her glazed eyes upon his face, that is all. He touches his fingers to the sleeve of her shift, and Johan sees it is only the linen he plucks at; as if he does not dare to touch the flesh and bone of her. As if he, too, cannot quite believe in her and avoids the moment he will have to face the matter plain.

'Katarina,' says Jacques again.

And this time he puts his hands gently to her shoulders and pulls her towards him.

'You are safe,' he says. 'Among friends.'

He wraps his arms around her and Johan sees that she closes her eyes as she rests against her brother's body.

Throughout the morning they attempt to persuade her to speak, but to no avail. They tell her about Rafe, and what a fine young man he has become. They bring out the dress she was wearing when she first arrived at the tenement – a simple dress, but edged with lace and silk ribbons. She does not wish to look at it, and when they press their questions upon her, she closes her eyes against their words, and turns her face away.

'Then we shall sit in silence,' says Jacques. 'Gathered, and guided by God.'

Katarina's eyes flicker to him then, and he smiles at her.

'Yes, sister, while you were lost to me, and I was bereft, I found truth in a despised people, and I am truly home. It is everything we were ever searching for – no need for clergy or for common prayer. I have discovered with great joy that God dwells not in temples made with hands.'

He pulls a blanket around her shoulders and crouches at her feet, fiddling with the woven wool as he speaks to her about his Quaker friends – the Peningtons, Thomas Ellwood and Anne Downer. His head nearly rests in her lap as he describes the joy of looking not to ordained ministers for knowledge and understanding, but to any person guided to speak when they gather together.

'Whosoever they be, they are welcomed and listened to – rich or poor, servant or master, man or woman. Can you imagine the beauty of such a thing, Katarina?'

She watches him now with interest.

'Each of us knows what it is to be lost in an ocean of darkness and death,' he says, taking her hands. 'But there is also an infinite ocean of lightness and love that flows for ever within us. And it is never so far away.'

They hold each other's gaze.

'Might that be true?' she whispers.

'I promise you, dear sister, it *is* true.'

Johan listens, unable to fathom quite why his heart is sinking so. Perhaps it is the air that gets to him – he can never breathe as freely here in the city as he does at home. He clutches his hand to his chest, as if he could shift the heaviness there. He has wished so fervently over the last days for Katarina to live, and now she does. So why does he find himself so heart sick? Surely it is gladness that his heart ought to be brimming with? Not only because of Katarina, but because he is here with Jacques – after all these months of uncertainty. Throughout last year he had been tortured by fear, convinced that his stubborn friend would perish if he did not sever his ties with Turnbull Street and escape the capital. But Jacques did not choose safety, or listen to Johan's anxieties. And he proved Johan wrong quite thoroughly. He proved him wrong by living, not dying. And proved him wrong by remaining in his garret on Turnbull Street, convinced his sister would one day return to him here.

Johan weighs the pride and wonder he feels at his friend's prescience. But they do not match the weight of his anger. It is all very well *now* to marvel at the miracles – that Jacques survived the plague and his sister has returned. It is easy to think *now* that Jacques was right to wait all this time. But, in truth, what kind of lunacy drives a man to do such a thing – all in the name of a ghost – when he has living friends that deserve his consideration? Johan feels the heat rising to his face as he remembers their argument last night – the unfinished business of it. *What if you had perished here in this garret last summer?* Johan had demanded of him. *What if the pestilence had found you and struck you down?*

Then you would not have been here to wash and wrap my body and take me to my resting place, had been Jacques' retort.

This has always been their fight: their separation, and who is more to blame for it.

Johan was sure he saw the glistening of tears in Jacques' eyes as his lover turned to fill their mugs with brandy; he has never once seen Jacques weep. But when Jacques returned with their drinks there was no sign of fragility – only a coldness there in his face.

Jacques makes the bed with fresh linen and sends Johan to scurry through the maze of tenements to the washerwoman with the soiled sheets. No sooner is he back than Jacques sends him out again – this time for roast beef and bread from the cookshop. *And don't spare the mustard.*

On his way down from the garret, Johan puts his foot through a rotten step, and topples against the mouldering wall – half-blind in the gloom. He yanks his boot from the splintered wood, angry at the wet walls that he finds himself compelled to touch for the purposes of navigation as he descends the steps; he does not see so well in the darkness these days.

Everywhere the stench of piss and shit! It is the thing he cannot bear about London – that there are so few places to be free of it. He longs to walk with Jacques between the elm trees in St James's Park. To get up early to watch the deer in the woodland beyond the palace. To spend an afternoon sauntering down Birdcage Walk. But those days seem a lifetime away; the city has now fallen into ruin and there is an irritation between him and Jacques that he has never known before.

And Katarina – how wonderful that she lives, but what will it mean for them all? He thinks of Rafe, and Isabel, and the love between them. And with a sinking heart, all over again (because I do my best to nudge him in that direction), he remembers his wife's warning: *things will be much changed when you return.*

As he makes his way out onto Turnbull Street, he welcomes the smell of smoke as he passes through the heat that tumbles from the entrance to the smithy. He lets the blacksmith's metallic hammering fill the space where his jumble of thoughts are tormenting him. Then he lets in the rattle of so many iron wheels against the cobbles, and the rap of the raker's clapper, and the vendor shouting himself hoarse about his mackerel and flounders. And beyond it all, streets away, he lets in the faraway lowing of oxen on their way to the slaughterhouse.

It is not long before Johan's nostrils are once again assaulted by the stench of cesspits and dung pots, and he presses his shirt sleeve to his mouth. It is no surprise to him that here the distemper spread like a fire. He wonders what Robert Hooke would have to say on the matter. And for a moment he longs to be home – in the quiet of his parlour, studying *Philosophical Transactions*, or Hooke's *Micrographia*.

The cook shop is crowded and hot: all four spits cooking joints over the fire. He will have to wait to be served, and contents himself with imagining, as he stuffs his pipe, the fatty mutton in his mouth, then the pink juicy beef, and the crispy-edged pork. He requests a flame from the proprietor, and as he pulls on his pipe – the relief of tobacco in his lungs – he weighs up his choices. He watches the overseer of the roast rub his face, neck and armpits with the damp cloth that rested until a moment ago across his bare shoulder.

By the time Johan gets to the counter he has made up his mind; he points to the blistering joint, asking for the fattiest part, and hands over his thruppence. He waits, flicking at the flies that land upon his beard. When the pork is passed to him he sprinkles the meat liberally with salt, folds the bread around it and takes a ravenous bite just where he stands, closing his eyes with the pleasure of the crispy, juicy meat and the subtle sweetness of the bread. The shop has emptied out a little and he moves to the corner to eat there in peace, to save his food from ruining on his journey back to the garret: it is raining now, and water bounces in the doorway.

The meat is hot, and the fat is tasty, and he thinks to himself that he likes *this* about London. Isabel would like it too. He has never managed to persuade her to visit with him – to meet Jacques and see the madness of the city for herself. But she always asks him for the details, and expresses her happiness for the love he knows here, made possible by their marriage of convenience; a marriage that saved Isabel from disgrace after she was found in the arms of another woman; a marriage that has given each of them their freedom. Just as Jacques has brought Katarina to life for Johan, so Johan has brought Jacques alive for Isabel, and Isabel for Jacques. The two loves of his life have never met. But he has brought them together in so many ways, and on numerous occasions. And as he chews on a mouthful of meat and bread, and thinks about home, his throat seems to close against the effort of swallowing.

His thoughts are interrupted by a scuffle at the counter – a man hitting a child so hard that he stumbles across the grimy tiled floor, and lands with a sickening thud against the wall at Johan's feet. Instinctively, Johan bends to the child.

'Leave him!' orders the man, and Johan pulls back.

As he feels the gaze of every hungry customer upon him, he wishes that he had not bent for the child in the first place. He wishes, in truth, that he had not dallied here to eat his food while it was hot, but had taken it outside into the rain. What would it have really mattered if the bread had become a little soggy? He feels an impulse to leave. But all the same, he cannot help glancing down at the child – no older than Edward. The boy struggles to right himself, and Johan sees that he is full of confusion. He feels anger swelling within him, and looks to the child's father who orders mutton at the counter.

'You sir, are a coward.'

Johan does not know where the words come from, but the man in question seems to be in no doubt as he turns to Johan with a sneer.

'Am I now? Is that what I am?'

Johan bends to the child and lifts him to his feet, brushing down his clothes gently, squeezing his small hands for the briefest moment, giving him a smile that he hopes says all manner of things. Then he stands and takes a step towards the man at the counter.

'Yes, sir, that's what you are.'

With an agility he did not know he possessed, Johan ducks the man's first punch, and sidesteps his second. He raises his fists as he has seen men do, but only to protect himself – or so he thinks. But before he knows what he's doing he has aimed a blow at the man's face, and he feels his knuckles connect with a stubbly jaw and the sharpness of teeth. After a brief stumble the man comes back at him with a roar, fists flying, and Johan finds himself on the dirty floor, with the child now looking down at him. The proprietor steps around the side of the counter – a great swinging fellow with sweat dripping from his face – and he takes hold of the man's arm and holds him back.

'Enough!' he says. 'Unless you wish to find yourself in the gutter.'

Johan stands, face stinging, and brushes crumbs of greasy food from his breeches with trembling hands. He does not care to look at the man, or the child, or anyone else in the cook shop, and so he takes his leave – and without any beef for Jacques. The food he has just eaten is unsettled in his stomach now, and he wonders if he will bring it all up onto the cobbles. What a waste that would be.

He buys Jacques a hot pie from a hawker, and fetches a quart of buttered ale from The King's Head on the corner. Katarina is unlikely to eat anything solid before she has taken a good long drink of something nourishing, and so buttered ale seems a good place to start.

By the time he ascends the steps to Jacques' garret, he is trembling so violently he fears there will be no buttered ale left for Katarina. What was he thinking, to start a fight with a man like that? What on earth was he trying to prove?

It is the look on Jacques' face that tells him how bad it is, and straightaway Jacques reaches out for the pie and the ale and Johan stands there in the honeyed sweetness of Jacques' room with strewing herbs beneath his feet, feeling that if he never had to leave that room again then it would be too soon.

The following day they receive a letter from Isabel. It is short, as if she could hardly spare the time to write those few scant lines: *Harry, Edward and Rafe have the plague. The village has agreed on a quarantine. Not a soul is to leave, and not a soul is to enter. I will try to write again, but am forced to rely on the kindness of others to arrange posting.*

Johan is trembling then, all over again.

'Stay with me,' says Jacques, standing in front of him. 'You cannot help your boys by travelling home to them. You told me I was out of my mind to stay here in London when it raged all around. By some stroke of luck I have survived, and now, I know why – for Katarina and for you. We can leave this place together, and find somewhere better for all of us. We can go to where our new Quaker friends meet, and make a life for ourselves where we can follow our own wills and be true to our hearts. What good would it do for you to return now to Eyam? Why go headlong towards that pestilence when it rages? They have decided as a village: no one is to enter, and no one is to leave. Your fate is sealed, surely?'

Johan feels no shame when he starts to cry, and Jacques shows no sign of frustration. He simply wraps his arms around his friend and rocks him until his sobs have ceased.

CHAPTER THIRTY-FOUR

Leah

*M*other never said the things I thought she might – the things I thought myself: that if I hadn't told Father about the eagle stone then the babies might have lived.

Father did not speak of sons, souls or blessings. And he did not gather us to pray for salvation – neither theirs nor ours. He brought Mae and me into the kitchen and told us, 'You are never to speak of this monstrous thing.'

He looked between the two of us, waiting for our promises, and both of us gave them. I glanced at Mae when he turned away, as if I might catch some sign in her face of what exactly it was we were promising never to speak of.

He took the dead babies from the house, and when he returned so many hours later, empty-handed, I could tell from the mud on his boots that he had been walking across the moors. The rain had been lashing down and he left peaty puddles wherever he stood. And I wanted to ask where he had taken them.

All night I lay awake, listening to Mother keening into her pillows, muffling the sound that seeped all through the house regardless. Mae came from her bed to mine, pushing herself into the curve of my body and, for once, I didn't turn away from her.

The next morning when Father went to Stanley, Mother told me to fetch Isabel. Although I knew I'd be in trouble if Father discovered my disobedience, I did as she asked. I ran all the way, hammered on the door and told her the babies had come too soon. Isabel came running, the eagle stone around her own neck now, bouncing there against her collarbone.

In the bedchamber, Mother said that her heart was weary, and then, as I listened from the doorway – Mae clutching at my coats – she spoke of sons joined together at the chest. I tried to imagine such a thing.

As if they wished not to be parted, she said.

Perfect in every other way, she said.

So many little fingers, she said.

Isabel sent me away to make a caudle. And from the kitchen I heard her singing to Mother, the tune holding steady beneath the rise and fall of Mother's cries.

When Father returned, he brought all the rage I had imagined him bringing. He called them witches most vile – throwing the words across the bedchamber, and Isabel from the house.

He brought a storm to every moment, and the day stretched on as if it would never end.

All through the night, the trouble was there nudging me awake. But by the time the sun rose in a sky of blazing crimson, a blessed calm had descended upon Father, and therefore upon us all.

He closed the door to his bedchamber and told us Mother needed her rest. He asked us to pick flowers from the garden for Isabel, and to take them to her with his letter of apology: he was most sorry for his words and actions. He had been distressed by the loss of his sons, and asked for her forgiveness — perhaps, in a few days, he said, when Mother has regained her strength, Isabel would be so kind as to pay a visit?

But three days later, Mother was in the ground.

CHAPTER THIRTY-FIVE

Early Summer 1666

That Rafe, Harry and Edward are laid low with the plague is not so much a thought in Mae's head, but a bird trapped in her ribcage, forever taking flight.

Don't let them die. Don't let them die.

Not a thing feels quite as it should. The stairs are a spongy moss beneath her feet. The milk smells of boiled onions, and the skillet takes every ounce of strength to lift. Even Sam strikes her as changed. *Has he always been so tall? Was his hair always the colour of straw?*

She remembers the time that Johan pressed his glasses to her eyes — how the world lurched away from her, fuzzy and strange. It is just the same now; when she rises from a chair, or her bed, or scales the steps in the pantry, she feels as if she is falling and falling and might keep falling for ever.

I flutter my warnings to her best I can — that this is the

start of it. And I hear the echo of my words beating through her thoughts: *this is the start of it.*

Father is changed, also, but only in that he has become much more himself. He brims with choler, unaware now of his troublesome hands. He grinds his own herbs, and works late into the night. They skirt around one another, pretending they do not. And Mae retches silently when she vomits, so he does not suspect her methods.

His energy for demonstrating to Sam knows no bounds, and the apprentice tires long before his master. Father's fingers do not slip on the knife, and the pestle and mortar behave in his hands. The quarantine, so threatening to some, has gifted Father a feverish excitement.

It is God's doing, he keeps saying. *God's wish.*

She tries to intuit how things unfold in Ivy Cottage, determined to somehow *feel* bad news before it has a chance to surprise her. As if it might be bested that way.

I try to distract her from it, as if the bad luck that has befallen the Frith household might somehow make its way here, if we are not careful. I try to distract *myself* from the stuffy chamber where the three boys lie, whimpering with pain and sweating with fever, wetting the sheets beneath them. The air in that chamber is full of a mother's fear, and that fear is thick at Isabel's throat as she watches the buboes at her sons' slender necks grow larger by the hour. She does not slice the swellings with a knife as Father advises, but coats them with an oak bark paste. She has instructed Gabriel and Frances to stay at all times downstairs, insisting that they sleep in the parlour. She shouts out to them when she wants for something, and they leave whatever she has requested upon the stairs. And when she hears Frances weeping in the kitchen, but cannot go to her, she sits at the top of the stairs and sings – loud enough so that all her children, in all the parts of the house, can hear her.

The clock strikes three in the morning. She may have been awake for hours, but there is also the sensation of waking – of slipping through from another place. Mae realises she has been dreaming of sleeping, and dreaming of waking, dreaming of this bed and this chamber. And she wonders now whether she is truly in the land of the living at all, or whether she only dreams of lying here. Even in the darkness, with nothing to lurch unnervingly, the world seems to be sliding away from her.

She thinks of the lost arrangements between herself and Rafe – the things they agreed now forgotten as he lies in his sickbed. He cannot go now to the Talbot boys; no key will be forged and thrown across the wall for her. Resentment runs through her, but her guilt does too; how can she begrudge him such a thing when he ails so?

She sits up, listening to the creaking of the cottage's bones, her hollow breath, the smooth, rounded call of the owl outside. Pushing away the sheet and blanket she eases herself out of bed and, barefoot, feels her way in the dark out of her chamber and down the stairs. The task is almost beyond her, and she leans against the wall to steady herself – to reassure herself that it only *feels* like falling.

One, two, three.

She counts each step – just a whisper, but loud enough to make herself real in the darkness.

Four, five, six.

She forgets about the second to last rise, and it cracks beneath her. Motionless, heart fluttering, she waits. And then, after a moment, settling, she descends into the kitchen.

In the darkness, groping, she checks the door to the garden and finds it locked. Blindly, she feels at the rusty nail in the doorframe. Then, shuffling through the kitchen she goes to the front door, grasping the cool ironwork in both hands, pushing down, urging it to open. It does not, and, without hope, she feels for the twine and key at the nail there too – her fingertips soft against that little stub, jagged and unadorned.

The air in the kitchen is warm, and thick with the smell of charred wood and smoke.

It is simply a roar they hear, no words, and nothing else to indicate what occurs. Mae had been scraping hot ashes from the bread oven, and Sam had been looking for an empty jar, but now they look to one another, eyes darting back and forth towards the lobby. When at last the door is thrown open, the rain comes lashing in with Father.

'How *dare* she come leaving her spells at my door?'

They stare at him, agog. Water drips from the rim of his hat until he slings it upon the table, scattering camomile flowers – weightless as dust, soft as feathers. He thrusts the contents of his open palm towards Mae, stepping close enough that she can smell the grease on his hair. A broken jar – its pieces dirty with soil, sticky with oil, wet from the rain – is settled in his hand like a dead thing. A coin glints amongst the mess, and she dares to look him in the eye. She shakes her head, trying to tell him, *I know nothing of this.*

'That woman thinks herself fit to meddle with me! With my household! With my daughter!' he says, taking the coin between finger and thumb, sharing the clumped pieces between cupped hands. He steps towards Sam and shows him, too.

'A spell,' he says. 'Hidden just out there in the soil, waiting to trip me up!'

'Where are your things?' Sam asks, as if trying to change the subject and remind Father of the butter and the cheese he had been to fetch from the Kings Arms.

'Ruining in the rain,' Father says, and Sam goes to retrieve them.

He brings the wet basket of food into the house and closes the door, locking it and returning the key to Father.

'Just a silly spell,' says Sam. 'My sisters do them all the time, for some fancy or another. If it's not a coin in a bottle then it's looking in the ashes in the morning, or putting a sprig of something beneath their pillow to see who they might be marrying.'

His words are cloying, obsequious, and Mae suspects his insides are churning just as hers are churning. She reaches for the table to steady herself.

'You sicken,' Father says, glaring at her.

She shakes her head.

'I am quite well . . .' she mutters, knowing she mustn't take to her bed, or give Sam any cause to think her ill. For *that* really would be the start of it.

Father leaves the broken jar and the coin on the hearth,

and fetches *Malleus Maleficarum* from the parlour, dropping the heavy tome on the table with a great thud. He opens the book, turns the pages. Then, leaving Mae and Sam glancing between each other and the open book, he unlocks the door to the garden and disappears out into the pouring rain.

What is he fetching?

She thinks of leaving, *right now*, as a matter of urgency. Of thrusting herself through his tiny window and falling to the ground. Of running and running if her leg bones have not broken. Sam fidgets, looking towards her with sorrowful eyes, his mouth opening and closing with lack of certitude. And before either of them manage to speak a word or to make a move towards anything useful, Father is at the door again, eggs in hand. He reaches for a porringer, lays it on the table, and cracks the eggs into it. He peers at the pert globules, squinting, scrunching up his face in concentration. Reaching for a knife, he points at one of the eggs with the tip of it, bringing the porringer to Sam, holding it up to the light of the window.

'You see those hairs? You *see them*?'

Sam nods.

'Witchcraft,' Father says.

Sam shakes his head.

'*Yes*. What else? What trickery can magic human hairs inside a hen's egg? And what do you suppose would happen if you were to eat such a thing? The hair of a witch putting down roots inside of you?'

Sam swallows, eyes wide.

Father turns to Mae.

'I never heard of such a thing,' she says, quickly.

'You think it chance? This—' He points at the broken

jar dribbling oil onto the table, the coin glistening. 'And this vile . . . '

He proffers the porringer of eggs, the contents all shiny and sliding. Mae shakes her head, unsure what to say.

'She lay with another woman,' Father says, turning back to Sam.

Mae falters. Her head is splitting in two – a pain dividing her brain into equal parts. Her mouth is dry as ash, and for a moment she cannot feel the flags beneath her feet.

Father is throwing Isabel's name around like a dirty clout, strewing *that* story about – two young women stripped of their shifts and stockings and modesty. Women who forgot themselves quite joyfully, and needed reminding.

'She repents nothing. She has *played* at it, to gull the fools in this village. But behind our backs she laughs at us,' says Wulfric. 'And goes about all manner of evil. *This* for one thing.'

He jostles the eggs in the porringer.

'My family is lost because of her,' says Father. 'My boys that never lived, my wife and daughters attainted. I have never heard of a midwife deliver so many dead and deformed infants. And yet not a soul in this village cares to challenge her. Do you know why they do not challenge her?'

Sam shakes his head.

'They are bewitched. They open their doors to her, inviting her into their parlours and kitchens so she may press upon them her potions and spells. Everywhere around us in this village there is evil and trickery. It has simmered beneath the skin of so many here around about – and now we face God's punishment because of it.'

It floods from him, and Mae sees how he lets it go – not so much carelessness, as confidence; how bolstered he has been by the plague tightening its grip on the village.

'God sees to all things, does he not?' says Father. 'Let justice roll on like a river, righteousness a never-failing stream.'

Sam and Mae exchange glances.

'Isabel Frith will soon know what it is to lose her sons. And those children of hers will be buried out in the fields where they belong. And as justice rolls on, she will lie beside them.'

A moth distracts him, flitting from beneath the shelf of crockery and making straight for his face. He bats it away, sloshing an egg onto the floor, its yolk splitting.

'Blasted things!'

He clatters the porringer onto the table and stretches for the creature, trying to close his slow fingers around it. It dances in the air between them and he tries for it again, slipping in the spilt egg, sliding to his knees with a cry of pain.

'Clean this mess,' he says to Mae, stepping up from kneeling, unfolding himself. 'And put this filth on the midden,' he says to Sam, pointing at the contents of the porringer.

The boy scurries out the door, quick as a rat.

Father takes the large flat spoon they use for measuring herbs from its hook on the wall and strikes at the moths that cluster beneath the shelves, thwacking the polished bone against the huddle of creatures. Some take flight – a great tumbling of fluttering wings – and others fall, broken, to the floor. Father stumbles about the kitchen, slapping and stamping – crushing the dusty bodies into smudges of silver brown. Then he goes through into the pantry, and as

Mae cleans the egg away and collects the dead moths that are scattered across the stone flags, she hears the *clack* of the spoon against the pantry shelves.

The back door is open still and she cannot help but look to the garden wall – the great impossible height of it. She would never get over it, but still, in her mind's eye, she *does*. She scrabbles upwards, pulling herself over the top, hanging down briefly on the other side, all the time the woods beckoning – urging her to let go.

She wipes at the dusty marks on the walls, as Father continues his frenzied activity in the pantry until the long-handled spoon of polished bone splinters into pieces. He comes through into the kitchen, rolling his sleeves, and splashes water from the trough outside across his neck and face. He stands there for a moment in the sunshine looking refreshed, full of vigour, and I wish I could steal a little for myself.

I am weakened by his morning massacre. I have carried his story and my own shame for so long. Surrounded now by so many broken wings, who is to carry me?

CHAPTER THIRTY-SIX

Wulfric's Diary

August 24th 1662

It is an affront to us all, and a great travesty for this village, that Reverend Thomas Stanley is to resign his living – unwilling (like any pious man would be unwilling) to accept the Book of Common Prayer being forced upon us by our papist king. Stanley says he takes some comfort from the hundreds of other ministers all across the land who refuse the oath also. He promises me, and his other faithful parishioners, that we will find a way to meet in collective worship, no matter the imposition of a new rector. I have considered confiding in him about the evil in my own household – the foul truth that has become my existence. But last night I dreamed that an angel stitched my lips together – so I will heed your warning. Not all men have the courage to do what you have asked of me. Stanley is a pious man, and your faithful servant. You have called him to minister on your behalf. But you have called on my courage for a purpose more urgent.

Speaking of courage, I confess to a small moment of doubt when Leah struggled against me. I did not expect that after Florence. There had been no resistance at all from my wife – as if she knew in her heart what must be done and that she would be delivered of the darkness when the deed was over. But the demon within Leah was sly – feeding her flagrant disobedience. Her denial of prayer! Her accusation that God is cruel and not to be worshipped! I caught her spitting in the milk, and later when I went to see, it had indeed gone sour. I knew she meant me ill. I saw in her eyes a look of Florence – the kind of cunning that would best me, given half the chance.

When you struck her down with the coughing epidemic, I understood it was an invitation and saw what needed to be done. She swallowed only a few mouthfuls of thornapple tea before the devil knew it was snared. I saw its cunning in her face – her attempt to pluck at my heart strings. She played at being a daughter – to make me forget what she truly was. But I felt you beside me then, your promise of salvation flowing once more like gold through my veins.

Never have I needed you more – and you did not forsake me, Lord. Did you feel me tremble? Not from fear I promise you, but from joy.

I have felt a beautiful peace return since Leah was placed in the ground beside her mother. It reminded me of how it had been after Florence was released. All around me is settled once more. And I do believe her sister feels it too. There is a quietness in the household that is truly a blessing – as if I am held in the bosom of Christ, suckling of his love.

CHAPTER THIRTY-SEVEN

Early Summer 1666

*S*am and Father sit across from one another and conduct their afternoon lesson by the fire, because Mae has stoked it up ready for the hare pie. And also because the rain has continued for days and everything has a dampness about it. Sam mirrors Father's posture – elbows resting on his knees, leaning forwards with his hands clasped in front of him.

They speak of sleep.

'The benefit of sleep need no proof, for without it no living creature may endure,' Father says, beginning the lesson, reading from Thomas Cogan's *The Haven of Health*.

They speak of Ovid and Metamorphoses, and the 'great chain of being'. It takes Father several attempts to explain to Sam the mystery of night-time transformation: that sleep is a midpoint between life and death, between the physical body and the soul, between a waking reality and the higher realm where God resides. Sleep provides an opportunity for alteration, and communion with the heavens.

Cradling Gervase Markham's *Country Contentments* in his arms, Father instructs Sam that adults must sleep well bolstered up, resting for the first few hours of the night on their right-hand side, and only then may they turn to their left.

'Old people must sleep in a chair, and children on their backs. And not one of us is to sleep grovelling on our stomachs.'

Father describes how the commodities of a proper sleep will perfect digestion, sharpen the mind and nourish the blood, heart and liver. So too will it restore the balance of heat and moisture in the body.

'Eating before bed leads to overheated bellies and provokes nightmares – especially true for children, due to the frailty of their stomachs and their watery organs.'

They discourse on the foods that can aid a restful slumber by sweetly moistening the bowels – oats cooked in warm milk, bread and dried fruits soaked in fortified wine, mixed with a little cream.

'Calm and honest contemplations are always the best way to procure oneself a good night of sleep,' says Father.

Mae closes her eyes at these words. She is mixing water into flour and suet, bringing the pastry together on the table – a little roughly to my mind, but perhaps she does not care if it spoils.

'Past misdemeanours can steal slumber in its entirety, and a fretful mind will hinder it greatly,' he continues. 'Prayer is advised because God provides the gift of sleep, although a man of medicine assists God in such matters.'

He rubs his hands together – the rasp of it like the sound of paper on paper.

They speak of the soporific syrups that might provoke a heavy sleep, how they can be made from poppies or the moss of an ash tree and that *once made, they keep well for years*. Father describes the process of harvesting the ingredients, infusing and straining them. They speak of the merits of bathing the feet in camomile water in the evening, or inhaling the vapours from aniseeds steeped in rose water. Father instructs Sam in the matter of soothing decoctions – to be made from mandrake, houseleek, purslane, cowslips, parsley, endive, tobacco, lily and henbane. These liquids can be wiped across the neck, face and temples to aid a restful slumber.

Sam's lips move, repeating the names of the herbs beneath his breath and Mae hears the hiss of his whispered *houseleek, purslane, cowslips, parsley*. And they tumble like a rhyme through her mind for the rest of the afternoon.

She grinds suet into the minced hare and parsley, and thinks of Anthony Skidmore lying in his sickbed just as Rafe, Harry and Edward lie in theirs. First thing this morning Anthony's mother sent his sister, Mary, up the road with a freshly killed hare to say thank you for the pills. Mary had stood for just a moment in the kitchen, and told them shyly that *Anthony sleeps much better now*. And as she was speaking, the hare hung limply from her hand, its silken ears brushing across the stone flags.

For the third time that day there is a knocking at the door. Father has sent Mae away to her bedchamber on both previous occasions, and so, pastry half-rolled, she chooses to take her leave to avoid giving him the satisfaction of commanding her to go. She slaps her hands one against the other, dusting the air with flour.

From her bedchamber Mae can just hear the murmur of a woman's voice coming from below. It sounds like Isabel, but she supposes this is only wishful thinking. She cannot see the doorstep from her small casement. As she listens to the timbre of their voices, picking out the familiar, she becomes certain it *is* Isabel. And all of a rush Mae is full of fear that she has come bearing bad news. Surely Isabel would not have left her sons' sickbeds if they were still alive? Would she not send Frances for medicines?

Mae pulls off her slipped shoes and sets them down. She creeps from the room and, taking a deep breath, reaches for the door to Father's bedchamber. Without permitting herself to think about it at all, she opens it, steps inside, and pushes it closed behind her.

On tiptoes, she moves across the floorboards to the little square of daylight. The rain has been falling against the open window all afternoon and the floor beneath it is wet. She leans out a little, snatches a glance below her, then comes back inside, and waits, listening, hardly able to bear the thought of what she might overhear.

Mae curbs her terror with the repetition of her ragged breath, and a rhythm on her tongue: *houseleek, purslane, cowslips and parsley.* Looking towards the wooden chest in the corner of the room, she thinks of the shift and coif Father has hidden there: her burial garments. She thinks of the winding sheet, of his intentions, and it takes her breath away. Johan flickers into her mind – the steady ticking of his clocks, the circling of his planets. *Come home*, she thinks. *Come home.*

She realises that Isabel and Father are saying goodbye, their voices stilted and polite. There is the clunk of the door closing and Mae throws herself to the window, leaning out as far as she can.

'Isabel,' she whispers, and Isabel swivels, eyes wide and searching. Her face collapses when she looks up and sees Mae, and for the briefest of moments it is as if she is about to cry.

Isabel thought you dead, Mae, I want to tell her. *She did not believe you were resting.*

'How does Rafe?' Mae asks.

Isabel shakes her head in disbelief. 'Reviving – the others too, I do believe!'

Mae smiles for the first time in days, and for a moment she thinks *herself* about to cry.

'Here! This is for you,' whispers Isabel.

And with no greater warning, she throws something upwards. Effortlessly, it travels from Isabel's hand into hers: a key. The women smile with wonder at one another, and then Isabel is hurrying away from the cottage. Mae retrieves herself, pads quietly across the floorboards and opens the door. The stairwell is dark, but she does not wait for her eyes to adjust. Closing Father's door behind her she slips into the safety of her own bedchamber, mouth dry from fear, arms tingling. She searches her pillows for the one she knows is in need of a little repair and prises the key through the loose stitching, pressing it down until it is lost in a cloud of feathers.

It is fortunate that Father prefers not to look at her, for Mae is sure when she descends the stairs into the kitchen that her deception is a flame across her face, all blaze and crimson, and that the heat of it rises off her. She is a comet, burning through the house, and it is a relief when Father takes Sam away into the parlour. She has to force herself to return to her duties, to attend to the mundane: to squeeze suet and meat together between her fingers.

The pastry comes together into a pie, and she pushes it into the oven, sealing up the gap around the door with a little clay, rushing the job. She clears the table and sweeps the floor. In the pantry she scales the steps – carefully, room swaying – and checks the multitude of jars. Back in the kitchen, she rummages through the contents of drawers – all the little parcels of pills labelled in her own hand, and some now in Sam's untidy scrawl. Ignoring Father's raised voice and rantings from the other room, she checks the whereabouts and quantities of the bezoar stones, crushed pearls and coral.

She will be a thief in the night, blind in the dark, and she makes a note of what she needs to pilfer from where. If he sleeps tonight, then she will away before morning, and she cannot help but imagine how furious he will be when he finds his most precious ingredients gone. He will surely set to shouting the place down – just as he is shouting now. Mae looks away from the shelves and stops to listen, his words coming through to her in snatches.

She thinks herself . . . all three of them spared . . . darkness at work . . .

She knows of what he speaks – of *whom*. Exhaustion surges upon her, and she sits in her chair by the fire. She feels as heavy as one of Marshall's stone slabs, and when *that woman*, and *Frances* tumble from the parlour she feels even heavier.

Father's face will be contorted, bitter with bile, spittle foaming white in the corners of his mouth. She expects him to come barrelling out of the parlour, full of venom, but he does not.

The pie is out the oven and nearly cold before he emerges. But even then he does not want to eat, leaving the house and telling Mae, without looking at her, to *feed the boy.*

They eat hare pie at the table, and it seems as if neither of them has much of an appetite. Her head is full of pain, her eyes playing tricks on her. Sam is ashen, all the summer stolen from him. And along with Father's saucer of pie, the silence sits between them, filling up all the space where usually, with Father absent, they might have talked between mouth-fuls. Sam might even have tried to make her laugh. But it is beyond them today, and Mae wonders at all the lies Father has knotted together in Sam's mind. What tangles he will have made. And what chance will there ever be of unpicking them?

As she wipes their plates she asks where Father has gone. And Sam says *Stanley*; the old rector's name a woeful whisper on his lips.

Mae lies awake as the long summer day finally gives way to the night. Father has been in bed since just after the church bell rang ten o'clock. It rings now to tell the village it is mid-night. She waits another little while, sits up, and reaches for her pillow. Feeling for the loose stitching, she rummages in the feathers for the key, shaking off her doubts. She dresses clumsily, snatches the long strips of linen from beneath her pillows, and slips from her bedchamber.

She holds the key between her teeth and uses her hands to steady herself on the stairs. In the kitchen, she moves as swiftly as her befuddled limbs will allow. She collects together the small jars of coral, pearls and bezoar stones. The jars of tobacco and coffee are too large for her to take, so she transfers some of their contents into pieces of cloth, tying the corners together. She takes the silver coins from the little tin, and feels for several parcels of pills which she had earlier pushed to the very edge of the drawer.

She also takes the cheese, butter and bread from the food-safe, and goes to the parlour for Father's leather bag – wishing there was an alternative to this particular larceny.

Back in the kitchen she fills the bag with her things.

In the lobby, she pulls her boots on – lacing and tying them quickly. She lifts the bag and puts it across her shoulder. She takes the key, and, careful of every tiny movement, slips it into the lock. Taking a breath, she rotates it. Without any resistance it turns, and the door is open.

The warm summer night washes across her face. The nearly full moon skims the rooftops, coy behind a scattering of lacy clouds.

She closes the door and locks it. Six steps and she is at the gate – smooth wood beneath her hands. Then she is through it, heels to the cobbles, stepping lightly. She only thinks as far as the cave and all the things she hopes have been hidden there. But I think further than that. I think as far as the morning and what Father will make of the empty house. Will he claw for the key, checking that it hangs still around his neck? Will he rattle at those tightly locked doors, and strip the blankets from her empty bed in the hope of finding some clue? What sorcery will he imagine has allowed her to escape?

What will he do with his fury?

After a few minutes, she takes a left past The Nook. She thinks of Marshall – all salt and sweat, and how the lines in his hands are stained with soil. She thinks, too, what the village says about him now – that he steals from the dead, helping himself to whatever he fancies from their parlours and pockets.

Further along the lane she notices the candlelight long before she reaches Ivy Cottage. Someone is awake upstairs, and the urge to knock at the door when she reaches it is almost too strong to resist. She feels a rush of doubt, thick and syrupy. Her legs are leaden, as if her very own limbs do not approve of her fleeing.

What am I doing?

I cannot go.

I cannot stay.

What choice do I have?

Already she is slow with whatever he has trickled into her. And all through the day he has been laying the foundations for what he intends to come – telling neighbours, in between gossiping about Marshall, that she *ails with some distemper.*

She tells herself – *I am away, I have escaped!*

Reluctantly, she walks on. She can smell the blackthorn in the darkness, the elder, the oak. The trees are casting moonlit shadows across the path.

Something moves in the meadow to her right. She swivels to look, her eyes making sense of shifting shapes in the gloom. Ann Skidmore, her waist-length hair falling like a veil around her face, is leaning into the task of dragging a wrapped body across the uneven ground. Mae thinks of Anthony Skidmore, and his sister Mary, and wonders who it is inside the winding sheet. She stares, shocked at the sight of a mother dragging her child in this way.

Move along girl, I try to warn her. *Move along.*

She pulls herself from the sight of poor Ann Skidmore, and turns towards the shadows ahead – the waiting trees, the delf, the cave.

At the entrance to the cave she slips the bag from her shoulder and lets it slither to the ground. She steps through the entrance, the temperature dropping and the smell of damp earth filling her nostrils. In the pitch dark she navigates with her hands on the wet stone, feeling her way towards the back. At the place where it narrows, her left hand reaching high along a little ledge, she finds a pile of linen. A smile stretches across her face as she lifts the bundle into her arms. Blindly – unsteady on her feet – she makes her way back outside.

Hidden amongst the clothes are a pair of scissors, a small purse containing some coins, six hardboiled eggs and a piece of cooked beef. She wonders whether it was Isabel or Rafe that gathered these things together, and if it was Isabel what exactly she knows.

She slips the eggs and beef into her bag, and takes the scissors into her hand. They open with the kind of grating sound that makes her shiver. Lifting them to her head, she makes the first cut, feeling the loose slither of hair across her fingers. But then she hesitates. The thoughts are blockish, slow but obstinate – she had sidestepped them on the lane, but here they are again. She thinks about the quarantine, the lives she puts at risk by breaking it. She thinks too of Isabel – how she leaves her friend at the mercy of Father if she goes. She imagines what Isabel might have risked arranging a key to be made — what she will have offered the Talbot family to keep them quiet. She hefts the weight of the purse, and contemplates the generosity of the cooked beef.

If I could force her into her waistcoat and breeches and chase her out the village, then I would. But she thinks still of Father — of the venom that seeps from him. How skilfully he would spread his gossip, turning the village against its midwife. What did he discuss with Stanley just this afternoon? It would be so simple for him to sow seeds of doubt in the minds of their neighbours. To stoke up the fear that smoulders through the village as Eyam stands alone — women and men burying their dead in shallow graves that litter the fields and meadows. All around it is a tragedy. But for Father it is a gift. And she cannot let him make the most of it.

Standing at the entrance to the cave, scissors in hand, she grapples with it all over again. If she cannot go, and she cannot stay, then what is left? Her thoughts are shadowy, blurred at the edges, drifting away from her as she grasps for them.

Slowly, the answer comes to her. The idea is not altogether new, but its weight is new. She breathes the cool night air, weaving the *how* together in her mind, promising herself she can make it work.

She puts the beef and eggs and coins back into the pile of clothing, and returns them to the little ledge where she found them. Back outside the cave she slips the scissors into the bag and turns towards the steep descent into Eyam Dale. Although she cannot see it, she knows it is *just there*. She lifts the bag across her body and falls to her hands and knees. Slithering backwards, she descends into the valley below, grasping at the familiar rocks to anchor herself – to slow her downward scrabbling.

When she reaches the bottom she turns in the direction of the stream. There is no moonlight at all beneath the forest canopy, and she walks with her hands stretched out in front of her. Soon her fingers find the plant's broad head of tiny flowers. Its mousey smell is quite distinctive, with its very own shade of indigo blue. She kneels, feeling for the scissors and the parcel of coffee beans. Emptying the beans into the bottom of the bag, she lays the cloth in front of her. Cutting foot-length pieces of thick stem, she piles them up. They will be oozing an oily yellow liquid, and the stems will be spotted red – some say with the blood of Christ.

She wraps them up and puts them with the other things in Father's bag. Her mind is scattering – rising up out of Eyam Dale, returning ahead of her to the cottage. Her heart pounds at the thought of it – at the notion of him having a sleepless night, poring over his books by candlelight, or praying in the darkness.

She stands, slinging the bag across her shoulder. *Have faith*. Finding her way to the stream, she crouches by the water. She lets the refreshing coolness run across her fingers, and she rinses the hemlock from her scissors.

CHAPTER THIRTY-EIGHT

Leah

As soon as Mother was dead, I realised how much I loved her. I could not forget the eagle stone betrayal; often it was the last thing I thought of at night, and the first thing I thought of in the morning. Once she was in the ground, it didn't seem to matter that Mae had been her favourite. I just wanted everything to go back to how it had been before she died. I couldn't bear Father's prayers – thanking God for his wisdom, his mercy, his love. What mercy? What love? I would not pray, no matter how many times Father beat me. And I refused to say a word in church – I turned myself to stone until the service was over.

I did not antagonise my sister quite so much. I did not pull her hair, or put spiders in her food. I did not wake her in the night with a pinch or a kick. But I did not look at her either, I did not speak to her; I behaved, from then onwards, as if she did not exist.

I went in search of Mother. I found her clothes in the wooden chest in Father's room and pulled them on. When Father found me curled in the bottom of the chest, he ordered me straight away out of her things. When I refused, he fetched a knife from the kitchen and cut me from the linen – nicking and slicing my skin as I wriggled and struck out and fought against him.

After he had burned her shifts and petticoats, her aprons and coifs, I still drifted through his bedchamber, picking her hairs from the floor, looking for her ghost in the glass of the casement.

As the months passed by, and she slowly disappeared, I didn't go to his bedchamber anymore. But if I was sick, I would stray to that room – to the chest in the corner – looking for any tiny sign of her that I might previously have missed. And it was there, after she'd been gone two years – when I was ailing with the coughing epidemic, and burning with fever – that I found his diary. I could not read well enough to make sense of it, but that did not diminish his rage when he discovered me.

He reached out for the diary, and because it had become a habit to refuse him anything he wanted, no matter the consequences, I let it drop to the floor. He took my wrist and dragged me back to bed.

Later that evening, he came with his medicine. I had always been a child that liked medicine – the little bottles, the bone spoon, the brief moment of attention. Though I was furious with him, I opened my mouth when he told me to, with no fuss at all.

CHAPTER THIRTY-NINE

Early Summer 1666

The cottage is perfectly still, and Mae thinks it too good to be true. She pauses on the threshold, the night air groping at her back, warm on her hot neck. Turning, she closes the door, easing the heavy handle. The key swivels smoothly, silently, just as it did before. Darkness is seeping into everything, and fear pulses through her body.

Crouching, fingers shaking, she unlaces her boots and eases them off. She presses them right up against the wall, careful to return things to their rightful place so not a thing can catch his eye.

Closing a hand around the thick strap of his leather bag, picking it off the floor, she takes one step and then another, feeling her way. In the kitchen, her gaze is drawn to the place by the hearth where she knows his chair to be. Making out its simple shape in the gloom, a wave of sickness washes over her; for a moment her fear gulled her into thinking he was sitting there. But it is just the folds of his discarded cloak.

At the table, with trembling hands, she begins to empty the bag, taking from it the wrapped stems and Isabel's scissors. She puts aside the long strips of linen that would have been binding her breasts by now had she left. Fleetingly, she evokes an image of herself in Rafe's clothing, travelling as the crow flies, following the fayre until she catches it – chasing fire-eaters and sword-swallowers, conjurers and gamblers, trumpets and drums. How easy it is to see herself amidst that fire and smoke – she can almost taste it in the air, as if her heart knows the choice she should have made. Doubt swirls, and she has to force herself to continue with the job in front of her, invisible and blind in the darkness.

Convinced that any moment she will hear his footfall in the chamber above, she reminds herself to be careful. One befuddled moment and her plans will slither away from her. Persuading herself to work slowly, with rigour, she returns the small parcels of pills to the shallow drawer where they belong. Into the tin that nestles in the corner of that drawer, she trickles a handful of silver coins – every tiny sound jangling her bones. Feeling as if she will never have an appetite again, she puts the cheese, butter and bread back into the food-safe. She unties the parcel of tobacco, returning the contents to its large jar in the pantry. She replaces the jars of crushed pearls, bezoar stones and coral.

She takes the coffee jar from its shelf, and into it she scoops beans from the bottom of the bag, knowing that the rich, pungent smell will still be drifting through the house in the morning; all she can do is trust that Father will not notice. Several coffee beans slither away from her, scattering across the kitchen floor. She cannot waste time crawling on hands and knees in search of them; she will have to find them when the sun rises. Pressing the stopper into the jar, she returns it to the shelf. And then, with everything else in its proper place, she returns Father's bag to the parlour.

Back in the kitchen, unable to look about herself for the stray coffee beans or any loose knot of tobacco that she may have left behind, she gathers in her arms the wrapped stems, strips of linen, and Isabel's scissors. Heart pounding, she navigates the stairs.

At times it is as if the house groans under the weight of its secrets, but tonight it is drowsy with a heavy hush, and Mae finds her way to her bedchamber as silently as a spirit, with just a moth fluttering in the darkness ahead of her.

She undresses hastily, pulling on her shift and night coif. Reaching for the loosely stitched pillow, she pushes the key into its thousands of feathers. She slides the scissors and hemlock behind the chest in the corner of the chamber, and tries to swallow the dryness in her mouth. The blanket and coverlet are old friends and she slips beneath them, grateful to be held for a little while, lying back, *well bolstered up to procure a restful slumber.*

It is a futile thing to hope for rest, but still she plays at it by closing her eyes. There is not a single calm and honest contemplation in the whole of her head, and she fancies that even milk of the poppy would do her fretful mind no good tonight. Sleep teases at her, luring her away for short moments of time – to hemlock-filled dreams from which she struggles to wake, breathless and suffocating.

It is a relief when daylight creeps into the far-off skies. She dresses – shift, petticoat, apron, stockings, slipped shoes. She picks up the wrapped hemlock stems, light as straw, the weight of them belying their power. She does not dare pray for help, even to Mother, given her intended sin. But still she mutters an entreaty to the silent house: *please let him sleep.*

Descending into the kitchen, she feels the day and all its possibilities snaking around her like the twisted vines of white briony – hopeful as those bride-like flowers, foul as the bitter berries. Resentment floods through her when she thinks of what she is driven to, as if, after all, she is proving him right. But there is nothing to be done but press on – tangling and untangling the hours ahead of her, making promises to herself that she cannot be sure of. She tells herself that Father knows nothing. That the parsley in the hare pie will hide the taste of the poison. That Sam will take his leave after eating because he always does. That Father will doze after their evening meal, drowsy from milk of the poppy. It all tumbles through her mind. The parsley. The poison. Milk of the poppy. Father will sleep; Father *must* sleep.

And when it all seems impossible, she tells herself, *one thing, then the next thing.*

No sooner does she have a knife in her hand, than she hears him stirring overhead. Did she disturb him, or has he also lain awake, waiting for the light, ruminating on his own intentions for the day?

The room shudders around her, and she steadies herself with a palm on the table, waiting for the feeling to pass. She hears his footfall, and looks at the wrapped hemlock stems waiting in front of her. She must whittle parcel into poison, and she must do it now before the opportunity is stolen by the day beginning.

She peels back the linen, revealing the speckled stems which, if only glanced at, might pretend to be rhubarb for a tart. She slices a sliver from every end, then cuts the stems in half. There is nothing to do but wait as the oily yellow blood beads at every cut.

Her attention flits to the stairwell, and it is some reassurance that Father has never known how to move silently around the house – has never had cause to practise such a thing.

She fetches a small jar.

Eventually the oozing becomes dribbling, and she catches the precious drops. She wraps the stems again, hiding them in the largest cauldron on the highest shelf. She wipes her hands on a damp cloth, and hides that too.

She is lost in the rhythm of stitching a split seam and sewing plans together when he opens his bedchamber door. Putting his shirt to one side, she rushes to the pantry and drinks a long draught of ale. She takes another mug-full, forcing the swallows. Then she pours Father one, and cuts two slices of bread and a little cheese. She hears the dry rasp of his hands rubbing together, and the scraping of his chair on the stone flags as he draws it closer to the small fire despite the warmth of the summer day. She takes his ale to him, then his bread, and sits across from him with her own saucer on her knees.

She has to force her mouth to chew and her throat to swallow. She also has to force herself to look at him, and she clenches her fingers so he will not see them trembling.

After they have eaten, she listens to the sounds of Father preparing her daily medicine in the pantry. It is the last, and oldest, routine, and once upon a time it had us lining up as if it was a great game to start the day — Mother at one end, and *little mouse* at the other. Sometimes he gave us a tincture on the tongue, at other times it was a syrup, or one of his herbal waters measured out into a mug. Occasionally, there was the riddle of a mystery ingredient — although he never bested Mae with that particular game. We had all enjoyed the daily ritual. Perhaps because all that time ago we glimpsed in him a streak of goodness. Perhaps because it felt like a father caring for his family. Mae tries to remember whether that was ever true — that he cared. And if I could advise I would suggest she cease contemplation on the matter; it confuses things to recollect in this way: Father's love of himself has masqueraded as all manner of kindnesses.

'Because you ail a little,' he says, proffering the spoon.

Before it reaches her mouth, Mae knows he has chosen his precious *Water of Life* for a reason. Not because it is a restorative, defending against all pestilence. Not because it comforts the spirits and bolsters the heart. Certainly not because it is the very best or the most expensive — usually reserved for his wealthiest patients. He chooses it because it overloads the senses. It is a mouthful of discord with balme stalks, burnett flowers and rosemary. Turmenstill and sundew. With red roses, red fennel and mint. With white wine and cinnamon. With ginger, cloves, saffron and nutmeg. With aniseed and treacle. Would she taste the palm of Christ, or a little meadow saffron, in that festival of flavours? Would she taste the thornapple? She cannot imagine that she would. She takes the spoonful he offers, and swallows it down as if she thinks nothing of it. Then she clears their saucers away, and finishes her mug of ale.

When Sam knocks at the door a quarter of an hour later and Father pulls the key from about his neck, Mae slips away to the stairwell. She leaps up the stairs to her bedchamber, and drags the chamber pot from beneath her bed. With her belly so full of ale, two fingers down her throat and the expulsion is swift and violent. It burns the inside of her nose, and she wipes her mouth with the back of her hand.

It is a miracle to have got away with this cunning for the last three days, although it must surely feed his darkest suspicions. Often, his eyes have been upon her in the kitchen when she reaches for the table to steady herself. Repeatedly, he has offered her the chance to rest, and she knows she vexes him by pressing on, *somehow*. He surely wonders what trickery is at play – searching for answers in a world beyond the realm of their own, while all the time the answer to the riddle swills in a hidden chamber pot.

The afternoon is full of the same promises, over and over. *One thing, then the next thing.* Father *will* drink his milk of the poppy, and eat his poisoned pie. He *will* sleep because she will ensure that he sleeps. And when he sleeps he will not notice the stiffening of his fingers and toes, his arms and legs. He will not notice how the poison creeps along his limbs – all the time drawing closer to his heaving lungs, and beating heart.

'Nature marks each growing thing with an indication of its curative benefits,' says Sam, responding to Father's request for a definition.

They discuss the Doctrine of Signatures.

'God has provided in nature the cure for all illnesses,' says Father. 'If only man will look carefully enough.'

Walnuts heal headaches and other afflictions of the brain – the undulating shell resembles a human skull when the hair is removed, and cracking it open reveals a brain in miniature, illustrating the doctrine quite perfectly. Equally wondrous is the stench of wound wort, undeniably like rotting flesh; it is no surprise its leaves make a powerful poultice for festering wounds.

Father lists further examples and Sam repeats them as Mae takes milk of the poppy from the pantry shelf. She gives the bottle a shake, removes the stopper, and pours a good dose into the bottom of Father's mug. She reaches for the pie, but her hands are shaking so severely she can hardly slice it. She brings every scrap of attention to the task – cutting three pieces, each diminishing in size. She lifts the pieces of pie onto their waiting saucers. The largest piece is for Father, the second largest for Sam and the smallest for her. She stares at her piece, wondering how she will manage to sit in the kitchen and eat alongside them. How will she take them their ale without spilling it on them?

One thing, then the next thing.

She scales the steps in the corner of the pantry and reaches for the cauldron, tipping it towards herself so she can retrieve the small jar. The few precious drops of hemlock milk will be coating its insides, pooling thickly in the bottom. She brings the jar back down the steps with her, taking her time, not trusting her limbs.

The saucers are lined up like an accusation. Looking at them, heat rising through her body, she is suffused with doubt. He must consume all the poison, for there will be no second opportunity and a lacklustre attempt will reveal all to him.

He must eat the whole piece.

But if his stomach gripes, as it sometimes does, he may not finish the pie at all. And then he will turn to his apprentice, passing Sam his unfinished meal. *Because you are a growing lad.*

Fear grips at her as she muddles through the difficulty. The saucers of pie blur in front of her, dancing about on the shelf. She squeezes her eyes shut, rearranging the fragments of what she needs to do, piecing them together this way and that.

Deep in that whirl of thinking – hardly aware of stepping backwards and knocking against something – she senses the bottle toppling before she sees it for herself.

She lunges for it, but isn't quick enough, and the milk of the poppy falls into the pail of ale. She snatches for it, but it's too late. The sleeping draught is all but gone: lost in the ale.

Heart clamouring, thoughts flailing, she is convinced of her doom; it is the only ale they have, and ale is the only drink to be taken with supper. The small jar of poison is in her other hand, and sweat is beading on her top lip. The shelves around her are moving like serpents. She squeezes her eyes shut again, back to thinking, blocking out the sound of Sam and Father's quiet discourse in the kitchen.

There is nothing for it, but to give them the ale. Sam will get a strong dose of milk of the poppy, too, but he will surely be home before it takes effect? He will sleep safely in his own bed, aware of nothing but the fact that the day was long and the ale a little too strong. She fills their mugs and is just about to take them through into the kitchen when she makes another decision. Taking the stopper from the tiny jar, she pours the thick drops of hemlock milk into Father's ale. He always finishes his ale – he'd never give the dregs of *that* away.

She takes their ale through to them, Father's fingers touching hers as he takes his mug. The kitchen is stuffy, and she longs to throw open the door to the garden. Does Sam not long for it too? Or Father? She glances at them – supping with long swallows.

In the pantry, she cuts some soft white cheese to go with the pie.

Every step back into the kitchen is an effort, requiring her concentration. There are feet to pick up, and feet to put down. There are saucers to keep level and hands to keep from trembling. There is an expression to find, and wear across her face. And there is warm, muggy air to coax into her lungs.

She passes Father his piece of pie, relieved it does not matter whether his stomach gripes, or not. She passes the second saucer to Sam, and returns to the pantry for her own, bringing a mug of ale for herself too, because it would seem strange to sit and eat without one. She pulls up a stool. Bringing the ale to her lips she pretends to drink. She breaks off a piece of pie and puts it into her mouth, looking from Father, to Sam. The two of them are gazing at the ash in the hearth. She forces her dry mouth to chew, but still the food feels solid in her throat when she swallows. She falls into a tumble of thoughts, and has to pull herself away from them as she realises that Father has spoken to her. She lifts her head and looks at him.

'You sicken,' he says, and his words are an accusation, as if he is tired of trying to make it so.

She finds that she is nodding.

'Yes,' she says.

She looks down at the saucer in her lap, the almost untouched pie. Before she knows what she is doing she lifts the saucer to him.

'Would you care for this? I must lie down for a little while.'

She does not ask for his permission, knowing she will not need it – that he has been hoping for this for days.

'Give it to the lad,' Father says, nodding.

She notices Father's mug – not quite empty. She imagines the hemlock, and milk of the poppy, swirling together like a storm in his stomach.

He will sleep, she tells herself.

Turning to Sam, she offers him the thin sliver of pie from her saucer, and he takes it with a muttered *thank you*. She stands, puts her saucer onto the table, and heads for the stairs, needing every last scrap of strength to lift herself from one step to the next.

It is done now, and if all falls around her she will drop herself from his window, broken bones or no. She will run to the wet cave for the things she knows are there. She will stop on the way to warn Isabel. *Go to him no longer! Find your medicines elsewhere!*

She slips beneath the coverlets.

Eyelids heavy, she listens to the quiet murmuring of conversation downstairs, wondering what they will discuss now she is out of the room. Will Father be grappling again with tales of deceit? What could he say of Mae now, though, that is not true? If he speaks of trickery and evil, could she honestly deny it? That darkness he is so fond of speaking of is all around her. Her body is heavy with it. Her senses smothered.

She sinks into the soft bedmat – falling, and falling. And somewhere, as she drifts, in the very back of her mind she wonders whether he hasn't bested her after all. *Did* she give them milk of the poppy? Or did she only imagine it? Was it some other remedy that fell into their ale? Why is it *she* who falls now into sleep?

CHAPTER FORTY

Wulfric's Diary

May 30th 1666

So it is true that the whole progeny is tainted. That if the Mother is a witch, then the daughters are witches too. She kept her visions and black magic so well hidden – but still I feel a fool. I was blind to what lay before me, and I feel such shame at the depth of her sin – flaunting her lust in your house where any one of our neighbours might have seen her. In your house!

I have been waiting for some sign from you as to how the deed should be done. But I cannot wait much longer. Clearly she has the devil on her side. What wickedness has she brought to bear, under my very nose? Wickedness that I cannot yet see? I am fearful – afraid for my soul if she has her way with me.

Are you angry with me, Lord? Have I failed you? I ask for your forgiveness if this is so. And I ask for you to show me plain – is the plague that visits us here an indication of your anger at me or at the evil in the village? What do you show me with the onslaught of this pestilence? You show me innocents taken. And you show me the devil surviving. Do you not? For this is what I see – the distemper that you have brought upon us, like a sore storm, is not enough to purge this place of evil.

What can I do, but offer my word that I am your faithful servant and will not be bested by the devil dressed up in petticoats?

With Sam in the house I must be careful. I have done the deed right in the past – and I know it pleased you, Lord. I will be sure to do the deed right once more. We are so close, are we not? Although, when I imagine her gone I do not find that my heart settles as I thought it would. You fill my dreams with new concerns – or old concerns, dressed up in new robes. Will her death be enough? Will it resolve the matter? I think not. It is not just Florence who has made witches of my daughters, but that despicable midwife also. What evil will she continue to spread in this village after Mae lies in the ground? If not my own daughters, then which innocents will she entice to do her bidding? And what of her own progeny?

CHAPTER FORTY-ONE

Early Summer 1666

*J*t is the moth on Mae's face that lures her back into the realm of consciousness. Brushing the creature away, remembering, she pushes herself to sitting. She listens, but hears nothing. A feeble daylight loiters at the window and she does not know whether it is still the evening or whether the morning has crept up upon her. Going to the casement, she looks for the sun, and finds what is left of it there in the western sky. She thinks it through – that she has not slept for more than an hour or two, but if all has gone to plan then the deed might be done. It hardly seems possible, but she forces herself to contemplate it. *Then what?* She had not thought beyond the stopping of his heart – she had not thought of his body and what she would do with it.

Slipping out of bed she goes to her jug and basin – dipping cupped fingers into the water and lifting them to her lips. For a moment – parched – she stands there, dipping and swallowing, feeling the cold liquid in the very depths of her.

Her whole body is alert for any tiny sound coming from elsewhere in the house, but she can hear nothing beyond the damp murmur of her breath, the water dripping from her fingers.

Does he sleep? Is it over? Or . . . ?

Wiping her wet hands on her apron, then wiping her mouth, she thinks through the possibilities. She fetches the key that lies hidden in the middle of her pillow.

From the top of the stairs, she sees light from the kitchen washed across the bottom step. She descends, careless about the creaking and groaning of the timbers as she goes. She stops halfway to listen, speaking briefly beneath her breath.

Please, Mama.

After a short wrestle with her courage, she enters the kitchen.

Father is in his chair by the hearth, head lolling backwards, eyes closed. She allows herself to hope, but as she watches him she sees the gentle movement of breath. The disappointment rushes over her, but she reminds herself how all through the day she promised herself this: *Father will sleep.* It is just as she intended.

It is then that she sees Sam asleep also, precisely where she left him. Eyes darting from one to the other, a wave of sickness rolls over her at the thought of what she has done — of the mess she has created.

Crouching beside Sam's chair, she shakes his arm gently, whispering his name. But he does not stir. The corner of his mouth is wet with saliva, and his breathing is heavy. She wonders at his poppy-dreams, carefree and endless.

'Sam,' she says, a little louder this time.

She puts her fingers to the side of his face and taps. Then again, over and over, harder and harder. Giving up, she puts her lips close to his ear, repeating his name as loudly as she dare.

'*Sam.*'

Father stirs – head lifting, lips muttering. Mae rises to her feet, nauseous, mouth dry. Her mind gabbles – that if the poison has worked then his limbs will be paralysed. He'll be unable to move, but perfectly capable of speaking. Of shouting and accusing. Of disturbing the peace, and having Sam do his bidding.

She runs to the pantry and grabs a handful of cloths. She throws them onto the table and rummages through them, plucking one out and scrunching it into a ball. She looks through the rest for something long enough for the task she has in mind. Failing to find it, she runs to her bedchamber and fetches the long strips of linen that she used to bind her breasts.

After summoning her courage, Mae takes a step towards Father, swallowing her fear. She puts her fingers between his lips, prising his teeth apart. He twists his head away from her, sleepily. She pushes the cloth into his mouth, and his eyelids flicker. He begins to make muffled noises – short sounds like faraway geese. Quickly, she takes a long strip of linen and stretches it over his stuffed mouth, pulling it tight and tying it behind his head. His eyes open slowly, and she watches him, with horror, discard his sleepiness.

His eyes dart about the room. He lifts his head and looks at her. Together, they realise the situation: he cannot move his limbs at all. Before he has a chance to gather his senses – to calculate the only action available to him – Mae wraps a second strip of linen over the first, tying that, too, behind his head. But then perhaps he *does* calculate it, for he groans and moans, looking fiercely at Sam with wide, watering eyes.

If Sam stirs now, then she is surely for the noose. She brings her hands to her face, covering her eyes for a moment, wishing to hide from it all. She thinks of her key, and the clothes in Cucklett Cave. And she looks at Father through her fingers – quiet again now. He is trying to calm his breathing – struggling to find the air that he needs. She feels a rush of pity, despite everything, and an urge to untie him – to open the door so the fresh air can rush in and he can heave it into his lungs. But she quietens the dutiful daughter – that part of herself that looks to placate him even now.

She takes a step towards him, crouching down so she can look into his face. She supposes their fear is equal, and this is a strange place to find herself. The silence sits between them, potent and feverish, until he looks towards his apprentice and starts up his furious moaning. She thinks of pressing a pillow to his face, finishing what the hemlock has started. But her insides revolt at the thought of it. It is not the idea of Sam waking and bearing witness that is so terrifying, it is the thought of Father twitching beneath the weight of her hands. Of feeling his last movements – of snuffing them out. She does not want the memory of that – she could not live with it. Reassuring herself that the hemlock will kill him eventually, she tries desperately to think of what to do with him in the meantime. She could drag him into the parlour; but his angry moaning would, from there, be heard easily by Sam when he wakes. She knows, as she thinks it through, that there is no alternative but to get Father to the privacy of his bedchamber. And her heart gallops at the impossibility of such a task.

She strides to the lobby and pulls on her boots, tying them with trembling fingers. She unlocks the door, closing it as quietly as possible. She locks it, lest any desperate neighbours come visiting.

The sky is a bright blood-orange, and a gusty wind is blowing a gale through the trees. She runs – not caring about the clatter of her boots on the cobbles, or whether she is seen fleeing through the village. Up the hill, and left past The Nook.

She finds herself at Ivy Cottage so quickly it's as if the moths have flown her there.

Mae looks tinier than ever. Her eyes are ringed with grey, dark as storm clouds, and her face is full of fear. *Is this it? Is she leaving?* There are plans that Isabel has been pulling together now that – *finally* – she has heard from Elizabeth. Her friend, full of remorse, sent not only a key for Bradshaw Hall, but an invitation to her house in Brampton. *If you feel in danger,* she said, *then you must come. Come right away, if you need to.* It would be a safe place for Mae, reasoned Isabel. A *perfect* place. And it is such a relief to see her stood on the doorstep now; she'd been afraid that Mae would disappear into the night and be lost to them for ever.

'Come hither, step inside,' says Isabel.

'I need your assistance!'

Isabel reaches out to take hold of Mae's arm, but Mae shakes her head, stepping away from the open door, making it quite clear she is resolved to stay outside. She lifts her chin and looks Isabel straight in the eye.

'You must come right now.'

'What *is* this? I am not dressed for coming out,' she says, indicating her house clothes. 'Let us talk inside – Rafe has told me everything. I have an idea – how I can help.'

Mae brings her hands to her face. 'There is no *time*.'

Isabel's fear ignites, all steel and flint. She has never seen Mae this way before. Her mind scrabbles with possibilities, but she keeps quiet, reaching for her boots. She pulls them on, stretching as best she can around the hindrance of her pregnant belly, breathless by the time she has tied the laces.

She steps out of the house, pulling the door closed behind her. Mae strides away into the colourful evening, and Isabel tries to keep pace, taking the weight of her belly by placing both hands beneath it, pain shooting between her legs and over her hips.

'Bounding after you is beyond me,' she says, short of breath.

Mae half glances back at her, but says nothing.

'*Mae*,' says Isabel. 'Slow down. I am coming as fast as I can.'

'We must get Father up the stairs,' says Mae. 'We will have to lift him. He . . . '

She does not look at Isabel, but to the lane ahead.

'Is he sick?'

Mae shakes her head, then seems to think about the question again.

'He—'

'He *what*?'

'He's dying.'

'So . . . he *is* sick?'

Mae shakes her head, but it is more of a twitch, like an animal trying to get free of something.

'What's *happening*? Something is very wrong, and I wish for you just to tell me . . . '

Isabel wonders if it is Mae who sickens. The fear she felt on the doorstep swells within her. It is the same feeling she had when Johan first left for London, and when the boys first ailed. It floods her again now, filling her full to bursting. Despite the surge of questions flowing through her, somehow she falls into silence, her loose hair whipped about by the wind as they pass The Nook and turn right onto Church Street.

At the gate Mae stops and turns, waiting for Isabel to catch her up.

'Sam sleeps, so be quiet,' says Mae.

Isabel tries to fathom what on earth that means as she follows Mae down the short garden path. Cheeks flushing with heat, she waits patiently while Mae unlocks and opens the door. They step into the dark lobby. Without saying a word, Mae disappears into the kitchen. Isabel shuts the door and raises the back of her hand to her flushed cheek. Wiping the sweat from her forehead and nose, she follows Mae. In the dimly lit kitchen she struggles to make sense of the scene in front of her – Father lolling in his chair, slumped to one side, gagged and wide eyed.

'Lord help us,' she whispers.

'We must move him,' says Mae. 'Lest Sam wakes and sees what I have done.'

'What *have* you done?'

Father starts groaning, and Mae pinches his nose, putting her face close to his.

'Quiet!'

He does as she says, and she releases his nostrils.

'What madness is this?' Isabel whispers, hand covering her mouth.

'Lift him with me.'

Isabel glances at Sam, who is also lolling back in his chair, and her mind fights with what's happening, struggling to make any sense of it.

'*Isabel!*'

With all the forbearance she can muster, Isabel puts aside her questions, and the two of them work as one. They grasp Father's bony limbs – lifting, tugging and heaving. They are hindered by baby and belly, and by Mae's tiny frame and weakened state.

Persevering, they struggle with him to the bottom of the stairs.

'Let me go first,' says Mae.

'We'll never do it like this,' says Isabel.

'We *must*.'

'Fetch a sheet.'

Mae runs up the stairs, disappears momentarily into her bedchamber and returns with a bundle in her arms.

Father growls, fixing Isabel with a furious stare. Horror prickling her neck, she leans down and pinches his nostrils closed. He quietens, and she releases him, gesturing to Mae for the sheet.

'Help me get it beneath his arms, and we'll tie it at the back.'

Together, they grapple with the task, knotting the sheet securely once it is wrapped about him. They take hold of the linen, and pull him upwards. With a flow of encouraging words, Isabel urges Mae onwards, up the stairs. Every few steps they pause, standing in the near-darkness, gathering their strength before continuing. Isabel's mouth is dry with fear, and she tries to ignore the sound of Father's head knocking in angry protest against the stairs, and the muffled words he tries to form behind his gag. When they reach the top, Mae opens the door to his bedchamber. Isabel looks to the casement window and the darkness beyond it, remembering the last time she was here in this room.

They drag him, and he glides easily now across the wooden floorboards. When they reach his bed they take a moment, drawing breath.

Mae closes his bedchamber door, and Isabel goes to the casement and struggles to get the rusty thing to close. Looking out across the village, at the candlelight flickering here and there, she wonders what other madness is unfolding tonight.

Mae pulls back his bedlinen, and when Isabel has recovered her strength they lift him onto the bed. They untie the sheet and lay him back. He shakes his head from side to side, letting out muffled cries. Mae unties his boots and agitates them, with some effort, off his feet. She arranges the covers over him.

'What *is this?*' Isabel asks.

'I gave him a dose of hemlock.'

'Enough to kill him?'

'I am hoping so.'

CHAPTER FORTY-TWO

Early Summer 1666

Johan makes his way south through Clerkenwell, and it is not just thoughts of home and the stench of the river Fleet that unsettle his stomach, but the feverish urgency to see his friend, Tom Loomes: crafter of lantern clocks and table clocks, microscopes and lenses.

Late into the night, long after Jacques and Katarina were fast asleep, Johan had listened to the steady ticking of his thoughts. What good would it do to return home now? Much better to stay here and be somehow useful – to negotiate two apprenticeships so that Rafe and Gabriel might leave for London sometime later in the year. With Katarina returned, Rafe cannot stay with them in the north. But if he has an indenture arranged alongside Gabriel – a favourable indenture at a reputable clockmaking house – then Isabel might not feel she has lost the boy entirely. And they would be looked after properly at the Loomes' place. Tom may have been brought before the Clockmaker's Guild on occasion for employing more apprentices than is permitted (business has been brisk ever since the Fromanteel's horological breakthrough of the pendulum clock), but he is a kindly soul, and his dear wife Maria feeds the young men well. An indenture for the boys would surely please both mothers, and spare Isabel the pain of Rafe's returning to Katarina.

This is what he tells himself — the arrangement is to appease Isabel. But, in truth, he wishes for the contracts so Rafe and Gabriel might *live* — as if their names on parchment alongside the signature of the best clockmaker in the country — admired once by Cromwell himself — could put them beyond the reach of any plague. As if death cares only for the idle and the uninspired.

And over breakfast (a draught of ale), Jacques told Johan to take his leave and conclude the matter as he saw fit. He reassured Johan that the clockmaking house in Lothbury, at the sign of The Mermaid, was open still for business — he passed by it himself just a few weeks ago.

'So you think it a good idea?' Johan asked.

'There is no harm in it, I suppose,' Jacques said.

Johan did not ask Jacques about the hesitation in his voice — reluctant to hear it translated into words. He reasoned with himself that Jacques had his own bit between his teeth — all of a sudden desperate to get Katarina away from Turnbull Street to a place where she might recover. For the last ten days he has been progressing his plans — packing up his garret little by little in preparation for taking them all to his Quaker friends in Wycombe.

Johan understands the logic of what Jacques says — *I know*

*your heart is heavy, Johan, but you cannot return to Eyam. Let
us make travellers of ourselves and see where it takes us* – and
has found himself agreeing each time Jacques requests an
answer from him. It *does* make sense to him. He longs to
be away from these sordid tenements, and for Jacques to be
away from them too.

But although he agrees, he cannot quite get swept away
on the tide of Jacques' enthusiasm. He does not only think of
the baby coming, and of his poor boys, who he might never
see again (*no, they will live! they MUST live!*), he thinks too
of the small child in the cookshop, and the thundering of
his angry father. Every night for the last week that strange
man's face has loomed into the darkness of Johan's dreams,
reminding him of a person he cannot quite place – of a
matter that is yet to be settled.

Slipping on the wet wood of the White Friars river stairs, he
slithers, ungainly, onto the narrow jetty, blushing beneath
his beard at the jeers of the watermen. Seconds later, their
chorus abandoned, they shout for Johan's attention with a
discordant barking of prices and enticements: *You look like a
man in a hurry! Surely you want the wherry to yourself? Oi! Here
sir! Only sixpence for the pleasure! Oi! Oi! Don't listen to that
thieving bastard! Let us be off! Quick sir! Step here, sir! Step here!*
Johan confirms his destination and pays the waterman –
tuppence for himself and tuppence to spare the wait for a
fifth passenger. The waterman gesticulates crudely at his
competitors, shouts at Johan to *sit the fuck down* and, standing, guides the wherry free from the clustered, jostling
boats with his oar. Then he sits, and begins to row across

the flow and chaos of the river – amongst the other scull-ers, the faster oars, the tideboats and Western Barges. The passengers speak a little of the intense summer heat – what it will mean for the price of hay later in the year, and the doublets the watermen must surely wish to peel from their backs as they row to and fro across the water all day. They speak of the Margate Ale at The Dog and Duck, and how refreshing it is. And they do not speak of the bloated corpses that drift past them in the water.

He ascends the river stairs at Paris Garden, passing The Dog and Duck, thinking of that Margate Ale, and promis-ing himself a draught on his return. Striding away into the liberties of Southwark there are houses still shut up – crosses painted upon the doors so there can be no mistake. Even the bigger, flat-fronted houses with gutters and gardens have not escaped this insult. Nor the playhouses and the inns – their casements boarded up. He thinks of summer evenings in Paris Garden, and the joy of the entertainment there; not the bear baiting (where the great stage is lowered to create a pit), but the lively comedies that provoke a laughter so raucous, and a bellowing so boisterous it is as if the bears and mastiffs have found their way out of their cages and into the throng of bodies to enjoy the spectacle.

When he finally catches sight of the sign of The Mermaid, he knows before he gets as far as the premises itself that it is not only his wife, and Jacques, who possess a little pres-cience. He understands with a rush of sorrow that the heavy stone in the pit of his belly had been forewarning him of *just this* – the locked workshop, and the empty rooms above where the journeymen and apprentices used to board: not a single casement thrown open.

He hammers his fist upon the door, listening to the silence within. Walking backwards into the centre of the street – his boot catching on the uneven flint – he cups his hands around his mouth.

'Tom! Maria!'

He looks to the casements for signs of life. Then, shaking his head, he fetches three crates from outside the bakery and piles them one atop the other. Not entirely trusting them beneath his weight, not entirely caring, he steps up and peers through the squares of grubby glass into the large workshop. The sun is hot on his back, and his shirt clings damply to his skin. He cups his hands around his eyes to better see, and there, inside, is a perfect stillness – tools abandoned upon the table tops.

All hope sinking, Johan closes his eyes, letting the truth of the matter settle. There will be no apprenticeships arranged today, nor any other day. Not here, at least.

With no certainty, no bond, what does he have? And what is he to do now? Sup a Margate Ale and wend his way across the river with its bobbing corpses?

With the sun burning his neck, eyes closed and head resting against the casement, he feels the beat of his heart there in his chest, pulsing now in his head also, and down the length of his arms, all the way into his fingertips. It beats in his groin too, and in the thickness of his thighs and the aching bones of his feet. As if his heart has broken into so many lost pieces.

Without intending it, his mind drifts home and to matters

that may already have come to pass: terrible matters. When he cannot bear to think about those matters any longer he tries to think of nothing at all – feeling the sun on his skin, and the sticky glass beneath his forehead. But his sons are as insistent in the cloisters of his mind as they are in the flesh. They leap up at him, with such zeal and zest that he is suddenly convinced they are alive – that it is *their* hearts he feels pulsing through his body. He squeezes his eyes shut and imagines it is so. Before he knows it, he feels Isabel's heart there also, and the tiny heart of the child within her. He feels *all* his children, and all their beating hearts. So, too, the frightened, bird-like fluttering of Katarina's, and the slow, steady drum of Jacques' – brimming with love. There is no chaos between them, no discordant clatter: just one steady beat.

It is then he remembers his dream. It was Wulfric there in the gloom, not the father from the cookshop. He thinks again of Isabel's warning that things will be much changed, and remembers all she has said about Wulfric over the years. He thinks of his own cowardice – how keen he is to stay on good terms with people, and how he shies away from trouble. What if Isabel has had it right all these years about Florence and Leah? What if Wulfric *is* what she says? And as he thinks now of Mae – a panic rising at the thought he has abandoned her to some hideous fate – he finds that he cannot imagine the beating of her heart at all. He pushes himself away from the casement, stepping down from the crates. He runs his hands through his hair, and reaches for his unlit pipe – placing the comforting stem between his lips.

All of a sudden it is not the beating of hearts he feels but the ticking of a clock – its insistence, its steady promise, its tightened spring winding down.

He walks away from The Mermaid along Bartholomew Street, striding at a pace as if he can free himself from the notion in his head. But it follows him all the way to the Dog and Duck, and all the way back across the river. And then it follows him all the way to Turnbull Street: *tick, tick, tick*.

CHAPTER FORTY-THREE

Early Summer 1666

As Isabel leans over Father to untie the gag, she is appalled to find herself there in his bedchamber, her hair drifting across his face as if they are lovers. Her hands are shaking uncontrollably and her thoughts are leaping skittishly from one thing to another. She is nauseous from the exertion of heaving Father up the stairs. And low in her belly, every time the baby moves, there is the sensation of bone against bone.

What would Johan think if he could see her now? Would it soften him to know that this is Mae's doing? Or would he think both of them mad, each as guilty as the other?

But Johan is not here now, she reminds herself, a little bitterness there in the thought. She weighs the possibility of keeping it from him – birthing a secret that ticks between them like one of his clocks.

They *are* mad, surely?

Isabel's hands feel weak, and useless, as she continues trying to prise apart the stubborn knot; feeling Mae's fierce desperation in the tightened twists of linen that will not yield beneath her fingers.

'Leave him as he is,' says Mae, her voice wavering.

But Isabel shakes her head. It would calm her nerves, if only a little, to remove the gag. Without it, she may be able to pretend that he is simply a man in his sick bed. She gives up on the knot, though, and yanks the gag downwards so it is a loop about his neck.

He is struggling to spit out the clout that is stuffed in his mouth, grunting like an animal. When Isabel reaches her fingertips to the soggy cloth, pulling so it unravels limply upon his chest, he gasps at the muggy air.

Isabel wonders at the slow progress of the poison.

'Can you speak?' she says.

But he slides his eyes away from her in mute disgust.

She looks to Mae.

'How much did you give him?'

Mae shakes her head, eyes wide and calculating.

'Eight drops.'

'Is that enough?'

'It *should* have been enough.'

Isabel imagines the hemlock creeping through his limbs towards his heart and lungs, but then retreating – too weak a dose to reach its destination. Might life be returning to his limbs as the two women stand dumbly by? She imagines his capacity for cunning, a chill running through her.

'It should be over by now,' says Isabel.

'*I know.*'

'We cannot just stand here like women in waiting.'

With a rush of urgency, Isabel's womb tightens. As the tightening deepens she dissolves into the undulating pain. When she emerges, breathless, heat prickling at her face and neck, she regrets closing the casement. She glances towards it longingly, but at the same time imagines all that occurs here in this bedchamber tumbling out onto the street below and into the village of loose, wagging tongues.

The ticking of a clock like the lantern clock in her parlour at home starts up from nowhere, marking out the seconds with its ghostly heartbeat. It is so distinct that Isabel looks around herself, just to be sure – unlikely though it is that she has overlooked such an object in the chamber.

When her gaze travels back to Father, she sees that he is staring at the ceiling, breathing steadily.

'Do you wish to pray for him?' Isabel asks.

Mae gives a tiny shake of the head. 'I must get rid of Sam,' she says, pushing wisps of hair beneath her coif. 'And then we can decide what to do.'

The kitchen is painted with a gentle apricot, the last of the day's light. On another day she might have been full of wonder, for this setting-sun colour that seeps around the kitchen is Sam's colour. Kneeling beside him, she touches her fingers to his arm. She says his name, and he stirs. She says it a little louder and his eyes flutter open, but then fall directly shut.

'You fell asleep,' she tells him, speaking into his confusion of waking. '*Sam.* It is time for you to go.'

His eyes stay open this time, and he regards her steadily. She stands, stepping away from him, fetching his cloak from the lobby. When she returns, he is sitting in the chair still, rubbing the heels of his hands into his eye sockets. She passes him his cloak.

'Are you sick?' he says.

'I'm feeling better after sleeping. Father is unwell, and has gone to his chamber to rest.'

'I've been asleep so long,' says Sam.

'You must've been tired, and the ale was strong, Father said so himself.'

Sam nods, bending to tie a bootlace that has come undone. He stands, takes his time with his cloak, and all the while that she watches him, she is also in the chamber above. She sifts the possibility that the hemlock was too weak, or that Father did not drink it all. She glances to his mug that waits on the hearth, and sees it is empty.

What more can she do?

What else could she give him?

She thinks of the poison cabinet, and the key that hangs around Father's neck.

Above them there is the sound of footfall, and although she dare not ask God for anything, she asks Mother to hurry Sam on his way.

Eventually, he steps away into the summer evening. Mae does not wait for him to reach the gate and offer a wave of farewell. She steps backwards into the gloom and locks the door.

In the kitchen she takes the scissors from their nail. She is careful to take every step on the stairs slowly and deliberately. When she opens the door to the bedchamber Isabel is leaning against the wall, her forehead pressed there.

Father is a man of stone, cold and resolute, as Mae puts the scissors against the ridge of his collarbone. She cuts the twine and grasps the keys. She snips at the linen gag. Father does not move, but his eyelids close in a long, slow, blink.

She returns the scissors to their place in the kitchen, and takes the wet gag to the pantry and adds it to a small pile of laundry.

Fetching her steps and leaning them close to the poison cabinet, she climbs. Then she brings the tiny key to the brass lock. The cabinet's shelves are dotted with carefully labelled jars and vials. Meadow saffron for Mary Banes' gout. The devil's turnip for Isaac Wilson's digestion. Palm of Christ for the miners' wounds. Valerian for the sleepless village. Henbane for its rotten teeth.

Thornapple for the murder of witches.

Fingers trembling, she picks up that jar. It is lightweight, its glaze cracked, the wax plunged hard in its neck. As she hefts it in her hand and feels the pitter-patter of tiny seeds within, there is a shout from upstairs – sudden, sharp, like the slip of a knife. She flinches, the jar jumping away from her, smashing on the floor and scattering its contents.

Another shout, fierce as a battle cry.

The kitchen glares at her in the late evening light as she dithers there, afraid to climb the stairs. She looks to the toasting fork hanging on the wall and reaches out for it. It is weighty, reassuring in her palm. She imagines plunging it in soft flesh – recoiling then at the thought, knowing she would never dare. But even so, she takes it with her.

She creeps up the stairs, vision blurred and fading – her body betraying her. Pushing open the door, her heart clamouring like a blacksmith's hammer, she looks to his bed.

He lies there, quite still.

Another shout comes from Isabel, who is leaning against the wall as if the cottage needs holding up – as if all its blocks of stone are about to crumble around them.

'Is the baby coming?'

Isabel shakes her head and Mae knows she is lying. She looks towards Father, steps towards the bed, tries to fathom what to do. The coverlets rise with his shallow breaths.

Why is it taking so long?

The horror of what she has done – of what she *is* – washes over her. Her hand comes to her mouth, stifling a cry. Isabel turns from the wall to look at her. Sweat glistens on her brow. The air between them feels thick with uncertainty, and Mae takes a deep breath, desperate to clear her mind.

'He says there's a darkness in me.' Mae looks at the toasting fork in her hand, then crouches to slip it beneath the bed.

Isabel shakes her head.

'He says it came from Mother.'

'*No,*' says Isabel.

'But *thou shalt not kill,*' says Mae.

'And yet *he* has, has he not?'

Mae nods, thinking of the thornapple seeds scattered beneath the pantry shelves. 'He confessed it in his diary,' she says, looking to the chest in the corner of his chamber.

'He *confessed* it?'

'But what if he was right about Mother? What if he's right about me?'

'If there's darkness within you, it is *his* doing. There was no darkness in Florence, only goodness. Do you remember how kind she was?'

Mae does not reply.

'You remember how jealous Leah was of you? How spiteful? That child, God rest her soul, could stretch her vexation for days on end, and yet your mother still overflowed with love for her.'

It is true. Everything she says about me is true.

'Florence was always ready with a kind word, and a gentle touch with those gentle hands,' says Isabel. 'What part of her do you fancy was beset with darkness?'

'All the dead baby boys . . .'

'Babies die,' says Isabel. 'I have no calculation to make sense of it. But I am certain it is not the evil women among us who are denied the blessing of a living child. The infants taken from Florence were indeed all boys. But it is only your father who has ever sought witchcraft as an explanation for this sorrow. He has turned your family's loss into a catastrophe. And the man is a fool.'

Mae wants to believe it, but doubt as well as shame has become her shadow.

'I smell things no one else can smell. See colours just like Mother did. These are *peculiar* things – what is at work if not some magic?'

'You think yourself *a witch*?'

Mae looks down at the floor, thinking through the diversity of Father's accusations and how they have been tumbling from him ever since he discovered her notes and rags hidden beneath the blackthorn tree.

'If you think yourself a witch,' says Isabel, taking Mae's

hands in hers and pressing them to her stomach. 'Then curse my child! Let us see what you're capable of!'

'Don't *say* that.'

Mae shudders at the thought of it – of causing harm with just a thought, or a muttered word, or a careless brush of her hand. She thinks of all the ways she might summon evil without intending it.

'You cannot let his lies fester within you,' says Isabel. 'You cannot fear them, or they will follow you everywhere.' *Already* they follow her everywhere; they are her burden, her shadow, her chains. And Isabel is wise enough to see it. 'Do not let him tell you who you are.'

Mae looks her in the eye.

'Curse me!' says Isabel. 'If you think you can. Let me *show* you who you are.'

Mae shakes her head, trying to pull away.

'Do it!'

And before Mae can stop them, the words are out of her mouth. Isabel slowly nods, and Mae pulls her hands away. There is no time to dwell on what has just occurred, and together they turn towards Father, noticing first his blinking eyes, then the slow rise and fall of the bedclothes.

'The last time I saw your mother, we were here in this chamber together,' says Isabel. 'Your father called me *witch most vile*, and threw me out of the house.'

Mae remembers, just as I remember.

'What is it he says?' Isabel asks, glancing up at the rafters. 'Let justice roll on like a river..?'

'Righteousness, a never-failing stream,' says Mae.

Isabel slips a pillow from behind Father's head and

without the smallest hesitation presses it to his face. She leans the weight of her body upon it, and the weight of all that has come to pass. Outwardly, she does not flinch; she holds steady. Inwardly, she fights her instincts to honour life and bring gentleness to all she does. She is a midwife of souls – so often the first to touch the hot squalling newborn flesh as it enters the world, but just as often the last to hold the brittle scraps of what remains at the end. Neighbours send for her not only when a child is on its way and the mother needs delivering, but when a life is ending – when the circle is closing. She attends the moments that weigh down a human life, and there is a quiet gravity to her ushering of that life. I have been filled with awe at how she shifts between worlds, unaware how close we come, she and I – how we almost touch in those moments when a life slips from her hands.

But she has never snuffed out a life before, and the moment takes its time, as if it might go on for ever; as if *this* is hell and they are trapped together in its fiery heat.

Then she straightens, looking down at the impression her hands have made in the pillow. There is the sound of water trickling, and she steps away from the bed and hitches up her petticoats, looking to the floor. She glances at Mae, drops her petticoats, takes the pillow from Father's face and places it back behind his head.

It is done.

CHAPTER FORTY-FOUR

Early Summer 1666

*J*ohan leaps up the stairs to the garret, unconcerned
about the gloomy light and rotten steps, and throws
open the door. The decision he has made will be met with
resistance, and he limbers like a cart, thoughts swaying. His
words are starting to tumble from his mouth, but Jacques
has risen from his stool and strides towards him, brandish-
ing a letter that he waves in Johan's face.

'The boys!' Jacques says. 'They have recovered!'

'*Recovered?*'

Jacques pulls Johan to him, and Johan closes his eyes,
the better to feel the relief that burns through him, and
the comfort of the arms that tighten around him. Breathing
in the smell of lavender, mint and meadowsweet from the
crushed herbs beneath their feet, and the beeswax-honeyed
scent of Jacques' skin, he grasps a handful of Jacques' shirt,

and a fistful of his hair, holding him close – wishing they could melt together in the heat of this happiness.

When eventually he opens his eyes they are blurred with tears, but through them, over Jacques' shoulder, he sees Katarina at the window, and realises that she is looking at him. Blinking away his tears to see her better, he smiles at her, and she returns that smile. He takes it as a sign of encouragement, but when he beckons her, she does not move. She does though offer him something else: a glimmer in her eyes that Johan has hitherto not seen.

'We must away for a good meal – all of us,' says Jacques, releasing Johan. 'Not beef and mustard at the cookshop, nor stewed mutton at The King's Head. We must go to The Bear, for goose and woodcock and oysters.'

Despite himself, Johan laughs, thinking how good that meal would be washed down with some sugared wine. He longs for the simplicity of a celebration, the joy of matters concluding.

'And you can eat toasted cheese and fruit,' Jacques says, cupping Johan's face, smiling wildly.

'First,' Johan says, looking into Jacques' eyes, remembering the words he had prepared. He takes his lover's hands, squeezing his fingers in his own. 'First, we must talk . . .'

'What must we talk about?'

Still, the broad smile brightens Jacques' face, and Johan is all of a sudden so tired – exhausted at the thought of a discourse that will flood them all with disappointment. He wonders whether the conversation can wait – whether there is truly any harm in filling their bellies with good food and wine, rather than their hearts with bitterness.

But the promise he made to himself floats to the surface of his thoughts.

'I have made a decision,' Johan says, pressing on into choppy waters, thinking of the watermen rowing back and forth across the river all day, averting their gaze from the bobbing corpses. 'Tom Loomes' place is boarded up – all of them gone.'

'Come and rest,' says Jacques, pulling Johan towards the bed so they can sit on the edge of it.

'Did they leave then, after all this time?' says Johan. 'I cannot imagine it. So what can we think, but that they perished? Our dear friends who introduced us . . .'

'I am so very sorry to hear it.'

Johan shakes his head.

'But it gave me clarity, Jacques – and I know you will not like it.'

He regards the freckles across the bridge of Jacques' nose and across his cheeks – those constellations he knows so well.

'What is it I will not like?'

'What comfort did poor Tom and Maria have for one another? What words did they share when they knew what they faced? It was all I could think of when I looked into the empty workshop . . . in what manner did they cherish one another? I did not mind so much that they were gone, only that . . .'

'But *what is it* I will not like?'

'You know what it is, Jacques – that I must return to Eyam.'

It is as if the whole garret slumps at his words. Jacques hangs his head, and the air that leaves his lungs comes in one long sigh, followed by silence, as if he will never take another breath. Johan understands it is not just his lover's head that hangs, but all thoughts and plans, and every hope he had dared to nurture.

'I know what you yearn for . . .' says Johan, '. . . to leave here together.'

'We were *agreed*,' Jacques says quietly, imploringly.

'But I must be with Isabel and the children.'

'They have shut themselves away.'

'The *village* has shut itself away, and what courage they demonstrate all together. You have seen what the plague will do to a city – the multitudes that would be sure to perish if the plague made it to Sheffield. *Think*, Jacques. It is a great sacrifice . . .'

'I do not dispute it. But you need not flee to that nest of pestilence! It is not a sacrifice required of you, and you do not serve your family or your village by returning.'

'I *would* be serving them by returning; that is precisely it. I cannot prevent them, or myself, from dying if that is what comes, but I must be there. I promised Isabel I would return, and that is all that matters.'

Jacques tries to turn away, but Johan grasps his shoulders, squaring up to him.

'I'm sorry – it's not *all* that matters. But it *does* matter. Just as you matter, and Katarina matters. So you must come with me,' says Johan. 'Katarina too. Find a place nearby to stay. I do not expect you to come into the village, but let us travel north together. We must all find a way to keep our promises – to ourselves, and to each other.'

Jacques shakes his head again. 'I have made arrangements for us to travel to Wycombe—'

'*Un*make those arrangements.'

'But the quarantine! It is there for a reason—'

Johan's hands play at the base of Jacques' neck – stroking the soft linen of his collar and the solid line of collarbone. Everything about him is symmetry and balance: every angle, every curve. If Katarina had not been watching from the window then perhaps Johan might have unbuttoned his belligerence, and gone in search of the part of him that wavers, the part of him that is curious and forgiving.

'It only makes sense that people cannot leave,' says Johan. 'Visitors cannot go in only to come out again. But of course I can enter the village – as long as I then stay. *Have faith*,' he says. 'We have all come so far. There is nothing that you cannot leave behind in London, and there will be no indentures for the boys here. You wish for Katarina a place where she can recover; everything points us now in the direction of Yorkshire where the Society of Friends gather in their multitudes. Let us go to them there – let us find the peace and truth we have for so long been seeking.'

'So then let us *all* go to that place,' Jacques says. 'Come with us to safety. I will pack up my warehouse and make arrangements. We can write to Isabel. But do not go back there when we are all so close to a new beginning.'

'Isabel is my *wife*, the mother of my children – of all our children.' Johan glances at Katarina as he says this, and Katarina reassures him with a gentle nod.

'And I suppose I am of no consequence,' says Jacques, trying vaguely to shake free of Johan's grasp.

'That is not true, and you know it,' says Johan. 'You have the lion's share of my heart, and Isabel does not ask for it to be any other way. But my bond with her, my promise – I will not break it.'

'You rescued her from ruin – she is saved! And grateful!'

Johan shakes his head. 'You understood the arrangement. I will always be her husband and protector. She will always be my wife. I have made you no promises beyond it, Jacques. Isabel has kept her word to me, and has never stood in the way of the time you and I spend together. We owe her our gratitude, not our bitterness. This is the bargain we made, and how we have been rewarded because of it!'

Jacques sighs, dropping his gaze to the floor. 'You do not need to go directly, though,' he says. 'Wait another week, at least.'

Johan shakes his head. 'I have explained why I must go. And, besides, there are other things to consider.'

'What *things*?'

'A long story.'

Johan thinks of the shorter version – the unlikely simplicity of it.

'So, spit it out, or tell me as we eat and sup,' says Jacques, slipping from Johan's grasp and joining Katarina at the window.

'We should finish our discussion first,' says Johan. 'And see then if we still have an appetite.'

Jacques glances away, looking briefly at his sister, then out of the casement, as if he cares not for the weight of what is coming. I do not care for it either: this story that has been so little spoken of. And I wonder how he will manage to tell it.

'It is a mess! And it sounds like madness when I try to find the words.'

I think of Mae, and how she searched for a way to tell the

obscene truth about Father to Rafe. How she struggled to find words safe enough, or clean enough, or simple enough. How there were no sentences that did not sound like a fabrication.

'Just say the words, Johan.'

'Give him time to speak,' says Katarina, looking up at her brother. 'Be patient.'

Jacques smiles, reaching for her hand.

'I have shut my eyes to something unspeakable,' says Johan. 'And silenced my wife from uttering the truth.'

'What truth?' says Jacques.

'The village apothecary, Wulfric, a man of medicine and high regard. Isabel has long suspected he killed his wife and daughter, and I have done my best to look away from the situation, unwilling to believe it.'

Katarina and Jacques watch him closely, their eyes identical, so too the attentive tilt of their heads.

'I have always resisted Isabel on this matter – but now I worry her fears are justified.' Johan pauses, shaking his head, gathering his thoughts around himself. 'What a fool I have been!'

'And what of it? Why is it so pressing now?'

'Mae is his only child left living. Isabel fears for her safety, and I think her fear is justified.'

'But what can be done? Will you accuse the man? What proof do you have?'

'I do not know what can be done, but I'm certain of one thing – I am no use here in London.'

Jacques looks at him impassively.

'So you still think me a coward?' asks Johan.

Jacques comes from the window and puts his palm to Johan's chest.

'You have a *good* heart, my friend.'

'But a weak one?' His tone is accusing.

'What you speak of demonstrates great strength. I do not think you a coward.'

'You have said as much before now.'

'I do not remember that.'

'Well, I *do*.'

'Then forgive me, for it isn't true. If I've ever suggested such a thing then it was surely in a moment of vexation, when my heart was as hot as my head.'

'I must tell her that I believe her – that I see what she sees and was wrong to dismiss her. I do not wish to do that in a letter.'

Jacques places a kiss on Johan's lips, lingering there.

'I will not flinch from duty,' says Johan. 'But nor do I wish to flinch from love. We must find a place for all our promises.'

Jacques smiles, nodding, kissing him again.

Out of the corner of his eye, Johan sees that Katarina is moving from her corner at the casement, and he glances towards her. She looks up at him with watery eyes, dark as the night sky. And then she is stood at his elbow, and it is as if she is looking at him for the very first time – taking in every line and whisker of his face. He smiles at her, his own eyes watering, and she rests her head against his chest, and wraps an arm about his waist.

CHAPTER FORTY-FIVE

Early Summer 1666

It is only when Mae stands at the door to The Nook she realises she is not wearing her boots, but her slipped shoes, ruined now with mud. When Marshall answers the door, she knows that she must have woken him, for there is a shadowiness about him that she does not recognise, and he rubs at his eyes as if trying to be free of it. Perhaps there is a strangeness about her also, for when he looks at her, his gaze lingers on her face in a way that feels odd. She wonders if it is her guilt he notices – drifting off her in the breeze like the white dust that lifts from the miners as they walk through the village after a long day beneath the ground.

'Father is dead.'

His face reveals nothing.

'Will you dig him a grave in Cucklett Delf? I can pay you.'

They only ever share the most necessary of words, so she

knows there is nothing unusual about the way she speaks to him, but still every syllable feels cumbersome in her mouth.

'And can you come for his body? Isabel is sitting with him, but her baby is on its way.'

Marshall nods, pulls on his boots and steps outside, reaching for the shovel which leans against the rough clay of his home. The touch of his hand on her shoulder as he passes is like a burst of song in her body. She grasps his hand quickly, bravely, and says, 'How do Joan and William?' He nods by way of reply, briefly, before stepping away in the direction of the delf.

'I pay no heed to village gossip,' says Mae, to his back, rushing the words before her courage fails her. Marshall pauses, turning to look at her, a grateful smile twitching at the corners of his mouth. Watching him walk away in the direction of the delf, she looks for the dip of his subtle limp – more familiar to her than his voice, more comforting.

She finds Isabel in the parlour – the dark shape of her leaning against the fireplace, palms flat on the stone lintel, her slow, deliberate breath like the wind when it whistles through the thatch.

'Let us chase the ghosts away – light candles,' she says, standing up, rubbing her lower back. 'And then let us burn some sage.'

Mae knows that Isabel's child is coming, and she wants no part of it.

'Your baby will be here soon,' she says. 'You need to go home to Frances.'

Isabel smiles away the suggestion.

'It'll be here tomorrow, no doubt. Plenty of time to get this house cleansed of all it has seen.'

Isabel reaches to the shelf, just an arm's length away, and pulls at *Malleus Maleficarum* until it tumbles to the hearth, splitting on the stone – its loose pages sliding between them across the floorboards. Then she cries out, turning back to the wall, leaning there with her silver hair obscuring her face.

In the low grey light of the parlour, Mae builds the fire as Isabel paces the room. She lays a torn page on top of the dried twigs, and watches how easily it is destroyed. Mesmerised, she takes another piece of the brittle paper and feeds it to the flames. She keeps at it, and Isabel comes to stand behind her. Together, they watch as the fire eats up Father's monstrous book, page by hateful page.

From the pantry, Mae brings all the candles she can find and lines them up on the lintel, the windowsill, the little table, the bookshelf. After she has lit them she sees the parlour as she has never seen it before: aglow with the warmth of bitter orange and butter yellow. Then she brings a thick bunch of sage to the fire, so it singes and crackles. She circles the room with the smouldering herb, searching for every space where evil might try to hide – every crack and corner. Taking a candle with her to keep the herbs burning, she moves into the lobby, pausing at Father's cloak and boots. In the pantry she is careful not to miss a single shelf, letting the wraiths of smoke touch each jar and package and wooden box, and every bottle in the poison cabinet. She ascends the stairs, shadows following. She waves the pungent scent into every corner of her bedchamber and high into the rafters.

In Father's bedchamber she re-lights the sage and drifts it slowly down the length of his body. Hand trembling, mouth dry, breath ragged, she tries to reassure herself that he really is dead. *He is gone.* She brings the crackling leaves to the flame time and again, until there is little left but blackened spikes in her hand and a trail of ash over his coverlet.

In the corner of his chamber, leaving sooty smears on everything she touches, she rummages in his chest, pushing aside his breeches and shirts, his diary of secrets, the shift he had purchased to bury her in. She lifts out the winding sheet – *her* winding sheet – and with a flourish shakes it out, letting it settle on the floorboards next to the bed. Stepping onto it, she pulls back his coverlet and blankets, exposing the length of his body. She regards the soft undulations of his clothing – the folds of shirt and flannel waistcoat, the creases in his stockings, the billowing of his breeches. She glances, too, at the sharp features of his face: his pointed nose, his jutting cheekbones, his prominent brow. Leaning across him, wrapping her hands around the far side of his body, she pulls him towards her, rolling him off the edge of the bed – leaping backwards as he thuds onto the winding sheet.

She neatens his limbs, pulls the winding sheet across his body and tucks it tightly. She ties it beneath his feet, and above his head. The shape of his face is barely discernible now beneath the layers of cloth – all sharpness gone, all prominence diminished. He has been reduced – shrunken to an unrecognisable parcel of bones and flesh.

*

In the parlour, Isabel's bed gown lies in a heap on the floor and she plucks restlessly at the top buttons of her shift. Mae notices the eagle stone nestling at her throat, and remembers – just as I do – the day that Father cut it from Mother.

The church bell rings for eleven o'clock.

'Perhaps you should return to Frances,' says Mae. 'I can wait here for Marshall.'

'I wish to stay.'

'But I do not mind waiting alone.'

'I do not wish to leave you.'

'But the baby . . . ?'

'It does not matter where it is born!'

It matters to me, Mae wants to say.

'We should eat a little something,' says Isabel. 'Before it gets too late.'

Mae takes a candle with her and lights the fire in the kitchen. She feels uncertainty rippling through her and takes her time, half hoping for the cry of a child – a healthy, living child, with all its limbs – as she busies herself with kindling and flame. But even she knows that a child does not come so simply into the world.

She fetches mugwort and cloves from the pantry, and puts them together with a cup of white wine into the smallest cauldron. She sets it over the fire to boil, and drinks a mug of milk while she waits. When it is ready, she pours the mugwort decoction and takes it through to Isabel, glad to offer her something she has not requested.

Back in the kitchen, she lowers four eggs into a cauldron

of water and slices bread at the table. Looking around, blinking slowly, she notices the room does not swim and sway so much now. She feels a little more *here* – not yet so solid as the cauldron, but more solid than the water.

She lifts the steaming eggs onto a saucer, and takes them with the slices of bread and butter into the parlour. Sitting at the table, she peels away the scalding shells and spreads soft egg onto crumbly bread. She holds out a slice to Isabel, and together they eat.

'I hear a clock ticking,' says Isabel, between mouthfuls.

Mae swallows, savouring the creamy, buttery flavours.

'What do you mean, you *hear a clock* . . . ?'

'All evening it has been in my head – *tick, tick, tick!* I told him the child would not wait for him – but did he care to listen? He risks our good fortune by staying away when he has always been my charm.'

'You are worried about this child?'

'A woman always worries about her child.'

Isabel strokes the loose folds of her shift, then drops slowly to her knees with a low groan.

A little later, Mae hears the soft wood of the gate outside and the click of Marshall's hobnails on the stone path. Isabel is lying in front of the fire as if she needs the heat. She has been asking for sips of water, which Mae has brought from the cauldron in which she boiled the eggs, and as fast as Isabel drinks it, it beads upon her face and in the space between her breasts. She does not seem to notice when the front door opens into the lobby, and ahead of Marshall comes Frances – a great bundle in her arms.

Marshall walks through into the kitchen without a glance towards them, and Frances comes straight to Mae, her face full of condolence.

'I'm sorry to hear of your loss – I did not know your father was sick.'

Mae shakes her head.

'The plague?' asks Frances.

'It was not the plague,' says Mae.

'It was very sudden,' says Isabel, looking up from the floor, wisps of damp hair framing her face. The three women regard one another for a short moment, and then Frances pulls Mae into her arms, drenching her in coltsfoot-yellow.

'And now the baby is coming,' says Frances, turning away, looking to her mother.

She goes to Isabel, kneels beside her, rests a hand on her shoulder. She draws breath as Isabel draws breath. She rubs her mother's back and, when she glances up, every curve of her face flickers with candlelight.

'It will not be long,' says Frances.

'I should speak to Marshall,' says Mae.

'You are not to go with him,' says Isabel.

'Mama?' says Frances.

'Mae must be here for the birth of this child. I do not want her going with Marshall to bury her father.'

'But *Mama* . . .'

'There are things you do not understand. Wulfric has been neither good nor kind, and Mae suffered greatly at his hand. She will not wish to go into the night to bury the man, and Marshall will not care whether he finishes the task alone. So, let us not get simply swept along; we must have our own wills, and find our own way.'

Frances nods, looking slowly at Mae, who nods also.

'Do you have some spare sheets? A bolster or two?' asks Frances. 'And set some water to boil.'

Mae finds Marshall in the dark of the kitchen, his hat in his hands. She leads him upstairs to Father's bedchamber.

'I've prepared him for you.'

'Are we to go now?' Marshall asks.

'I'm needed here.'

She puts the candle down on the floor in the middle of the chamber to afford them both a little light, and as she does so she notices the toasting fork where she left it earlier. She snatches a quick glance at Marshall; he too is looking at the oddity of the object there beneath the bed. She goes quickly to the wooden chest and busies herself there.

'I do not need to know where you bury him,' she says.

After opening his mouth to speak, and then closing it again, Marshall gives a nod and Mae turns back to the soot-smudged linen. She spends longer than necessary choosing which sheets and coverlets to take downstairs – arranging them neatly, as if there is a need for neatness.

She does not watch but listens, instead, to the sound of Father being taken from the chamber. Then she lifts herself and goes to the window to collect the sounds of him being taken from the house: the clunk of ironwork, the solid nudge of the door closing, the click of Marshall's hobnails on the cobbles. When eventually she raises her gaze, he is halfway gone – just a shadow further up the street, his hobnails fainter with every step. She pushes the casement open a little further, leaning out to watch Marshall disappear into the gloom, dragging Father behind him.

She takes the pile of linen, and three bolsters from her own bed. On her way through the kitchen she puts everything onto the table, and lifts the large cauldron over the fire. Then she rejoins the women in the parlour, closing the door so they are cocooned in the heat and flame of the birthing chamber.

Frances spreads the sheets and coverlets in front of the hearth, positioning the bolsters. Isabel comes to them on hands and knees, like a cat searching for the warmest spot. Frances ties a clean apron about herself, and passes one to Mae.

'A woman's womb is like a purse, with its opening at the bottom,' says Frances. 'A child cannot be born until the womb is fully open. Feel here.'

Frances touches Isabel's foot.

'Feel how cold she is.'

Mae nods.

'Now here.'

Frances briefly wraps her hand around the curve of Isabel's ankle, gesturing for Mae to do the same: cold again.

'As a woman's womb slowly opens during her travail, she chills from the feet upwards. By the time her legs are cold *here* – the womb is fully open.'

Mae nods.

'You have cleavers?' asks Frances.

'Yes.'

'Then soak some in a little of the boiled water. And bring the cauldron in here with some fresh clouts.'

Mae goes for the things as instructed, and when she returns Isabel is lying on her side with her head resting against the bolsters.

'Come,' says Frances, gesturing to Mae.

'This often helps with the pain,' says Frances, showing Mae how to press her thumb and forefinger into the soft parts of Isabel's ankles.

Frances unties her bundle and spreads it across the floor. She reaches for an earthenware bottle and pulls out the stopper, filling the air with the scent of thyme.

Isabel pushes to her knees, moves from kneeling to crouching, puts her hands beneath her belly and blows impatient breaths so forcefully that the walls dance with shadows. She groans, and a gush of liquid soaks the sheets beneath her. The smell is the colour of tarnished silver, and Mae becomes lost in the swirl of an altogether new scent; it is the just-sharpened steel of a scythe; it is powdered stag horns.

Frances moves like water, lifting her mother's shift, pouring oil so her hands glisten slickly. The rest of the world has ceased to be – there is only the smell of their bodies, and the heat of the fire, and the certainty of where they travel.

It has been quiet for some time. And when Mae looks to Isabel she sees that her eyes are closed and her breathing is slow and steady. Even the candles are still.

'Is she asleep?' Mae whispers.

'She is resting a little,' says Frances. 'It won't be long now.'

They share a cup of hot water, sipping it slowly.

Frances whispers prayers to St Margaret, asking for

the safe delivery of mother from child, and scatters herbs onto the floor between them – crumbling the sweetness of meadowsweet, hyssop and mint. The church bell strikes a singular chime, and Mae marvels that she did not hear it ringing for midnight.

When Isabel stirs, they offer her mouthfuls of dandelion root cake, gritty with hemp seeds. And they eat a little themselves.

Soon Isabel rises on her elbows.

Her growl is guttural, thick in her throat. It fills the room – this sound of heaving stone up a hillside, of lifting a mountain.

It goes on, and on.

And all Mae and Frances can do is draw breath – breathing for Isabel.

Whenever she slumps against her bolsters she gulps air into her lungs, gasping and panting. But before she seems ready, she is pulled back to growling, as if some furious animal has her caught in its spell.

Frances strokes her mother's leg.

They wait, and together we witness.

Wave after wave.

Isabel's hair becomes wet with sweat, her face flushed, eyes bright.

'Be ready with a clout,' says Frances.

Mae dips one into the cauldron, wrings it, lets the steam rise away.

Isabel cries out.

Her opening bulges – skin stretching – and Frances presses a clout against her.

'Here,' Frances says, moving aside, motioning that Mae should come closer.

Mae wants to pull away – shadows of doubt creeping towards her from all corners of the room.

I can't, she tries to say, but Frances is tugging on her sleeve roughly, persuasively, and Mae finds herself kneeling between Isabel's legs.

'Press the clout against her,' says Frances. 'And press gently against the baby as it comes, so it is born slowly.'

Isabel lets out another cry, and Mae feels a surge at her palms.

'It is coming,' says Mae, full of fear, looking towards Frances. 'You should—'

Frances nudges Mae's hands briefly away, revealing a glimpse of new scalp, and the drum-tight stretching of Isabel's opening.

'Press against the child,' instructs Frances.

Mae does as she is told, and together they watch the bulging curves of body and flesh; shifting skin; the insinuation of bone.

Just as Mae thinks Isabel's task is impossible – that a woman's body cannot give so much – the baby's head is born.

She smells the new smell again, all stag horn and sharpened scythe – tarnishing the air with silver.

'Hold here,' says Frances, and Mae cups the hot head in her hand.

Isabel groans, bearing down.

The child's shoulders shift a little into the world.

Mae's fear beats hard at her throat, and panic washes over her as Father's accusations flood her thoughts.

'*I can't!*' Mae says, moving backwards.

'You *can*,' says Isabel, lifting her head and looking directly at Mae. 'You will do no harm, I promise you.'

Isabel flops back onto her bolster and her voice spills from her in one long, continuous cry, as if resolved it is all she will give: there will be no more after this.

Mae holds the child's head, and the tiny shoulders come towards her, one slow pulse at a time. Then the arms slither loose and the baby falls from his mother's body in a rush of blood and liquid.

Mae stares down at the child in her hands – still as a pool, blue as a bruise.

He does not move, and she knows in her heart that what she fears has come to pass.

'Blow upon his face,' says Frances.

Mae does so, knowing it will make no difference. Jostling him in her hands, she wills him to live.

The baby is still. His face is peaceful. And Mae remembers the curse that Isabel drew from her – how foolish they both had been.

She blows more forcefully, a storm from her lungs.

Have *my* breath, she thinks. *Take it.*

And as if he hears her, and understands, with a tiny shudder he comes to life; he screws up his face, draws up his legs and lets out a warbling bleat of indignation.

CHAPTER FORTY-SIX

Summer 1666

The sun is burning in the cloudless sky, just as it did yesterday, and the day before, and the day before that. Mae cannot remember a summer like it. The heat finds her even within the thick stone walls of the cottage. Sweat beads on her brow all through the night. And the milk – no sooner drawn from the cow and settled in the pail – is forever too warm, too cloying, too sour.

The village smells of death: the pungent stench of rotting flesh.

Perhaps the shallow graves are too shallow. Or perhaps the grieving do not have the strength or the will to bury their loved ones quite as soon as they ought. It is not just the mothers who are guilty of this; I have watched miners and blacksmiths cling to their dead infants, unwilling to imagine life without the light of their child.

The village has been losing its children in their multitudes.

Since only Sunday: Jane, Anne and Jonathan Naylor. Elizabeth Glover and Roland Mower. Sarah Elliott, Robert Kempe and Godfrey Torre. Margaret Percival and Anne Swinnerton. John and Elizabeth Hancock: all the way up at the top of Riley Lane, where the village thought the plague could never reach.

Not all of them had mothers left to grieve them, or fathers to bury them.

Mae walks to meet Rafe at the mews, but he is there in the road, with Swift, before she gets that far. He is taller by the week – wearing Johan's breeches – and has taken to using a black ribbon to tie back his hair. He holds out his hand and she takes it. She looks then to the curled talons and yellow legs, the cream and bronze of the bird's breast. Seeking Swift's gaze, and finding it – or so she thinks – she reaches out to stroke the soft grey feathers of his back.

But it is not *Mae* that Swift looks to – it is me. Perhaps it is the moths that catch his attention – those that tumbled from the rafters and the underside of the pantry shelves to escape the cottage before Mae pulled the door closed behind us.

'You are quite well?' Rafe asks, searching her face. He asks this every time they meet.

'Look!' She gestures the length of herself, from coif to boots. 'I live and sleep in a house of herbs. What harm can come to me?'

Marshall – wearing his wide-brimmed black hat despite the heat – is in his garden with Joan and baby William. Mae passes Marshall a bottle of spice water, and he smiles at her, nodding his gratitude despite his obvious embarrassment; he is slowly growing accustomed to her gifts. He gestures for Rafe and Mae to clamber over the crumbling wall. At the far side of the garden, past the plum trees and the roses in full bloom, is a large, sprawling patch of raspberry canes laden with swollen fruit, warm from the sun. They eat the berries straight from the bushes in companionable silence; not quite greedily, but almost.

Leaving Rafe to skirt around the edges whispering endearments to his restless hawk, Mae and Marshall work their way into the maze of canes, drifting away from one another as they follow the enticement of riper, plumper fruit – from one plant to another. Soon, Mae cannot see Marshall at all, though hears the snapping of twigs beneath his boots and the scrape of his thick linen shirt against the dead wood. Mice and blackbirds rustle in the cool, green world beneath the canopy of foliage and Mae stuffs her mouth so full of fruit that it bursts with a whole summer all at once.

At Ivy Cottage they wait for Harry and Edward to be coaxed from the house, Johan calling from the doorstep, 'We will go without you!'

Gabriel talks to Rafe about the hawk – *what* he last ate, *when* he last ate and whether he would eat today. Swift rouses, ruffling his feathers, settling again with three quick swivels of his head. He is losing all patience with these bustling humans and their ponderous limbs, and flashes me an angry glare.

Frances comes from the house with the baby in her arms, and Isabel follows behind, rolling her eyes at Johan.

'They are on their way,' she reassures him, before turning to Mae, grasping her in the way that she grasps her own children – at least daily, for a breath or two; long enough to feel the life in them.

Eventually, the small boys tumble from the dark interior of the cottage into the blinding sunshine, hurtling up the lane together without stopping to say good day – their nursery gowns billowing white against the green of the hawthorn.

Mae feels Isabel watching as Frances passes her the baby, their fingers touching as she does so, wisps of strawberry-blonde hair brushing Mae's face. There is a subtle enchantment between the four of them now, as if threads of the purest gold have been woven between all their souls – strong as silk, sticky as spider webs. And Mae wonders whether this is how Isabel feels with all the mothers, and all the children she has helped into the world. And those too that have died? And Mae wonders whether it will be the same for her when she tends to the sick, and comforts the dying, and catches new life as it enters the world. She wonders, when she reaches into nature's cornucopia and plucks gratefully that which she needs – adjusting the tincture, infusion or cordial so its colour is *just right* for its purpose – whether she, too, will feel those sticky, silken webs of connection.

The baby is awake and fidgeting, tasting the air with his tongue, frowning at the brightness of the sky. I look down at them as Mae bows her head into that waft of new-child scent. She kisses his fat cheeks, liking the way his flesh gives so reliably beneath her own, and offers her little finger to his open palm so he can grip at her fiercely. She likes that too – the power in his little fingers, his sense of ease. She is drawn to it, like a compass pointing north. And I understand it completely, even if she does not quite yet: that all the tiny child knows is belonging – the simplicity of it – and he is, in all his innocence, pointing her home.

'How now, Mae,' says Johan, stepping down onto the path.

It does not trouble him, what he has learned of Isabel and Mae since coming home. He has settled himself against the knowledge that their courage reached the heart of the matter just a little before his own. He puts his pipe in his mouth and waits for Isabel to come outside before shutting the door.

'Let us be away!'

The family flows up the lane together: their new Saturday ritual. Frances and Isabel link arms with Johan. Harry and Edward race to and fro. Gabriel walks with Mae and Rafe.

And all the time, Swift is poised to fly.

Both of us, restless together.

Jacques and Katarina, coming from the village of Stoney Middleton, scale the opposite side of Eyam Dale, following the semblance of a path they have created over the weeks through the thick ferns and bracken. They cannot be sure that the Frith family are making their way at this very moment to the place where the trees thin, and the ground rises on either side of the dale – from where, across the deep ravine of trees, they will drink in the sight of one another and shout their news through cupped hands.

But they hope.

And they look for the hawk, straining their ears for Rafe's whistle.

*

Swift launches from the glove, and flies skyward, resisting the lure of the dense trees where the song thrushes wait. The warm summer air pulls us upwards, ruffling Swift's finer feathers as we soar until our loved ones below are only flashes of shift and shirt through the canopy of green.

Now, not even that.

I try to look back, but the hawk is neither perturbed, nor distracted. He takes us onwards to where the moths have gathered into such a plume that the dust from their thousands of wings, and the dust of my thousands of thoughts, catch the sun's rays like powdered pearls. I am at once surrounded by old thoughts and new. By thoughts so complete that I might once have considered them perfect. By inchoate thoughts, long forgotten. And brittle thoughts that I have not cared to handle. I am surrounded too, by thoughts as soft as a mouse, as simple as the church bell chiming, as reliable as the planets circling.

And then they are gone.

It is truer to say that I let them go. For it is *that* we're asked to relinquish. Not those we leave behind, not love, not belonging. But the burden of thinking.

The hawk keeps his yellow eye upon me, knowing what it is to be tethered and what it is to be free. And then, leaving me safe in the velvet flutter of a thousand familiar wings, he is gone. Swift as an arrow let loose.

*D*uring the remainder of the summer and the start of autumn, a further one hundred and seventy-seven villagers died from the plague in Eyam. The bravery and sacrifice of the village as a whole did indeed prevent the spread of the disease outside the boundaries of the village. The number who died in total was two hundred and sixty, out of a population of around seven or eight hundred.

My main characters (Mae, Wulfric, Isabel, Johan and Rafe) are entirely fictitious. But their neighbours, including William and Catherine Mompesson, Thomas Stanley (the exiled rector), Elizabeth Bradshaw and her children, Sam Chapman, and the many villagers mentioned, are real people recorded as living (and dying) in Eyam at the time. Marshall Howe was indeed the grave digger, tainted by rumours that he stole belongings from the dead. I have given Marshall the benefit of the doubt, and written him as a man of integrity. I have kept to the facts, to the extent they're known, with regard to the 'lockdown' of Eyam, and the arrangements that were made with surrounding villages.

It is unlikely that a small village would have had a formally-trained apothecary, so I made use of my artistic licence a little when creating Wulfric's character. A man called Humphrey Merrill was Eyam's herbalist at the time of the plague, and he died on the 9th September 1666, at the very end of the outbreak.

The scientific discoveries mentioned in the novel, the midwifery, the books, periodicals, as well as the developments within clockmaking, are historically accurate to the best of my knowledge. The same is true of the use of herbs (including the poisons) and the apothecary ingredients and products — the pills, tinctures, decoctions, cordials and balms. The chapters that take place in London depict the city as it was in the spring of 1666.

The Bradshaw family were not in residence at Bradshaw Hall during The Commonwealth and Protectorate, but for the purposes of the scene in Chapter Ten I have imagined them in Eyam during this time.

Catherine Mompesson, wife of the rector, died from the plague on 25th August 1666, the same day that Sam Chapman died. On the 27th August, Joan Howe perished, followed by her infant son William, a few days later. Marshall Howe fell ill with the plague, but survived.

Elizabeth Bradshaw never returned to Eyam with her sons, and Bradshaw Hall fell into ruin.

ACKNOWLEDGEMENTS

The generosity, encouragement and expertise I've encountered while writing and editing *The Hemlock Cure* has been wonderful, and I feel indebted to so many.

Firstly, to the fabulous team at Sphere: thank you for publishing this book with such enthusiasm and passion. Special thanks to Rosanna Forte, for your unwavering confidence in my story, for your vision and your beautiful editing. Thank you Emily Moran, Thalia Proctor, Millie Seaward, Vanessa Neuling and Rachel Cross. Thank you Micaela Alcaino, for your extremely stunning cover design.

Thank you to my agent, Ella Kahn, for your encouragement and sage counsel, and also just for believing in me. You really are the very best.

For reading and commenting on the manuscript, I thank: Rebecca Bonner-Wallace, Lance Burn, Val Chambers, Sophie Hunter and Jamie Voce. This novel would not be what it is without you.

Huge thanks to Renuka Russell for your invaluable herbal and botanical advice, and to Val Chambers for your insights into the religious history of the period. Thank you Roma Norriss for sharing your midwifery knowledge so generously. Thank you Francine Clifford and the volunteers at The Eyam Museum for conversation and guidance around the story of Eyam. Thank you too, Ken Hoare at Ham House, for your advice about stillrooms in the seventeenth century. I've had lots of help throughout the writing of this novel and any mistakes that remain are entirely my own.

I am grateful for the lovely support from so many, but especially: Bex Bonner-Wallace, Wendy Burke, Anna Caig, Anton Cannell, Jeanette Caw, Blossom Chambers, Chris Chambers, Charlotte Cooke, Karen Dunn, Ann Gornall, Merryn Gott, Cate Hammond, Sophie Hunter, Christine Kelly, Caroline and Angus McLeod, Sarah-Jane Page, Chrissie Poulson, Simon Seligman, Sarah Thompson, Jamie Voce, Ceris Vroone, Richard Wraight and Lou Wright.

Thank you Mum and Dad for those early lessons in creativity, and for all your encouragement.

To my daughters, forever a source of joy, inspiration and reasons to be grateful, *thank you*.

And from the bottom of my heart, to Lance, always.

I am indebted also to the many books I read during the writing of this novel:

Helen MacDonald's *H is for Hawk*; Lucy Moore's *Lady Fanshawe's Receipt Book*; Ian Mortimer's *The Time Traveller's Guide to Restoration Britain*; John Clifford's *Eyam Plague*, Miranda Kaufmann's *Black Tudors*; Sasha Handley's *Sleep in Early Modern England*, Nicholas Culpeper's *Culpeper's English Physician*; Daniel Defoe's *A Journal of the Plague*

Year (which especially inspired Jacques' letter in chapter two); Christopher S. Mackay's translation of Heinrich Kramer's *The Hammer of Witches*; Jennifer Evans & Sara Read's *Maladies and Medicine, Exploring Health and Healing 1540-1740*; Janet Arnold's *Patterns of Fashion 4*.